Dear Reader,

Destiny was inspired by those fascinating people we all
seem to know, the ones who meet their life's partner in
childhood and stay bonded for all of their lives.

In my next book, *Fearless,* Judith and Einhard come
together much later, at a dangerous turning point, a crisis
that demands both courage and faith in the future. That
faith is sometimes hard to hold, but we all need its power.
Fearless is the story of two people who suffered losses
and find their hope restored.

Judith's world was destroyed and the loss makes her
guard her feelings. The exiled princess pledges her service
to King Alfred, the last king to resist the Vikings who
ravaged her home. She will dare all for her duty, but she
will risk her heart for no one, least of all for the foreign
mercenary who refuses her.

Einhard, exiled for piracy, appears to have no morals, only
an unbreakable will. But Judith's disastrous attempt at
seducing the stranger into the service of her king spins out
of control. Einhard holds unexpected depths. He is a man
with secrets—a pain and a loss he keeps hidden. In that,
they seem soul mates.

But Einhard's quest is implacably opposed to Judith's, and
she must make choices that risk not only her duty to her
king, but the defenses over her feelings and her heart.

In *Destiny,* Berg and Elene shared the power of a
childhood bond. In *Fearless,* Judith and Einhard meet
at the turning point of their lives. They must prove their
courage and their faith. I hope you will join me to share
their story.

Helen Kirkman

PRAISE FOR HELEN KIRKMAN

"Dark Ages? In Helen Kirkman's hands, they shine."
—HQN author Margaret Moore

A Fragile Trust
"Kirkman's lyrically descriptive prose sustains an unusual emotional intensity. This one generates that rare urge to read it straight through."
—*Romantic Times BOOKclub*

"*A Fragile Trust* tells the story of a love so powerful that readers will never forget it…absolutely awe-inspiring and sure to be one of the best historicals of 2005!"
—*Cataromance.com*

A Moment's Madness
"This debut novel is rich with textural details of an ancient time, retelling with flair the age-old story of love trumping vengeance."
—*Romantic Times BOOKclub*

"*A Moment's Madness* is a mesmerizing tale and I was loath to put it down until the very last page was turned."
—*ARomanceReview.com*

Forbidden
"Very graphic and sensual, this tale is well-told and fast-paced from start to finish."
—*Old Book Barn Gazette*

"*Forbidden* will hold your attention from the vivid opening to the climax."
—*Romantic Times BOOKclub*

Embers
"The lush backdrop and intrigue-laden plot make for good reading."
—*Romantic Times BOOKclub*

HELEN KIRKMAN

Destiny

HQN™

If you purchased this book without a cover you should be aware that this book is stolen property. It was reported as "unsold and destroyed" to the publisher, and neither the author nor the publisher has received any payment for this "stripped book."

HQN™

ISBN 0-373-77054-5

DESTINY

Copyright © 2006 by Helen Kirkman

All rights reserved. Except for use in any review, the reproduction or utilization of this work in whole or in part in any form by any electronic, mechanical or other means, now known or hereafter invented, including xerography, photocopying and recording, or in any information storage or retrieval system, is forbidden without the written permission of the publisher, Harlequin Enterprises Limited, 225 Duncan Mill Road, Don Mills, Ontario M3B 3K9, Canada.

All characters in this book have no existence outside the imagination of the author and have no relation whatsoever to anyone bearing the same name or names. They are not even distantly inspired by any individual known or unknown to the author, and all incidents are pure invention.

This edition published by arrangement with Harlequin Books S.A.

® and TM are trademarks of the publisher. Trademarks indicated with ® are registered in the United States Patent and Trademark Office, the Canadian Trade Marks Office and in other countries.

www.HQNBooks.com

Printed in U.S.A.

To the memory of my father,
whose love and support throughout my life
I will always cherish.
Thanks Arthur. We miss you.

Also by Helen Kirkman

A Fragile Trust
A Moment's Madness
Forbidden
Embers

And coming soon from HQN Books
Fearless

N

Viking forces control
all of England north of
the River Thames

Saxon warriors fiercely
defend their king in
the last free land...
Wessex.

NORTHUMBRIA

MERCIA

EAST
ANGLIA

THE WELSH

River Thames

London

WESSEX

KENT

Andred Forest

Winchester

CORNWALL

England 875AD

CHAPTER 1

Kent, England—The Andredesweald, AD 875

ELENE HAD TWO ADVANTAGES—desperation and a spear. She also had a dress fit for a whore. She kicked back her trailing skirts. The man had a sword. Light glittered off his chain mail, off the deep gold fall of his hair. It sparked from him as he moved.

The warrior's sword, gold-hilted, rune-carved, was as yet undrawn, as though he thought he did not need it. She balanced the seven-foot shaft of grey ash wood in her hand. The leafed blade at the tip was strong enough to pierce the hand-linked steel across his chest.

He was shouting; Elene did not heed it. She would deal death rather than be under any man's power, *his*.

He ran, closing the gap between them, lithe as a grey wolf, fast. He was huge, a shape of strength, threat. His shadow was black. Behind him was the open space in the half-built wall of the fortress. Behind that was the forest.

She tightened her grip on the smooth wood. The distance between her and the warrior closed at a speed that defied reason. Suddenly he was within striking range.

He did not unsheathe the sword. *Why?*

No weapon. She would have to spear a man unarmed. The world receded around the glittering moving shape, the death-black shadow. She was close enough to sense realness, fast breath, heat, living muscle, the courage to face killing steel. For a critical instant she held back.

Her breath choked. She would have to strike him or she was gone. Back into hell. A captive. She could not bear that again.

He swerved. Left… She tried to follow with the spear point. He yelled, his voice harsh, so strong like him.

He lunged.

The madness made her strike, the point of the spear aimed true, straight at where his heart would be, locked to his movement—it was a feint. She realised too late. The twist of his body, supple despite his size, was too swift to follow.

He took her feet from under her. The spear scraped metal, ripped out of her hand. The point pitched into the dust. He caught her before she could follow. His arms imprisoned her, a solid leg pinned hers.

The feel of his body was pure heat, hard metal, heavy muscle, size. Such size. Weight. It was the way Kraka used to hold her. She struggled, insane.

"Keep still, woman!" The words came through, Danish mangled by West Saxon. She hit, her fist jarring against metal, on flesh hot with sun and exertion, fine skin. "Hell-rune…" Hell-fiend, sorceress. It came out in English, equally mangled. She realised what his accent was and went still. She swore. The language she used was the same, only the dialect was different, the pure Mercian that belonged farther north, in the broad midlands.

"You are English, then." The deep, richly accented voice held a thread of amusement, exasperation, the fierce intensity of the shared struggle. He was breathing hard.

"Will you stop now?" he enquired. She swallowed with a dry throat. The spellbinding shape of his voice had no significance. East Anglians were dead meat anyway, their rich open landscape lost forever to the Viking army, to raiders like the ones she had lived with.

"Well?" demanded the dead East Anglian.

She did not know why he was interested in her answer. He could kill her one-handed. He knew it. Her chance was gone.

For now.

"Aye."

He loosened his grip. The fingers of her left hand were tangled in the bright mass of his hair beneath his war helm. She had pulled bits of it out. She unclenched her fingers. Threads of pure gold stuck to her flesh. When he breathed, the solid wall of his chest pressed into her, metal and padding, and beneath it strong life. His hands, huge, heavy, eminently capable, burned her skin through the bedizened inadequate gown. He shifted a dense, thickly muscled thigh. His hands moved briefly across her back, the curve of her ribs, under her arms. Shivers coursed over her skin. Her half-clothed body slid down the metal-clad length of his, hardness and heated flesh. Her skirt caught between their tightly pressed legs, lifting. She yanked it down, vicious with fright. He moved. The material came free, dropped, covering the revealing flash of skin, the bright red shoes.

But he had seen the strumpet's dyed shoes of cheap leather, the curving shape of hidden flesh bared to the knee. He had touched her. She read the flare of heat in his grey eyes, beyond anger or vengefulness, as deep as instinct. Male. Her breath hitched.

He caught her arm, his hand warm, alive, the touch direct, shockingly intimate, more so because of the brief, naked moments when they had fought between life and death. Close. Deep inside her, sharp feeling uncoiled like a snake waiting to strike.

It was anger, the bitter melding of rage and fear like a killing frost. He kept his hand where it was. The heat of the feeling, the solid living touch of him, mocked her.

Her feet lighted on the ground and the dizziness hit her. She felt ill with exhaustion, the mad, fey strength of the struggle, spent. Her belly clenched. No food, no money, no hope of anything. All lost like her freedom. She made herself stand up straight. Not her freedom. She would do whatever it took.

"Lord, you have caught her!"

She stiffened with shock. She had not seen the others, or even realised they were there, that anything existed beyond the man who held her. She turned her neck on tight muscles.

The garrison of the unfinished Kentish fort surrounded her and the East Anglian warrior like a circle of carrion birds after the battle. Near her feet on the dusty ground lay the lost throwing-spear. Beside her captor's large boots lay the scratched linen bag of pilfered food, the leather bottle of clean precious springwater. Someone's ration of dried meat spilled onto the ground.

"She is dangerous, lord. We could have shot her, but…"

She saw the man with the arrow ready on string. The bow was still bent. *But the East Anglian with the flashing armour, the one referred to as the leader, had flung himself at her with a wolf's speed, shouting.* Her foot grazed the deadly spear shaft. The *lord* held on to her, a tightening of iron fingers on her bare arm, like a warning.

Like a sign of outright possession.

"She is a thief," insisted the man who could only be the garrison commander. The speech, thickly Kentish, alien to the richness of East Anglia, brought sullen murmurs of agreement.

"Of the armoury?" The lord's voice was flat. The captain of the garrison flushed. Elene should not have found the throwing-spear. They had been unforgivably careless.

"She speaks Danish."

This time her belly clenched with fear. The accusation was true. She spoke across them, shouting. "I am not Danish." She nearly spat it. She sought for calm, reason, for her voice to ring with conviction. "I was living in the forest. The Andredesweald."

"An outlaw, then. And—"

A *hor-cwen.* The appalling scarlet dress clung to every curve of her body like a second skin. Her flesh spilled out of it, her arms bare past the elbow, the curve of her shoulder exposed, the tops of her breasts. The material was thin, now travel-stained, ripped at the hem and—heaven knew what she looked like after fighting a warrior built like Beowulf the monster slayer. It required only the iron grip of his hand on her arm to hold her still. The strength seemed to pour from him in hot waves. He did not speak, but her accuser suddenly stepped back, bowing his head.

But it did not stop his vengeful gaze, the mixture of anger and thwarted lust. The same look, the same bitter fire burned in the eyes of every man in the tight circle that hemmed her in, trapping her from escape. She had made fools out of them all. She was a Danish whore. She consorted with those who had raided their land and killed their kindred and taken their families as slaves. Kent had suffered badly, ravaged by horrors.

It was nothing to what had happened in East Anglia.

The relentless pressure of the massive hand on her arm increased. The fierce, strong body with its merciless courage moved.

"I will deal with this."

She could feel the unslaked anger in the company of men around them, the resentment. There were a score of weapons. But the unexplained right over them the East Anglian lord possessed, the command, the unbreakable strength of his will was enough.

"My lord Berg."

Berg.

The circle of men opened to reveal a sunlit path that led straight into the heart of the fortress.

"Come," said the man called Berg.

Question, command or offer. It did not matter. The choice was clear—him or the pack of angry bated hounds on the scent. The lord in the brilliant armour did not spell it out. No need.

She tossed her head. The whore's dress rustled as she walked.

SMALL BOLTS OF PANIC DARTED through the pit of Elene's stomach. She should have stabbed the man when she'd had the chance, fled back to the dark forest. She looked at the enormous bulk in front of her, the sunlight flashing on chain mail. Her stolen spear had been strong enough to penetrate his protection. She could have killed him. Mayhap. She tried to imagine it—the fierce, terrifying fire gone from his deep grey eyes. Shivers raced down her spine.

He had charged at her with no weapon.

If he had not done such an insanely dangerous thing, the others would have killed her.

She followed in his heavy footsteps. They beat out a concentrated rhythm on the dusty earth.

She was weak and a fool, and she had got herself caught. She would have to get out of it. There was always a way out if you had the courage to take it.

Her captor led her to a bower. It was roughly made, the walls of wattlework, the furnishings sparse. But it was warm, with a fire to keep the cool wind of early summer at bay. The golden glow of flame accentuated the fading light outside. It would soon be dark. Darkness and the forest. Her chances, any chances, faded with the light.

The monster slayer named Berg waited at the door. She went inside. He clumped after. Then he closed the door. It was like a trap shutting.

His size filled the room. She could not see his face, only a glimpse of straight shadowed features. And the eyes. Grey as the battle steel that encased him. The rest was hidden by a war helm that was treasure beyond reckoning, a master smith's creation carved with boar shapes for strength, crested with an intricately carved, double-headed snake for protection.

Its splendour was barbaric, equal parts brute strength and a savage kind of beauty. Wholly intimidating.

Like him.

She had lost the spear. That left only the whore's dress.

He faced her. His dark blond hair spilled from beneath the helm, half-hidden by the curtain of fine mail that protected his neck, pouring down to touch a giant's shoulders. Unreal.

She watched the heavy swell of the breath in his chest, which meant he would speak.

Her heart pounded.

"What are you doing here?"

His accent pulled at her, the sound of a people who lived in a land so open that it had no beginning and no end, just distance stretching out like a long-remembered dream.

"I was thieving," she said. She no longer dealt in

dreams. Or memories. Besides, the man was nothing to her, only some great brutish lump. She would escape him. She looked straight back. "As you saw."

"That spear. Aye." His finely made mouth quirked. "I saw it." It was a mad kind of irony, just as it had been a mad kind of courage that had sent him running at her when he could have had her shot. Fool. It had been her intention to kill him.

She would not even contemplate what might have stayed her hand for that heated, fractured instant that now proved fatal.

"And food," he said.

She regarded the costly armour, the well-developed body, the rude health. He did not look like a man who had ever known hunger or the kind of desperation that stripped the soul.

"I was hungry," she said. "There is not a lot to be had in the forest."

The trace of amusement died, leaving his eyes flat grey.

"No. And there are other hunters in the forest."

His remark made her lip curl. If he meant the Vikings, he was wrong. Kraka's men were not so close, neither would they come near a West Saxon fortress. It was why she had come this way.

"There are wolves," she said blandly, "and wild boar."

His gaze flickered, but he did not pursue the subject. Just a lumpish fool.

She tried not to think of the depths in his eyes.

"What is your name?"

The dizziness and the tiredness washed over her suddenly. She thought she would drop. "El—" She choked over the next syllable. *Elgiva.* She had almost blurted out her true name, the formal name she had been baptised with. Why had she so nearly done that, now, in front of a stranger? It seemed unfitting…dangerous.

"Elene," she said rapidly. That was also true. It was the everyday family name her father had chosen for her, because he said she always took things head on. *Elen,* he had said, the word that meant *courage.*

She needed it now. The intense gaze of the East Anglian held her. He said nothing at all. She saw his eyes narrow. The intelligence she had sensed before became focused on her, and she thought for one insane moment that he knew exactly who she really was.

She was mad, driven to this state of distraction by hunger and fear and uncertainty. Her breath caught in her throat. But he turned away, so abruptly that the tiny links of steel at his neck made a small cold sound.

She let the breath out of her chest. He had no reason to know who she was. Had been. He was just some crude warrior she could outwit. An oaf. He had to be.

He sat down, the same deadly, metallic sound echoing in the silence between them. She tried not to shudder. She stared at him.

She would think her way out of this.

"What are you doing here, Elene?"

The sound of her name on his lips made her skin shiver, not with cold fear, but with a sudden unexplained heat. He filled her sight, raked her fragile senses. The rich shape he gave the word still trod on abandoned dreams. Her hands clenched. She hated that, hated *him* with his raw power and his flaunted strength.

She smiled. "What do you think? The same as your men—that I am a Danish *hór-kona?*" *Whore.* She smoothed the gaudy dress, the last weapon. It had been a gift from another man. Just like him. The East Anglian lord had touched her and he had desired her. He still did. Nothing could disguise that. She watched the hot eyes, the potent body. She would use that strength, that burning desire, if she had to. She knew how. She had been taught well, but she was on her own road now. He would not stop her.

She tipped back her head. The warm air of the small room, heated by the flames in the hearth, by the flames in him, slid over her exposed throat, over too much skin bared by the dress. "Tell me, what do you see?"

"A woman who would use a spear, like a Valkyrie."

A shield-maiden, a woman who had more power than a warrior, who could choose, if the warrior would fight, either his life or his death. A woman who was a link with other worlds.

She did not believe him.

He saw only the dress, the mad creature who now wore it. She moved her clenched fists, the thin material gaped.

"No." Stifled fury and long-held bitterness made her voice harsh.

"No?" The grey eyes held hers. "What then? Are you Danish?"

"No." She wanted to hit him. She sneered in her turn. "Does that make a difference?"

"We will have to see. The Danes are two miles away in

the shelter of the Andred Forest. I am here. Tomorrow that could be reversed."

"What?" Her throat closed. The Vikings were still at their camp, waiting for Kraka the Storm Crow to return. They would not move without him.

"You are wrong."

"Am I?" He turned his head toward her, the sharp glitter of his eyes as fast as a snake striking.

She took a step backward and shoved the uncombed mass of her hair from her face.

If her hand was not quite steady, she could turn even that to account. "You frighten me by saying the Danes are so close while I was in the forest." She swallowed, sought control. "But you cannot believe they will attack this fortress?" She had to get away. If Kraka's brothers caught her now. If Kraka—

"They will."

The nausea in her empty belly gripped. She felt all the rage and the blind fear and the madness that had driven her to spear-fighting.

"Don't."

Elene stared at his hand locked around the bare flesh of her arm. She must have lunged for the door without thinking. He had caught her. So fast.

She had promised herself she would think her way through this. She went still in his grasp. He was so close she could see the separate links of metal that made up his armour, the linen sleeve of his tunic beneath, the scattered dark gold hairs along the edge of his hand. He held her tightly because he had so much strength. The heavy ring on his finger dug into her flesh, gold, one more obvious symbol of his wealth. It was a unique symbol, carefully wrought, an eagle holding a fish in its claws. The ancient sign of the transition into new life.

The church said that the fish was like a soul.

"I would not set foot outside this fortress," he said. He took a breath that was measured. The shining net of steel rose and fell. "Unless you want to go back to the Viking army."

Kraka... How much did he know that she did not? What things? But he could not know what she was, *had been*.

"It was you who said the Vikings would come here." Her breath whispered across a strand of dark blond hair lying over highly polished links of steel, lifting one single thread of gold.

"I said they would attack the fort."

His breath touched her skin. Warmth. The same warmth that was in the bond of his hand. Small dancing shivers of hot and cold coursed through her flesh. His chest moved. Steel glittered.

"I did not say they would win."

He was so strong. She thought of that hand on her body in the courtyard, picking her up as though she were some child's toy. She had struggled; it had made no difference to him.

"Then you are saying you will win?" He would boast, as men always did before battle. She had been made to understand why. They had to make themselves believe they would win. It was their means of survival. Just as it had become hers.

"Would that help your choice?" His voice lightened unexpectedly, the same quick irony that had made those determined lips curve when he had spoken of the spear she had used on him.

"Aye," she snapped back. "It might."

Her decisions were spinning out of her control, the way they had when he had conveyed without words that the choice lay between him and the men of the garrison. Or the dark wastes of the Andredesweald. She could feel his living warmth, just as she had then.

"I cannot tell you that I will win, Elene."

She raised her head, looked at his face, into his eyes.

"I do not know how the battle will fall."

It was extraordinary that he would say such a thing to her. In his dark grey gaze she could read bitterness like her own, and over that a courage that was endless. The kind of courage that looked deeply and faced truths.

She thought of Kraka's troop, the harshness of it, the vicious lust for conquest. She thought of the vastness of the army waiting in the conquered lands of East Anglia, readying itself to strike at Kent, easternmost fringe of Wessex, the last English kingdom to hold out. Kraka's raiding band was only one small part of the army commanded by the Viking earl, Guthrum.

Truths.

"You will win," she said. She was not a believer in destiny. Not any longer. But the certainty was there. She wanted the East Anglian with the bitter eyes to feel it. She could not have said why.

The fire in his eyes caught, lightning fast. It transformed

his face, like a sheet of brightness, so that she could see beauty. The lightning flicked her. Hot sparks that made her skin glow where they touched.

He had both hands on her arms now and she was leaning against him, touching hard unyielding metal and warm flesh.

"That is not what a Valkyrie should say. She chooses the slain after a battle."

Her breath felt quick in her chest, her consciousness of him overwhelming. She did not want this feeling. Above all, she did not want to look at the light in his eyes. She had her plans. She had worked out what she would have to do, and he was nothing, just a man like any other, at the mercy of his own greedy desires. She needed his flaunted strength right now. She needed anything that would keep her from the Vikings in the Andredesweald. From Kraka. She would use this man for survival. It was how the world worked.

Her mouth curved. "A Valkyrie would offer the slain warrior a new life of endless battle and all the joys and the pleasures of the mead-hall. What more could a man want?"

She caught the edge of his fire.

"A thousand things. Things beyond reaching."

The pain lanced through her like a spear's thrust, pain for all the things lost that could never be regained, for all the things she had once dared to imagine and long for. Dreams. Long ago memory shot through with promise. Happiness. She blocked it out.

"There is nothing else," said Kraka's escaped mistress. "There is only fighting and the victory of the strongest. The division of the spoils. Bargains." *Bargains made in hell.*

"I am exactly what the men of this garrison thought me. We all make bargains to get what we want. I am what *you* think me," she said, straight into those dark grey eyes that held dreams. Dreams were dangerous. They had the power to crumble the solid wall of reality that enclosed her life.

"You used your strength to protect me." She leaned toward him. The ruined neckline of her dress slid across her skin without any of her contriving.

She would find her way through this.

She knew what she must do. It would be simple, and she had been so well taught. She was nineteen winters old and had survived the flames of hell.

Yet her heart beat hard. He was so big, so close.

Her hand brushed across his arm below the glittering chain-mail links. The muscle was thick, hard as the metal that covered his body. Her heart seemed to skitter. The strange, dangerous, frightening sensation shivered along her skin. She ignored it because she was in control.

Elene smiled. "I know what I owe you for your protection. I know how to pay."

Her breath must touch his skin. She was staring into his face, the stark shadowed glimpses she could see under polished metal incised with shapes of power. He had beauty. It was undisguisable. He had strength beyond that given to the most envied of warriors. She knew what all that meant.

"I know what you want…." She had known it, felt it. She touched it now in his vital living flesh. She watched his eyes. What she had sensed from the first moment was there in the dream-filled, fire-flecked darkness, the sharp flare of desire, bright. Heated. Like the flesh under her hand. Still metal hard, but hot.

She made the smile broaden, provocative, a challenge. She could survive his strength. Such heat burned quickly and then it was over.

She slid her hand over his bare flesh under the linen of his tunic. She sensed the breath he took to speak.

"I have not asked for payment."

Her hand stopped.

She knew what his desire was: all men were the same. She could feel its power beating through the tautness of his body. The shadowed air of the close room shimmered with tension.

She could see the brightness in his eyes. Brightness and…something else. Something stronger. She had not counted on the measure of his will. She felt out of her depth.

Yet the desire was still there, she was sure. Burning. That was what counted in the end. Greed. For riches or power or the appetites of the body. That greed was stronger than anything. She had such cause to know.

"I know what you want," she said.

"You have not the slightest idea."

The bite of his words cut, the powerful conviction. It made her insane with pain—not pain, anger. He thought he was better, because he possessed brute strength. Because he had never been as desperate as she. Because—

Because his eyes still held dreams and he had said it was possible to want more than what was real. She could not accept that. It would drive her mad. Her heart beat hard and her breath choked her. There were no dreams, none that lasted. Reality was all there was. She would teach him.

She brushed her lips against his, just the slightest touch, meant to inflame him, not to satisfy. She felt the warmth of skin, breath hard and fast.

"See? It is simple. It means nothing."

"Nothing?"

The hot brightness in his eyes suddenly filled her vision. Just as the leashed strength of his body filled her hands, harsh metal and living flesh. Even as she voiced the lie, her lips were still tingling with the print of his, supple and heated with virile strength.

"There could be nothing between you and me." Yet as the words left her mouth, her skin shivered with a different awareness, something tied up with the dreams and memory. Memory. None of her memories belonged with him. Nothing of her did. She could bed Kraka and feel naught. She could do the same with this man. She was going to survive, escape him when she could.

Easy.

"Nothing…" *Nothing but emptiness.* Emptiness kept her safe. But the thought was lost in the instant his lips took hers.

His mouth was heat, pure and burning. All touch, all sensation, was focused in the joining of their lips. The metal skin of his chain mail, the padding beneath, blocked out the feel of his body. There was only the awareness of latent power. She should be careful of such power but Elene could not even think of it. She could think of nothing beyond the feel of his mouth.

She thought she had understood. There had only been Kraka, but the lesson had been complete. It had changed who she was in ten terrifying minutes.

The person who existed now could survive anything and turn it to her advantage.

Except this.

A sound escaped her throat, then was quickly lost against the smooth slide of his lips. The fragile sound did not stop him. Rather, it prompted him to deepen the kiss. Because he knew it was not protest, it was craving.

She wanted his touch—it was like being bespelled. She wanted the power of his mouth, the hot subtle line of his lips against hers, moving with such fine skill, such fierce intimacy. Touching *her,* and not some *hór-kona.*

Fear kicked in at the edge of her consciousness. Kraka had only ever had the *hór-kona.* She had made sure of that. After that first time—

She would not think of that. Nothing touched her. Even though she was trapped in the stranger's arms, against the heavy mass of his body and she wanted him… The pressure of his mouth changed. A sharp jab of sensation knifed through the pit of her stomach. Heat. The heat that came from him. Her mouth moved against his. *She* moved, pressing closer, not just her mouth, but her body.

She knew by the faint rough sound in his throat that he felt that small movement. She sensed the urgency behind the kiss more sharply, although it was clear he still held back. His arms were around her, inescapable, intensifying the closeness that the involuntary movement of her body had made. He touched her through the garish material of her dress, seeking the outline of her body, finding every curve and hollow, making her burn as though he touched skin, and her clothes were no barrier at all.

Elene shivered. She must tear herself away from him. She had to because it was more than she could manage, more than she had known. Yet she could not make herself move. It was dark magic. Because she would not share the terrible spell of lust. Never.

She pressed against him, even though she could feel his tenseness. The fear blossomed and her breath caught against the enchantment of his mouth. But the urgency of his touch softened, as though he knew what she felt inside. As though that actually mattered.

His hands soothed, the strength bated. He touched her as though she were something precious and cared for. That was where the terrible power lay—not in his strength, not in some dark bespellment. His power existed because he could make her believe things she had cast away. Things that had cast her away.

Things beyond reaching.

If he could make her believe, she would be lost. She would never survive. The fear inside her head overwhelmed her.

She tried to steady her breathing. She would not let herself draw back. She did not move one single tiny muscle.

He was her living shield from Kraka's men who were so unexpectedly close, who would find her if she fled, who might attack, even here, tomorrow…. After tomorrow, as soon as it was possible, she would move on, escape. There would be chances, whichever way the battle went, and she would make the most of them. She made herself touch the heated skin of his neck, beneath the brilliant richness of his hair, beneath steel.

He pulled away.

She felt the withdrawal of that living sheet of muscle, the stark heat, the terrible strength. Of the warmth. Of the blinding enchantment of his mouth.

She tried to hold on to him. It was useless.

He moved back.

She waited.

"Elene."

She did not look up. "I can get in the bed."

"What?"

"Whatever it was, whatever I did wrong, it was noth—"

Nothing. It means nothing. She hesitated on the edge of the insane, dangerous challenge she had thrown out to him without the slightest conception of what it meant.

"The bed." She looked up, straight at the furious brightness of his eyes, even though he had won. The knowledge between them was like fire. She glanced away. She was not a coward. She had always been able to do what she had to.

She heard him swear. Worse than the Danish equivalent of anything Kraka would say. She heard the heavy tread of his feet. She knew the consequences of anger. Of refusal. She tried for a straight spine. Then she turned her head.

He had moved to the other side of the wooden table. His hands reached to tear off the fantastic helmet, as though it irked him unbearably.

"You may get into the bed if you want to sleep."

"But…"

The helmet came off. She was riveted by a profile of stark lines and shadows that drew the eye. No wonder he had such thoughts, such arrogance, such *dreams*. It was because he was a creature untouchable, beauty matched with strength beyond mortal measure.

He did not crawl through life's endless compromise like the rest of mankind. He must live and breathe in the heights, in some different world. He knew nothing. She despised him. He had not won their appalling challenge at all, because he did not have to live like— He turned around. In the brightness cast by the fire and the setting sun she saw his face.

She stifled the shriek, but it might just as well have been heard in the warm air. She took a step toward him. As though she could do something. As though he had been hurt just now. As though the scars were not old and un-healable. Several winters old. To carry that in silence, to know that such a cut was too deep ever to fade…

"I…" There was nothing she could say.

He looked at her with the forced patience of someone who had seen that reaction a hundred times before.

"You wanted to speak?"

The straight spine and the seeming carelessness that had eluded her before were suddenly there. She shrugged one shoulder.

"I could have helped you remove your helm before."

The fine mouth that had teased magic from hers twisted.

"Aye. That could have saved us both some trouble."

She met that terrible patience head-on. To her satisfaction, her gaze never faltered under his.

"No," she said. "It would not have." She sought for his name. "Berg." Then she added, "Lord."

The marred face might have been a stone wall. The idea of offering sympathy was impossible—even if she could remember how to do so. Instead, she gave the ruined stranger her *hór-kona* smile.

It had no effect, other than to make his eyes narrow in a way that sent quite different shivers over her skin. He had his hand on the door latch.

"Where are you going?"

"To dig a ditch and some ramparts. I have a spare half hour."

The unfinished mess of the fort. The Vikings in the forest.

"You should have told me. I would have brought a shovel."

"Nay, the spear will come in handy, like as not."

She thought of Kraka's brothers hiding in the forest, of all the death and destruction she had seen. She thought of how she had felt when she had determined she would use the spear in her hand.

He went out, with the battle shadows crowding round him.

He left food and the heat of the fire. His payment.

She ate his food and then she stripped down to her ragged shift and got into his bed.

More warmth than she had had in a year. She stared at the thatched roof. Thoughts, unbidden, of his hard body and his finely turned skin skittered through her mind. The ruddy gleam of his hair in the firelight. His hands.

She turned over in the empty width of the bed and closed her eyes. Her senses swam with the exhaustion of her headlong flight from the Danish camp, from days without enough food or proper sleep, from the relentless fear of travelling through the blackness of the forest. From not knowing where she was, or how to escape or whether she would live.

From the vivid disturbing memory of him and his unexpected warmth.

She sat up, opening her eyes. It was late. The warmth and the firelight mocked her. There must be very few hours left until dawn.

Not enough time to build a fort.

She watched the dark. Her own desperate plans twisted like serpents in her head.

They were alike in one respect, she and the East Anglian. Neither of them knew whether they would live beyond the morrow.

CHAPTER 2

OUTSIDE BELONGED TO HELL. Berg, former prince of East Anglia, covert representative of the Wessex king, strode through it, flame and smoke. The myriad fires used to harden the timber stakes split the gathering dark. The activity was one step removed from panic.

A pile of timber collapsed. It was followed by West Saxon swearing. Tempers snapped. Someone hurled a wooden, metal-tipped spade. There was only one valid response. He ditched the armour.

Hours later, when the garrison was so busy the men had neither the time nor the energy left to panic, Berg found the commander in the muted fire glow beside the gate.

"We are lost," said Waerferth. "The Danes will kill us tomorrow."

Sweat stung Berg's eyes, coated his bared chest and

back. Grime and smoke choked his throat and the pores of his skin.

Lost. Berg's gaze fastened on a carved stone tablet stuck on the gate. *Ælfred Rex hanc fecit* it announced to a waiting world in painstaking Latin.

Alfred *Rex,* king of the West Saxons, speaker of Latin and translator of arcane books, held Berg's oath. "We are not lost."

Anno dominicæ incarnationis dccclxxv…

"The Danes will c-come and—" Waerferth had trouble getting the words out. His chest heaved. If an East Anglian ex-prince could dig ditches and pass sharpened stakes through flame, it behooved a man of Kent to attempt to keep up.

Regni sui v, declared the inscription.

Four years of struggle gone. The fifth begun.

"They will not take the fort." *God willing.*

The other man made a strangled noise. Berg thought of the Valkyrie's offer of a shovel. More guts than Waerferth. "Or are you saying you have no courage?" He was not good with patience. "Even a woman could hold you off at spearpoint."

Foolishness. Every sense was on edge with the girl and her disturbing beauty, so deep, intensely female. The effect, with the *hor-cwen*'s clothes, enough to shatter restraint.

The whites of Waerferth's eyes flickered in the torchlight. "She is a Danish—" The man stopped. The stark consciousness cut through Berg's mind that he would not let Waerferth or anyone else touch the woman. Not if it came to bloodshed. He uncurled both hands.

"The woman is English." So she said. *Elene.* She spoke well, like a Mercian from the green lands of the northwest. A captive could be brought a long way. His mind saw the anger that lived in her, in those narrow slanting eyes, as intensely blue as the far horizon at home.

"Does anyone recognise her?"

"No." It was flat. The garrison commander knew everyone within a twenty-mile radius, that was his business. And one thing was certain, no man who had ever seen his Valkyrie would forget her. Shivers crossed his naked skin, the coldness of the night wind, like the wash of memory.

"Tell the men they can stand down." What was done was done. The Kentish garrison needed rest before the morrow. Waerferth sagged. Berg reminded himself that he represented a king, that people had once expended much effort on teaching him diplomacy.

"I am grateful for what you have done, that I can count on you tomorrow. So will King Alfred be when I tell him of your success. The reward will match your courage."

The white-rimmed eyes flickered. Fear, greed and coercion. What more could life hold? Waerferth vanished into the dark.

Berg stayed where he was, the woman in his mind so close he could have touched her.

What more could a man want?

A thousand things. Things beyond reaching.

He was a fool. A fool to think that anything beyond the reach of dust and sweat existed. She had seen that, the woman with the Valkyrie heart and the intriguing name that recalled lost things.

Yet it had not stopped him from wanting her, with a force that had possessed body and mind. So that he could have given in to that terrible desire there and then, just as he was, in armour and with the heated sun streaming in through the open window.

Except she would not have wanted that. For all that he had believed for one blinding moment that she had. But she had known. There could have been nothing different between the woman and himself than the commerce of a captor with a prize. He could not stomach that.

He reached the well that fed the fort and stripped off the rest of his clothes. The water was pure, sprung from somewhere deep beneath the Kentish soil, as vital as the weapons and the unfinished stockade.

The coldness stung skin heated alike from the physical work and thoughts of the girl. She was not a problem he could take on. He would not stay after the fort was se-cured. The other commission called him, the king's true mission, confided in secret, hidden from Waerferth.

Guessed at by the Danes?

He did not know. Just as he knew nothing of the woman who spoke Mercian and Danish and caused havoc with one glance, with the fineness of her face and her body and the coiling richness of her brown, unveiled hair. Who flaunted a dress not intended for the practicalities of trav-elling and painted shoes that had not survived many days in the Andredesweald.

Who she was, who she might be…

Elene.

The thoughts in his head were useless. Everything was

until after the battle tomorrow. Only then could any decision be made.

He straightened up, gathered his clothes, the sword and the chain mail *byrnie* he had left beside the well. He strode back toward the bower and the unknown woman.

Ælfred Rex hanc fecit.

The words carved in stone glittered in the light of the dying fires.

King Alfred made this, in the year of Christ's incarnation 875. The fifth of his reign.

Maybe Alfred's last. Who could know? The only certainty was that the storm that had begun in his own homeland six winters ago and had swept across the length of Britain was gathering again.

No one knew better than he did how kings' reigns ended.

Memory unravelled through time to the torchlit vault at Wimborne Abbey. To the oath that had been given to the newly crowned king of the only land in England that had not fallen to the Vikings.

Beyond that memory lay others. His hand moved to the ridged indentations on the left side of his face.

His oath to the living king was unbreakable, as was the promise he had once made to one now dead.

He walked back to the bower.

"Wake up."

Elene's body stiffened instinctively against the familiar heaviness of the hand on her shoulder. It was the stuff of nightmares. Nightmares that belonged to wakefulness, not sleep.

"Will you wake, woman?"

She registered the fact that the voice was English, deeply resonant, sparking with impatience. Not Kraka.

She turned her head and looked straight into the eyes of the East Anglian. Berg.

She had not meant to sleep, to be caught like this, helpless and befuddled with exhaustion. His hand burned through her flesh. It was night, the blackness split by the glow of the newly stoked fire in the hearth, by lamplight.

"About time. It will be dawn soon."

She moved, narrowing her lids against the fire's brightness that struck across her tired eyes. The bedclothes spilled. She was too proud to catch at them. Nothing changed what she was.

His hand stayed touching her, sliding with her body's movement across the top of her shoulder, beneath the inadequate line of her shift. Her skin tingled, suddenly and wholly and alive. She caught her breath. Her aching eyes widened.

She did not know what showed in her face, but the deep grey eyes flared, the way they had before. She sought for something to say, anything that would shatter the sudden overpowering tension in the small bower.

The tension between *them*.

"Get up. I have not much time." His hands hauled her into a sitting position.

"What—"

He let her go. She stared. He had his back to her. Light glowed off glittering skin like a dragon's scales, off steel incised with gold.

"The Vikings…" Her voice stopped. She stared at the width of his back, the fierce power in his movements. The impatience. Controlled. For now. But she knew Kraka's temper before battle. After it.

The East Anglian found whatever it was he was looking for.

"You might want this."

Her whore's dress sailed through the air over his shoulder.

She caught the dress, staring at it as though she had never seen it before.

"Put it on. Unless you want to go out in your undershirt."

"Out?"

She pulled on the dress before he could turn back round, before that fierce, heavy-lidded gaze could touch her.

"You mean the Danes are here?" Thin shards of panic stabbed through her chest, the hateful fear bred over months.

"They will be if you keep dithering. Are you set then?" He turned round just as she finished tying the last of the laces at the gaping neckline of the tunic. The force of his gaze was like something physical. Her hands shook.

He saw it. There was the kind of pause that lasted an age of time.

"Come. They are not here yet." The fierce impatience was gone from his voice. From his eyes. Not gone, controlled. He held out his hand.

She stared at it in disbelief.

He knew she was afraid, and this was what he chose to do, hold out one hand like a friend. Her stomach lurched.

"Come on."

The impatience that sparked from him like fire crept back. But he did not grab at her, just held his hand straight, as though she would want to take it.

He thought she was afraid of the Vikings. She was. But the other fears, the nameless ones that lived in the hidden recesses of her mind, stirred out of their place in the dark.

He believed she would take his hand.

She stared at his stupid, great ham fist. She could not take it.

His patience snapped. She could almost hear the control break. He caught her, shoving her through the door, his strength ruthless, efficient, the kind she was used to. They crossed a yard full of the sort of activity that covered terror. The cold predawn air struck the life and the warmth out of her skin. Out of her heart.

They crossed the endless space enclosed by the incomplete barrier of wooden stakes driven into the ground, smoke-grey, their tips sharpened to lethal points.

"Where are you taking me?"

"The stables."

Stables was an exaggeration. The area for the horses was as unfinished as the rest of the fort. They stopped. The darkness closed round them. She could scarcely see where he was, only the pale blur of flesh beneath the shadowed fantastical helm, small flashes of brightness from the moving sheet of metal links that covered his body.

But she could feel him. Not just from the press of his hands on her arms but from the intense awareness of him, heightened by the dark, by the sense of isolation that held the two of them apart from the scurrying activity on the other side of the yard.

Her breath came fast and her limbs trembled. He would sense that, as he sensed everything about her. He would know. He did not move. Just held her. His huge bulk cut out the traces of light, the sounds of people.

"Elene."

Courage. She tried to control her breath; to summon up every last ounce of the bitter strength life had taught her. He was so close.

"Berg! Lord!" Another voice, footsteps, hurrying, coming toward them. She released her breath.

"I will be there. Wait!" The command cut through the dark.

"Come here."

He dragged her farther through the shadows. When they stopped, he finally let her go, but it could not matter. There was nowhere to run.

He turned away, made some soft sound on the restless air. A dark shape materialised at his shoulder.

"What…?"

"You seem to have trouble finishing questions. This is the best horse I have apart from my own war stallion. Do not try taking mine because someone would kill you for it. Or the horse might kill you. He has bad manners. This one, however, does not."

"I—"

"Fortunately the horse does not look much, but it is hard to equal for speed and endurance. There is enough food in the saddlebags for several days if you are careful.

The purse here—" her palm was filled with soft leather over the intimately familiar jingle of coins "—holds enough to keep you and not enough to make you too great a target. With that, you can get to Canterbury."

"*Canterbury?*" To her it meant only one thing. The royal mint. The sheets of silver hammered out to an even thickness and stamped with the king's image. With the name of the moneyer. Coins. Her head spun.

"Aye, unlike here, the fortifications at Canterbury are finished. It helps."

"I suppose it does." The dizziness increased. "I really should have brought you that shovel."

He was nothing but shadows and small glitters of light. She watched the pale shape of his hand slide across the neck of the well-mannered horse.

"Nay. I told you. The spear will do for me."

She caught the faint gleam of his teeth, which meant that he smiled, even as the Vikings massed under the blackness of the forest. He knew the odds were that he would die. Kraka's volatile temper would have been in fits by now. She had forgotten people could meet horrors with that kind of understated courage.

Her gaze locked on his smile.

"Think you are good with a spear, then, do you?"

His hand stilled and he looked up. She could sense the hidden intensity in him that was needed before battle, the ruthless inward focus. But his smile only broadened.

"Aye."

She heard the deep sound of his laughter. The richness of it made the intimate dark close round them. So intimate it reached the hidden places inside her, the places locked against the world. Body and mind filled with the awareness of him and his vitality, with the controlled strength of him.

She straightened the neckline of her whore's dress.

"Let us hope you are as good as you say."

"We will soon see."

"Aye."

But it will be you who will see. I shall be gone, with this prince's gift. And not to Canterbury. I will never go there again.

The East Anglian looked at her as though he could read the thoughts in her head.

"Why would you make me such a gift?" Her reckless question shimmered in the air.

The movement of his massive shoulders brought shadows over silver light.

"The battle will go as God wills. I cannot see how that will be."

As God wills. It had been more than a year since she had heard such words. An eternity.

"I did not think you wished to go back to the Vikings."

"You think that will happen."

"Not necessarily. But if the dragon standard goes down and stays down, you will know." There was the sudden flash of polished steel as he thrust the leather reins into her hands. "If you see that happen, do not linger."

The nondescript horse that could not be matched for speed and endurance nuzzled absently at her shoulder.

The means to escape. Now…

"I have to go," he said.

"Are you so keen to fight your ill-matched battle?"

"I have never fought much else."

"And does that not stop you?"

"There are many things on which to base a decision."

She caught the glittering movement of the fine helm as he glanced at the sky. She saw what he saw. The night faded already. Day.

"Time to hand out the spears."

"I suppose it is." There seemed nothing else for her to say. Nothing that could encompass the measure of life and the prospect of death for two strangers. He turned away. Not another word. And she would never see him again.

"Wait!" She sounded like him yelling at churls. He would never stop for that. "Berg!" She did not want to shout out his name. He had no existence for her, just a shadow that came and went.

"Berg…" It was not a real name. He must be called that for his size. It meant mountain. Or protection.

He stopped.

She had no idea what she wanted to say, why she wanted to say anything. Why it should feel like loss all over again.

"*Wæs hal.*"

He stayed, pausing between shadow and light, an image of strength finely balanced and whole. Headed for carnage. The tension between them strung out so that she wished she could shatter it.

Or that she could touch him with the elemental simplicity he had offered before. But her hands were balled like fists.

Stay safe, she had said.

Nothing changed in his face. He walked back into the
unfinished fort, until the darkness swallowed him.

She was left alone. With the means of escape in her hands.

"Bʀɪʟʟɪᴀɴᴛ, ɪꜱɴ'ᴛ ɪᴛ?"

"What?" Elene's hands were trembling and sweat
pricked her skin despite the cool breeze. The wind
brought the sound of the screaming.

"The battle."

She could not at first work out where the piping voice
came from. Then she saw it. A small boy clinging like
some dreadful insect to the mound of earth she was using
for concealment. One more day and the mound would
have been a rampart.

Too late now.

Her hand closed round the rough wooden stakes that
made up half a wall. There was a stone tablet with an inscription. *Ælfred Rex hanc fecit. Anno dominicæ incarnationis dccclxxv. Regni sui v.* Her mind translated it without
thinking.

Some skills never faded.

Years of practice. Useless practice.

"Look. They are making the Vikings run now. See how
the king's men charge out from the fort?"

"Aye." The battle did not rage round the closed gate she
had gradually crept back to, but round the weak points at
the other side, the gaps in the walls.

"First they loose the arrows," piped the insect, "then the
spears, and then it is close quarters. Axes. Swords. What
about that?"

"What about it," she muttered, transferring both damp palms to the horse's reins.

"Tactics." A small chest swelled under a covering of grubby brown. "I know how it is done. Whoosh!" he added. "Chop. And then anyone who still has a thrusting spear can use it when the enemy is fighting someone else and his shield shows a gap." Twig-like arms demonstrated stabbing motions in case she had not understood. "See?"

"Brilliant." Someone should have trodden on him when he was smaller.

"Look at that!" He swarmed higher up the mound in a tangle of elbows and sharp knees.

"Not at the moment."

She stared at the inscription.

What was she doing here? The road to the west lay below her. She could get to it if she tried. If—

"*Girls,*" said the boy in disgust. He craned forward.

Perhaps he would get his head taken off with a tactical spear.

"Will you keep your head down? Do you not have parents who will be looking for you?"

"No." Suddenly the irritating cockiness was gone.

"I do not need any parents," he continued. "I am eight winters old already."

He did not look so old. He was undersized and scraggly. Did no one feed him?

"Oh, look at that!" He made whooshing noises. Swordplay, doubtless.

No parents.

She closed her eyes. She had to go. Not too far down

the western road. Not as far as Winchester. Because that was where her own parents had found refuge from the disaster of Viking-held Mercia. Mayhap. That was what they had planned. Or perhaps they had changed their minds and risked Canterbury and their far-flung kindred after all. Canterbury had to be safe if the East Anglian had sent her there—high walls, a cathedral, doubtless a working mint.

Nay. They had said Winchester. That was where they would have gone.

Her hands tightened on the reins. She pictured her parents' faces if they ever saw her again. In her mind, her mother always wept for gladness.

But it would never happen. They could never welcome her back now. Not after— She banished the thought.

No one thought too deeply in these times.

What mattered was that her parents were safe. She had made sure of that. She had survived what had followed and now escape was within her grasp.

She had everything she needed. She had gone through the saddlebags one by one. He had even left her a *seax*. The leather-sheathed blade hung from her belt. She put her foot in the stirrup.

"Mercy!"

"What?"

"The big one. The one with the fine armour. He—"

"*What?*" She pushed away, leaving the horse, swarming up the mound of dirt like the boy. Rubble spilled out under her feet and her hands, cascading downward, its roughness unfelt.

The boy swore with self-conscious ostentation. "Did you see what he did? Everyone said the king's men could not win. That was why not many dared to join them. But did you see what he did?"

She could see precisely what Berg had done. She could also see that in the first vital moments, the other one called Waerferth had not had the guts to follow him, and now that he tried, it was too late.

The insect-child swore again, this time out of fright.

"They are being driven back! They will lose after all. See? The standard is down. The Vikings will take it."

She stood up.

If the dragon standard goes down and stays down, you will know…do not linger.

From her vantage point, she could see everything. The whole course of the battle set out like moving pieces on a board game. But it would not look like a game down there. Hand-to-hand combat. Whoosh. Chop.

The child scrabbled backward, flicking earth and small stones.

Behind her was the horse and the road that led west. Empty in both journey and destination. Empty beyond redeeming.

All she had. All she would ever have.

It was nothing to her if people could not build forts in good time. Or if the ruler of Wessex was the kind of person who would put a Latin inscription in a place surrounded by Vikings.

Above all, a man who would furnish a complete stranger with the means to escape meant nothing.

"Wait!" screamed the insect child. "Where are you going?"

She slithered down the useless rampart in a scatter of dust and stones.

CHAPTER 3

IT WAS STILL POSSIBLE to survive.

If Waerferth could keep his men together. Berg tried to slow his breathing.

The initial advantage of penetrating the Viking lines was lost. But if the shield fort behind him kept its formation, they would survive.

But if the densely packed ranks thinned out, the Danes would pick them off. One by one.

He started yelling.

He thought that some, at least, of Waerferth's half-trained men understood. He would not have taken bets. Reactions in this kind of fighting were instinctive. Training might have helped.

If he had had time.

They would paint that on his grave.

Some clever bastard managed to lodge another axe in

the leather-covered wood of his shield. The weight of the three-foot circle of lime wood plugged with axe blades, the awkwardness, was beyond managing. Even for him.

There was no time to free it of weapons. No time too for halfheartedness like Waerferth's. He could see a figure in chain mail, helmeted, wearing looted gold. He threw the shield.

It took the legs out from whoever was wearing the *byrnie*. The man collapsed, yelling.

He hurled the spear at full strength. No time to see whether it hit because by that stage he was doing some yelling of his own. The advantage was there. Again. If this time they could take it.

Waerferth's men came through. The confusion in the Viking ranks was real. The mail-clad man, then, had been one of the leaders.

Berg bellowed encouragement at Waerferth and the rest of the line charged, but he could not follow. If the mail-clad Viking had been a target, so was he. He was caught as the Kentish forces pressed forward, passing him. He was cut off, isolated by the disciplined attack of what must be the remnant of someone's highly trained bodyguard. It was impossible to move, even to keep his feet.

He lunged, the sword fast in his hand, connecting, but there were too many round him. Something hit him and he pitched forward, rolling, tangling with the golden banner spread through the dust.

At least the woman would be gone, even if she had stayed this long. She would be somewhere on the road east. She would not witness the aftermath of this.

The axe aimed at his neck grazed the carved metal helmet even as he twisted. Fire-hardened steel, or the charms inscribed on it, turned the blow.

He thought some of his own men, scattered down the line to stiffen the garrison, would try to get to him. They would be better to stay where they were. There was no way out of this.

He struck back by instinct, but he knew he must be dead. The last thing he saw was the Valkyrie's face, white and wide-eyed, its delicate beauty unreal.

She had a spear.

"YOU STUPID WOMAN. You will get yourself killed."

Well, that was gratitude for you. Elene swallowed the urge to be sick. The spear point had missed. But it had certainly made her target move.

She shut her eyes as Berg the ungrateful scrambled to his great heavy feet and launched himself at the axe wielder. There was a kind of sickening thud.

She did not look. She got the point of her spear out of the ground. It swung wide in her unpractised grip.

By good fortune, the butt end hit someone Danish who folded up with a grunt. The impact jarred the ashwood shaft out of her fingers. But it did not matter. Berg had hold of her. And there were other people. English. Closing round them. Someone caught the banner, raised it.

Berg's grip tightened. Judging by the amount of noise he was making, he was hale and very much alive. She winced. Because of the unnecessary force of his grip and because he was bellowing down her ear. Something about moving. Fast.

The physical instinct to flee flared up inside her, an urge to survive beyond the mind's reach. Yet beside it was a determination that was equally primitive.

"Nay. I will not."

Her muscles stiffened against his hold. It was as though all the sum of her life had come together here. Beginning and ending. Like a circle.

"Let me go." She managed to get her hand round the hilt of the *seax* he had given her.

"Why? So you can die?"

Yes. The word was only in her head but he might as well have read it. She saw the fury in his grey eyes.

"Let me go." She did not know why it should matter to him what a whore did. But she knew he would stop her. It was as though they only had to look at each other's eyes, no words needed.

She lunged for freedom. But his grip on her was far too secure. He swatted her hand away from the knife hilt.

"Do not—"

There were severe limits to his patience. He picked her up, the way he had before. His arm under her ribs choking breath, metal links digging into her.

Her own fury ignited, born out of fear and despair and the images of hell unfolding round them.

"Wistan!" His yell assaulted her ears, reverberated against her body. Someone answered.

"Take her back to the fort. Make sure she stays there. Tie her down if necessary."

"I will not—"

"What is *that?*"

She stared, cradled in his arms.

It looked like a squatting frog. It was examining the dead axeman. Her stomach heaved. Even as she watched, a sticklike finger poked the body.

Dreadful boy.

Berg took a step. His fury burned. She could feel its frightening deepness.

"Leave him. He is only a child."

The boy's head whipped round. She made an urgent gesture at him and he fled, quick and uncatchable.

"Take her."

IT WAS DARK when he got back.

Elene had expected him much sooner. He had won. She had known that much for hours. Whatever was left of the Viking war band would have fled into the vastness of the Andredesweald.

It had not been necessary to tie her down. She knew when her chances were gone.

When she had thrown them away.

They had not treated her badly. Wistan had brought her food and had stared at her as though she were likely to produce some further weapon out of thin air and behead him with it. He was very young.

She had not bothered with the food. She had been too tired and her mind was too full. Spinning out of control.

The door shut against cold air. She lay in the bed and watched the East Anglian strip his clothes off.

It was such a familiar routine, seeing a man come back from fighting. She watched him set the sword belt aside with its fine buckle fashioned in the shape of a gilded wolf, slide the corselet over his head. Firelight rippled over the subtle weaving of the battle net, as though it were something living. Dragon's skin.

He shook it out and the thousands of riveted links sang. She watched him thread it over the crossed poles that kept it straight.

He started to take off the padded shirt underneath. Her attention sharpened, noting each movement with long-practised closeness for what it could tell her. There was always bruising, sometimes wounds large or small.

All she could see in him was the overwhelming strength that made everything seem effortless. Her hands tightened on the bedcovers. In the darkness.

He turned to the firelight. Oblivious. She might as well not have been in the room for all the notice he had taken of the shadowed corner where she waited.

He moved, intent only on what he was doing. So sure in his strength. Invincible.

Yet he had nearly died on the battlefield.

He discarded the padded shirt, the linen undershirt. Gilded light glowed on shadowed skin, on thick muscle over heavy bones. The terrible awareness of him tightened inside her. She fought it down; he was nothing. What had happened today on the battlefield had happened because of her own madness.

He reached for the water. The pitcher nearly slipped out

of his hand. She realised what the strength had blinded her to. He was unutterably weary.

She watched as the weariness was pushed aside.

He poured from the jug, plunging his hands, his face, into the bowl of clear water, the heavy mass of his hair. He came up, gasping. The water cascaded like liquid fire down his skin.

Small tendrils of sharp feeling uncoiled inside her. Incomprehensible. She had seen Kraka a hundred times. With the cold shield of indifference over contempt. With loathing. She turned away, biting her lips lest she make some betraying sound.

She heard the thud of his boots tossed on the floor, the rustle of clothing. She would not look at him. She stayed, staring at the dark, back in her own world of nothing. All feeling, all thought blanked out, unable to touch her.

She could hear his every movement. The bright fall of the water, the small splashes as it touched his skin, the hiss of the rushes beneath his bare feet.

She closed her mind against his nakedness. Yet her mind filled out the pictures the sounds made for her. Filled them with the glowing skin she had glimpsed when he had taken off his shirt, with the solid turn of muscle. Her breath tightened, despite all she could do.

He was quick, ruthlessly so. Yet she heard the sharp clash of the earthenware pitcher against the bowl, as though his weariness had betrayed control again, the muffled curse bitten off. The sudden silence.

She waited for a burst of temper that never came.

Elene turned her head. The breath stopped in her throat. She had not pictured that. She was used to Kraka, to his size and his heavy power. But Kraka had been nothing like this. She closed her mind on beauty; it did not exist.

It was like watching a flame. No damaged face because he was turned half-away from her. His body was straight. A single sweeping line of raw strength from broad shoulder to solid torso, from tight hip to flaring thigh. Fire and shadow. Perfection.

She used to dream about that. About a perfect man. About—she had not dreamed about *him* since he had abandoned her.

She had tried to block him out of her mind and there was no reason to think of him now. Or to think of this man, Berg. The sight of him in the half dark could not make her heart tighten with longing and her skin flood with terrifying warmth. With *wanting*.

He turned. The fire's glow caught everything, not just the fierce power and the rough-edged beauty, but the damaged face, the sheer exhaustion.

The intensity of the feeling inside her was more than she wanted. More than she could ever let herself feel. Her hands clenched. She thought he would see her, lying there in the dark, spying on him like a maid on her wedding night.

Her body went rigid, holding utterly still in the silence, every muscle stiffened with resistance. But all the time, the shivers raced across her skin. She held her breath. She thought his gaze touched her, lingered. The response inside her was instant, out of her control, bitter as pain.

But he had not noticed her. He turned away. The great hand picked up the cloth, weariness gone. Imagined.

Not imagined. Elene watched the awkwardness of his movement, the terrible effort that was not right for someone so strong. For someone perfect.

For someone with his ruined face.

The horrors of the battle stung at her mind.

She wanted to take the cloth out of his hand.

She had performed such tasks for Kraka. Not out of a desire to help, but for survival.

She watched the sharp play of muscle, the tight flesh. Power. Danger. Shrouded now by the weariness.

She did not want to help him.

She lay still in the darkness of his bed. The whiteness of the cloth blurred before her aching eyes as he rubbed it across the living gold of his flesh, soaking up the fire-red beads of moisture, the glittering path of the water across his burnished skin.

The wad of linen unravelled under the clumsiness of his great fist. He caught it, dragging the cloth across the broad plane of his chest with his natural impatience. She would not have been so rough. She would…

She stopped, at the edge of her own imaginings, at the impossible thought of performing such a task because she wanted to. For choice. For…pleasure.

The dizzying thought unrolled inside her head, with the bright power of something new, overwhelming, strong as though she acted on the thought now. As though she touched him. As though it was her hand that felt the rough dampness of the cloth, the smooth heat of his skin, the intimate richness of its strength.

Elene imagined touching him, tracing the solid contours of that living shape, the stark planes and the shadowed hollows, each thickened separate muscle. He seemed not blatant like Kraka, but infinitely mysterious, as though the differences between men and women could hold some secret pleasuring, some undiscovered meaning she had no knowledge of.

It was impossible for men to give pleasure. But even as that truth formed in her head, the memory of his mouth on hers seared through her. The fierce heat, the terrifying anticipation in mind and aching body. The bright feelings. All the things she felt now.

His hand moved lower, across the taut line of hips and belly, shadowed darkness… She turned, so abruptly there was no hiding it. He must have heard her, must have realised she was awake. She lay still, facing the wall, letting the blackness blind sight, thought, sensation, everything. The blankness obliterated past and future, just the way it always did.

But this time, the blankness would not come. She could still hear him move. Nothing would stifle her awareness of him.

Thoughts crowded her mind. Of him. Of his fine body and his scarred face. Of his urgency and his courage in the dawn light. Of the gift he had made that would have let her escape. Of the battle, the horror of it. Of the fact that for one instant he had been able to read her mind.

She heard the firm quietness of his tread.

She had thrown away the chance to escape.

The straw mattress gave under his weight. The chance had been thrown away because of him. Because she had seen him charging into the horror of that battle like a silver flame, with only death ahead.

Elene stared at the wall. She had given away the chance because of herself. She shut her eyes.

Perhaps he would think she was asleep after all. He had not made the slightest move in her direction, had not uttered a word since he had come back into the bower. She had seen his weariness; it was impossible that he was not injured in some way.

Sometimes Kraka had just slept, despite everything. She kept very still.

It was as though he did not know she was there.

He touched her.

The pathetic thoughts in her head were exposed for the lies they were. She had known all the time that the awareness between them was double-edged. Like a sword. She had known it long before his mouth had covered hers. It was as though she had known it before she had met him.

She sought the comfort of the dark. But the thoughts crowded harder. Thoughts of life and death. Thoughts of him. Only him. Her breath caught. She could feel his warmth. There in the darkness. Unmoving. Her mind played through all the things he had made her feel.

She kept her eyes closed, willing the blankness that had been her protection, like a warrior's shield. If only he did not speak, she would be able to stand it.

"Elene."

Her breath choked, making a small rasping sound like a desperate animal's.

"Come here."

She would not. She lay silent, her whole body rigid, curled up and away from him. He moved. She heard the rustle of the bedclothes, sensed the sheer solid weight of him. The warmth.

It enfolded her. It tingled down her spine, across her skin beneath the thinness of her shift, down the backs of her legs, her feet. She fought to control her breath, but it came out ragged and shallow and uneven.

His weight against her body was as solid as the wall in front of her face. As inescapable.

Living. She could sense his breath, in the press of his solid chest against her back, in the faint sharp sound on the edge of hearing. His breath came as hard as her own, as if the control that was so far beyond her power this night escaped him, too.

When she made some small movement, turning against the barrier of his chest, arm hard against his ribs, she heard the breath sharpen on pain, stop, then resume again in the uneven rhythm of hers.

She thought of all the blows that hard-linked steel could turn aside but not wholly stop the impact of. She thought of the battle and all she had seen in those few brief moments. She thought of the man with the axe.

She had faced death before, but she had not truly understood what must have happened inside Kraka's head when it had come to fighting. Now she'd had her own glimpse of battle. Except that Kraka had craved those horrors, despite the payment they demanded.

She did not. She wondered what Berg the East Anglian thought. Whether the same pictures of horror played through his head. Or whether he craved such things, like Kraka.

She wanted to pull away from him, but she could not. He was alive.

She felt the warmth of his body at her back. The shivers racked her flesh. She had run into the battle like a madwoman. In part for this stranger who held her in his arms in silence and stillness, despite the heat in his blood that she had tasted. Despite everything.

She had run into the battle because of him. Because of a few useless words in Latin. Because she had wanted death and it had not been there, and now it was too late.

Her body stirred restlessly, despite her will. Her naked feet tangled with the man who shared the bed with her, the rumpled shift twisted, the thin linen dragged tight, scarcely covering her, digging into her flesh.

She felt his hand move to free it. Her breathing choked in the sudden dryness of her throat. His strong fingers touched bared flesh, her thigh, the twisted line of the hem. She could not breathe at all now. His hand brushed skin, tugged at patched linen so thin it would tear. She bit her lip. His fingers caught against the small piece of metal she had sewn into the hem.

The movement of his hand stopped.

It was nothing, the tiny fragment of pressed metal that

he touched, a token of no value. Just half of a thin silver coin, commonplace despite its careful craftsmanship.

Nothing.

She remained still. The air in the warm room became thin, as though someone had stretched it out beyond bearing. His heavy fingers stopped moving, and he simply held the small metal token. He could not know what it was.

A broken penny. The only sign that remained of another life, one that was no longer hers.

She moved. She tried to stop the tightening of tensed muscles, but she could not. Behind her she heard the sharp intake of breath, as though she had hurt him again, touched some unseen wound from the battle.

She felt his hand draw away, dropping the token, releasing her shift.

His breathing slowed. The moment passed. It was nothing. Nothing…

Except his warmth was still there, inescapable as his touch. Silent. She lay in the stranger's arms. There was such stillness. It was like a dream and yet his strength and his power, the heavy warmth of his flesh, told her that it was real. That she was alive. They both were.

She lay and let his warmth flow through her skin. There seemed no barrier between them.

She knew that from the moment the night-dark gave way to day, the future would be there, the harshness and the danger and the lack of hope. She could not cut it off. She would have to face it. Just as he would.

It was impossible for either of them to go back.

CHAPTER 4

"WILL YOU WAKE UP!"

Berg had a wonderful manner with mornings. Elene wondered whether anyone had ever told him that.

She opened her eyes. There was something wrong with the sun outside the bower. The light through the open window was rich, like molten honey. Warm and enveloping like…

It was past noon. He was sitting on the bed. Her face was less than a hand's span away from his thigh. She stared.

"Good morning." She could not think of anything else to say. The thigh moved. It was encased in fine dark trousers that did nothing to disguise its shape. She tried not to remember its weight, its warmth. How it had felt touching her.

"Good it might be," observed Berg, "but as for morning…"

She watched a sun-gilded knee. The upper part of his thigh disappeared beneath the edge of a dark blue tunic. There was a lot of complex braid. She tried to raise her head, but it seemed stuck to the pillow like a lead weight.

"You could outsleep Morpheus. Has anyone ever told you that?"

My Viking captor. Did you not know? Except he would not have known who Morpheus was.

She forced her gaze upward over the deep blue tunic. It was of thin linen, not wool, because of the heat. Open at the neck. She could see the shadowed hollow of his throat, firm bronze skin below, the hint of dark gold body hair.

She had slept with him. That was what she had done. She had lain with him last night. All the heavy golden muscle that the clothing hid had touched her. She had done nothing to pull away from him. She had shared the warmth of his body until she slept. She could feel the heat rising in her face as though she were not a Viking's whore but some greensick bride.

Looking at him in the daylight made that sharing seem horribly intimate, far more so than a few straining minutes of appalling nothingness with Kraka. She blinked against the sun streaming into the bower.

"It is afternoon." *Scintillating. I could outtalk Cicero.*

He shifted on the bed. More of the thigh became visible, and she spied a gold arm ring, its brightness flashing past her eyes. She really had to get her head off the bolster, to preserve even the smallest illusion of control while lingering in a strange man's bed in the afternoon.

The precisely crafted leg shifted again, the whole of the powerful body. He spoke.

"What you did yesterday—"

"Yes. I know. I am sorry about losing the horse." The words rattled out of her. "I realise how valuable it was." She sat up; she probably looked pathetic. Her tattered shift hung off her body, showing heaven knew what. Her hair straggled in elf locks over her eyes so that she could hardly see through it. She thought she was shaking. Control.

"I am sorry for the loss."

She tried to keep her expression calm, whatever he could see of it. Perhaps it was futile to try and hide the despair resulting from twelve months of terrors endured, the kind of terrors that had made her seek death.

She watched his eyes, deep and beyond her reading, filled with the kind of determination that broke through Viking shield walls.

If only he would not ask about the battle.

"Aye. It seems there was a bit of a problem about the horse. But that was not—"

"About the horse, I—"

"I am not concerned about the horse."

She caught the full intensity of his eyes. She would not be able to bear anything he said about yesterday, about her crazed actions. She did not know, when he had not actually harmed her yet, why he was so much more danger-ous to her than Kraka.

She smiled. Confidence. "I did not intend to lose the horse and the provisions."

"Intentions are one thing. Life is another."

Her heart stopped. The words, the bright depths of his eyes, could have laid her own life bare. She had gone with Kraka through her own decision, because she would make no other choice. Her intention had held honour, which she had believed could sustain her.

She had believed all sorts of things. Once.

She looked away.

He stirred beside her. She could sense his power, closer. Shadow and light. She tensed, but she did not move—not one inch. The bright sun caught hard gold, warm flesh. She knew what would happen the instant before he touched her.

She made herself wait in the rough mess of the bed-covers tangled from her sleep, from his. She sensed the strong heat of him against bared skin. She felt utterly, intensely aware of her half-naked state. Her body stayed rigid.

But he did nothing else. Just let the heat of his hand rest against the subtler warmth of her flesh.

Like something shared.

She could not believe that.

She turned. The bedcovers slipped farther, revealing more of her bare arms and the shift that hid nothing. She refused to scrabble after them. She just stared at his hand touching her skin and let him see her gaze. Then she gave him the smile that shut out everything.

"So will you take your revenge on the horse thief?"

"Maybe."

"What will you do?"

The great shoulders rippled. She could feel his strength through his arm, through the hand on her shoulder.

"Hanging sprang to mind."

Her gaze moved to his scarred face. His eyes had flecks of darker grey in their depths. She had seen such eyes before. Somewhere. Her thoughts spiralled back, beyond her control, far back to childhood, summer and an endless sky. Freedom.

Madness.

She stared at the warrior's face, the stark lines and the ugliness of the old wounds, blank, intimidating, full of the same strength that was in his body. Brute strength. A fool would say there was nothing more. Nothing more—

She shook her head.

"You will not do it."

"Is that what you think?"

"Yes."

She thought something changed in the blankness, so fast she could not read it.

"Then let us hope the real thief is not so sure."

"The *real* thief?"

"We caught him. I have the horse and…most of what was in the saddlebags."

The surge and release of her breath swelled her flesh against the tight barrier of his hand.

"Then…"

"The thief is waiting for my sentence while contemplating his sins." There was a pause. "It could take some time. He had the look of someone who could pack a considerable amount into eight winters."

"The *boy?*"

"The hell-fiend. Where did you find such a creature?"

"I did not. He found me. He was watching the battle. He must have followed me onto the field and then fled. He is just a child." She half twisted toward him, the uncontrolled movement bringing her into shocking contact with the supple line of chest and thigh, the bright trap of his gaze. "He has nothing, no parents…" Her breath caught and her heart slammed against her ribs so that she wanted to draw back. She forced utter stillness.

"Nothing?"

She stared into his eyes, felt the heated trap of his body. "Is that why a person would end up on a battlefield?"

Her mouth went dry.

"Mayhap," said her voice, while all the time the truth screamed through her head. She was accustomed to emptiness; she could bear it. She had even created it, and it had helped her survive her world with Kraka.

What Elene had not been able to bear was what this man had brought: thoughts of other things, things that were dead for her and should stay so.

He did not understand. He was destructive, lethal. Not just because he could not understand, but because of what he thought, what he was.

She had to leave him. She should never have come back. Panic flicked at her. She fought it down.

"Yesterday was a mistake. Sometimes people can lose their heads, do something witless."

The grey-flecked gaze stayed on hers.

"It is over." She realised he would want some kind of assurance that he did not have a dangerous madwoman on his hands. "The mistake will not repeat itself."

There was silence. She looked away. But she could still feel his closeness surrounding her. He would not let it go. There was nothing else she could explain, but he would keep on in his ignorance until he had destroyed everything.

He stood up. She watched him stride across the room, heavy feet, hulking strength.

"What will you do?"

"Go to the victory feast, make a speech about the invincible power of the new fort. Get drunk."

His matter of fact words jolted her mind free from her spiralling thoughts.

"I may even pretend not to notice that there are several score more men at the feast than actually fought the battle."

"You do not mind that?" She did not have the slightest interest, but she would take any path that led off dangerous ground.

"It is a big fortress. It requires enough men to make up the garrison. Every pole of measured length requires four soldiers to man it. A distance of a furlong needs a hundred and sixty men. Try working it out. The fort needs people, and what the people need is to have faith in its purpose." He picked up a jewelled sword belt. "Besides, I have been trained in diplomacy."

"You?" The word spun out before she could stop it, her head reeling from the sudden reprieve.

"Aye." He looked up. The grey eyes were like light across windswept water.

"Well." Her voice was a thread, her hands fisted in the bedclothes.

He shrugged. "I cannot blame those who were afraid to fight. You do not know what has happened in Kent, all the raiding."

He pulled the belt tight, broad hands fastening the buckle at the taut line of solid hip bone.

"Or mayhap you do."

Looking away did not block out the sound of his voice, or the thoughts in her head.

"If they do not want Kent to go the way of occupied Mercia and East Anglia and all the lands north, they had better defend this fort," Elene said, the words spilling out. "If they do not, the Vikings will be masters of everything and everyone this side of the Andredesweald. The shadow of the forest will make this region inaccessible from Alfred's power base in the west. The east will be lost to Wessex. It is a strategy—"

She stopped speaking. She stared at the wall. What had she said? She sounded like someone from a Viking war council. She sounded like someone who had heard a Danish leader talking. Kraka the carrion crow. She did not want to admit as much to an Englishman who had just fought a battle. It was dangerous.

Berg the East Anglian did not need her advice on warfare.

She kept her gaze on the rough wattle wall.

"The fortress will survive now." His words were flat, utterly without compromise. "What people wanted was hope. They are desperate for that. Yet when they get it, they do not know what to do."

She fisted her hands. "And you would show them where their hope lies?"

There was no answer, only the scrape of the sword and the heavy sound of his feet.

"Or do you not know yourself?" She turned her head, the bitterness stronger than gall.

"I am not West Saxon."

It was not an answer at all. He had taken something in his hand, something huge that gleamed in the shadows. Wreaths of gold unfurled under his grasp, embroidered scales in sinuous lengths, white teeth, eyes that glowed like fire.

He gathered it up carefully, wrapping the embroidered face of the cloth inward, so that the flame-snake was hidden.

The storm king's standard, which had so recently presided over blood and despair. She wondered that the power of it had not burned the bower to the ground in the night.

Alfred, King of the West Saxons, who wrote inscriptions in Latin.

He took his burden away, grey linen, anonymous. He paused in the doorway.

"And afterward?" she said to his broad back and his jewelled belt and his arms full of magic. "After the feast?"

"We are going west."

West.

Then the door was shut and she was left to contemplate the meaning of the word *we*.

One thing was clear: she would not stay to find out.

SUPPOSE IT WAS TRUE?

Edmund, atheling and prince of the royal house of East Anglia, otherwise known as Berg, lay stretched full length on the ground. The hard contours dug against his shoulders, found every aching bruise from yesterday. But he could not go back into the hall.

It was impossible to get drunk when you wanted to.

The brightness of the stars was like something that could be touched. Even though the hills and the black bulk of the forest cut off the width of the sky. His mind saw the vastness of the flatlands at home and the limitless horizon.

He could not think of that. Home did not exist. Neither did...

If it was true.

He shut his eyes. It was not the pain of bruised muscles he felt.

Even as the hard ground dug into his flesh, disjointed images crossed his mind, past, present and future, until the face of the captive woman took shape. It filled his inner vision, vital and full of passion, yet cut off from him by a deliberate remoteness. The image was wholly and intensely beautiful, taunting.

I am what you think me...a Danish hór-kona.

He could feel her touch, body heat, see her face as it had turned to him this morning in his bed, the narrow eyes heavy-lidded, the skin flushed with heat.

They had shared touching. She had lain in his bed, her body spilling out of its flimsy clothes. A Valkyrie. She had stared straight through him. He still saw her smile.

The sounds of rejoicing floated to him through the summer night. The air was mild. His skin was heated from the drinking that could not bring the relief he craved from the force of his thoughts. Yet inside he was chilled, frozen like the corpses that still littered the field below. He would never get used to that, no matter how many times he saw it. He thought of those who had died. On this field and on countless others, across the breadth of Britain. Of those who still lived, and those who had wished for death. Perhaps.

He thought of the Viking called Kraka who was Earl Guthrum's man, and before that had served King Ivar. Mayhap. No one knew for sure. Deep inside, the black rage that had sought release for six winters stirred in his blood. Vengeance. The Viking called Kraka should have been there on the field of battle yesterday. He had not been.

There were many things to be learned.

Waerferth, set to gather local knowledge like a dog after a bone, had come up with the theory the woman must be Kraka's mistress.

She had decided to give him lessons in Viking tactics.

The moon's light and the glow of the stars dazzled his opened eyes. Moon glow held uncanny powers. But he could not use them. It was not his nature. For the first time he wished he were like Macsen, blood brother and uncanny Briton, who could pull knowledge out of the blank air.

He would find out the truth.

He sat up. The movement was pushed through pain, but that had never stopped him. He stood, forcing the stiffness out of muscle and sinew. Turning toward the bower where the woman lay.

He would not allow her to escape him a second time. Fate had brought her back. He knew that much.

And whoever she was, whatever secret she held he would take. She would not be able to prevent it.

THE APPALLING BRAT was still alive, neck as yet unstretched. Elene watched his small form scurrying in and out of the torchlight. He was cleaning out the half-built stables.

She wanted the much-disputed horse.

Why would the hell-fiend be shovelling horse droppings now, in the dark?

Punishment, doubtless.

He saw her.

"I thought you was dead."

"It seems not."

"You know, with the spear and all." He almost sounded disappointed, as though her violent end would have been more interesting. She bit her lip.

"I came to look at the horses. So, will they hang you?" He seemed keen on blood and guts.

"No. At least, I don't think so."

She caught a glimpse of the whites of his eyes. Stupid boy. "Come here."

She sat down on the wall bench. The child approached,

holding the aromatic fruits of his labours before him like an offering.

"Perhaps you could leave the shovel."

"I have to finish this."

"Just for now."

"He'll skin me."

Good lord.

She had to give the mountainous Berg his due. She had had no idea the little imp could be biddable.

"Sit."

He sat, obedient as a prize hound, and gazed up at her.

"What exactly did he say?" There was no need to elaborate on who.

"I am not to steal, particularly from defenseless women, I am to apologise to you and clean out the stables," he recited without actually stopping to breathe. "I must obey orders, forswear lying—"

"Clean your teeth?"

"Aye."

She choked.

The child blinked. "Do you know how to do it?"

"You need salt," she replied with suitable gravity. "Or a green twig."

"I could get a twig. I also have to honour those who themselves have shown courage and honour, even if they are an enemy, or dead." He picked up the shovel again.

"Honour those…" She followed his sticklike figure through the torchlight. She had a sudden vision of his knobbly fingers poking at the dead Viking to see whether it would move, and of Berg's anger.

"What sort of twig?"

"Twig? Oh, yes. I do not know that it matters much. Birch, perhaps, or ash. Something pliable. I am sure if you do all that, he will not hang you."

"Do you think so?"

She caught the flash of cleanable teeth.

"Did you hear the song they made in his honour? They were singing it in the hall. But he said the honour was due to the king."

"No. I mean, did he?" She thought of the standard spilling magic through his careful hands. She thought... No. She would not think of yesterday.

At that moment, she noticed the horse endowed with speed and good manners. No one knew she had come here. They were all at the feast. Making speeches, getting drunk, singing. There was only the child. She hoped he would be all right with his shovel and his twigs of unknown origin. Even Berg-the-hero would not harm such a creature, surely.

She hefted a saddle.

"Lady! What are you doing?" There was a clatter as the loaded shovel hit the floor.

"Taking my horse back."

"You cannot go riding now."

"I must."

A small pinched face stared up at her. A scrawny throat swallowed untidily.

"He will not let you."

"*He?*"

"I heard him. Telling everyone. You are...you are not allowed to go out."

I must obey orders....

Arrogant man with his dream-filled eyes. He would force her like anyone in the end. She knew it.

"I am going. Tell him I cleaned my teeth." She touched the horse.

"Lady!"

It was not the child's piping voice. It was another, still young, but belonging to one who had fought a battle yesterday and killed.

"You may not take the horse."

Several minutes later, back in Berg's room, Elene stared at the window. Wistan of the large muscles and the smaller brain had gone. There were disadvantages to being young. You believed things. He had even apologised for carrying out his master's orders. Then he had left so that she could go to bed.

Elene crossed the floor. She could fit through the window. She might get a long way even without a horse.

The room had somehow become cluttered. She nearly tripped over a set of gaming pieces carved out of walrus ivory. They were Danish, *hnefatafl,* a board game for dark winter evenings. It mimicked battle. There was a king who had to be protected from attack or taken. Part of the commander's share of the plunder?

She picked up one of the spilled pieces. The carved figure of the king. Well fashioned... She recognised it.

She sat down on the bed. But there were more things there, scattered where she had been sleeping.

She put down Kraka's brother's gaming piece.

Women's things.

For the captive?

Her hands played over a tunic, a gown, linens. Her fingertips brushed something hard. Cold. A brooch. The design was beautiful, divided into four matching fields, each centred on a white crystal surrounded by a complicated pattern of red garnets and green glass and gold beadwork.

On the inside was someone's name.

The world disintegrated.

CHAPTER 5

"READY?"

"Of course. You know how keen I am to ride this horse." Elene produced her blandest smile; it was not returned. Perhaps it was not wise to bait the giver of orders. He had spent the night on the mead bench, or under it. In the morning light, he had the look of a man who was paying for his sins.

She watched Berg's heavy fingers tighten on her reins.

She was wearing the looted dress. It had belonged to someone else but there was no longer anything in her to care about such things. She was wearing it because it was better than what she had. Because it was not the whore's dress that Kraka had given her.

The brooch was pinned inside it.

Berg had not remarked on the absence from sight of something made of gold and bright gems and brilliant expertise. Perhaps he had so much plunder he did not care. Perhaps he was still so ale-soaked he had not noticed.

She had to move west now that she had seen the brooch. That was all that mattered.

There was only one thing left to ask.

"What did you do with the child?"

"The hell-fiend?" The shaggy head raised. His eyes were as bleak as lake ice. "Sent him back to the village this morning with a flea in his ear."

Avoid lying, robbery and dishonouring the fallen.

"Did he clean his teeth?"

"I doubt it. Good job you did."

He let go of the reins. The horse sidled, but it was not that which sent the jolt through her. His hand touched hers in releasing the leather strap. Rough-callused skin. Heat. The searing memory of the greater heat of his mouth on hers. Clean and supple.

She brought the horse under control with skill learned since she was five winters old. Berg watched her.

Elene set her face toward the dark bulk of the Andredesweald. It was a long way to Winchester.

"*Still* there?"

"Aye, lord."

The hapless Wistan was in the front rank of trouble again. Elene slid down from her horse's back. She could not quite remember why she had wanted so much to ride it. Even though her saddle had been thoughtfully provided with sheepskin and she was used to following in Kraka's wake, she had had enough. It had been rough riding.

They were now in the forest. They had not followed the *herepath*, the road newly fashioned for the swift transportation of armies to feed the fort.

"…will not be able to keep up much longer," offered Wistan. How sensible. She hoped he was talking about her again. She tried walking. Across the clearing, Berg made exasperated noises.

"…blundering around like…"

Poor Wistan. She stretched her back. She could see a clump of pink and white wood sorrel under the oaks. It glowed in the shadows. She would go and—

"…gets caught by the Danes."

She froze. The exasperated one was not talking about Wistan.

"…time before some scout finds…"

The well-mannered horse snorted, butting at her hand, seeking attention. She was the other side of it. Berg, in all probability, could not see her. Wistan's solid form stood between them. Besides, she was doing nothing wrong, just holding her mount.

"Hush." Her breath was hardly a whisper of sound. She looped the reins tighter round her hand, stroked the horse's warm muscular neck. "Hush…"

Berg's speech was now so low she could catch nothing. Only a single word, one that had the power to send ice through her veins. *Viking.*

"That is how things will stay." Berg's voice, utterly decisive, no compromise, cut to her across the mild evening air. "Catch him."

Wistan left.

"Horse bothering you?"

Elene's hand jerked on the already tight reins, causing her mount's neck to arch and the heavy hoofs to shift.

"No."

She stepped back, but Berg was so close she nearly thudded into him. She swore. He caught the now slackened reins effortlessly, touching the horse with one solid hand. It made a breathy, indignant noise and then nuzzled its face against Berg's arm and shoulder, much the way it had tried to do with her when she had been distracted. Fickle creature. It subsided into pleasure under competent hands.

"It was trying to gain your attention."

Did he know? That she had been listening like a spy? Yet his eyes were utterly bland, like someone waiting. The cold fear prickled up and down her spine for quite other reasons.

What will happen? She wanted to shout out the question.

She watched his hand, sure, careful, as uncompromising as his voice had sounded from across the clearing.

That is how things will stay. He would not let her out of his sight.

The hand paused, held out the reins to her. For all she knew, Kraka was at their backs. Now. She wanted to scream, but what difference could it make? Whether it was Dane or competent Englishman, she was at someone's mercy either way. But she did not know whether she could tolerate it this time.

She had to get to Winchester.

She mounted the docile horse. He helped her.

THE PRISONER WAS BROUGHT IN as night fell.

It was the irksome boy.

"What on earth did you think you were *doing?*" said Elene. Berg's comments had been rather more blistering. The fiend's small shoulders hunched.

"Well?"

She received a second shrug and a mutinous glare. It was about as much as Berg had got.

"Do you have any idea how dangerous it was to have tried to follow us?"

The look of blankness could belong only to a small boy.

"Do you have no one who will be worried about you, who—" She suddenly realised what the blankness hid.

She had temporary custody of the prisoner. No one else seemed to know what to do with him. She dragged him away into the shadows of an ash grove before any of the men could see his tears.

"Is that why you did it?" she asked, when he had been hustled, snuffling, into a patch of black night.

"I did not want to stay there."

She sat beside him. "But surely someone must look after you?"

"I don't need it. I can do things for myself, all sorts of things. And sometimes people give me things. Or I can find things they throw out on the midden. Or I can earn for myself. I am good with pigs."

"I am sure you are."

Something moved in the shadows. Something blacker and surprisingly quiet for its size. She must have gone too far for her jailer.

Her charge sniffed.

"I like pigs."

The separate shadow among the ash trees stilled. Its form coalesced with the greater darkness. It might not have been there. But she knew it was.

"Most people do not take to pigs," said the boy. "But they do not understand what they like."

The shadow wavered. Elene watched it.

"Pigs can be very…interesting," she said.

Do not frighten him. Please.

"And I can do horses," said the boy.

She tried not to glance at the shadow.

"Perhaps we will not mention horses."

"I was not really stealing the horse I got from the fort. Not this time. I brought it here."

"So you did."

"Do not let him send me back. Please." The last word was no more than a hiss of sound.

"No one will harm you. But I cannot—"

"They hate me."

"Hate you?" exclaimed Elene. "Who? Back at the village? Surely not. Why would—"

"Because the man who got me was a Viking."

"A *Viking?*" Her heart went tight. Cold.

"That is why my mother had to leave."

"Your—" Her breath choked off. "She left you?"

"After the raids. She did try to stay, and the blacksmith was going to wed her. But in the end he would not, because she had me. He would have had to bring me up, a Viking's child, the child of those who had murdered his kin." The boy's voice paused, as though reciting words heard from other people, adults, and learned by heart.

"But…" There were no words. Only the horror unfolding so clearly she could see it.

Across the trees, the shadow moved, swiftly. The boy did not notice. *A Viking's child.* Her limbs were too heavy to lift.

"She thought no one would have her after that. She said she had to go. She could not take me with her. But she would have if she could."

The high-pitched voice wavered and the shadow spoke across it, claiming the child's attention, talking, saying things. Drowning the terrible words. But the boy needed to explain nothing else.

Not to her, the Viking's whore.

Elene had to speak in her turn. Offer some comfort for the boy's sake. It did not matter what she felt.

"How could they have treated her like that?" Her voice came out high-pitched. The child stared at her in shock. "It is vile!" she yelled.

"Elene—"

She clapped her hand over her mouth before any more sounds could come out in front of the white face of the child.

"It is all right." The dark figure had hold of the boy, drawing him away.

"I am sorry." The words struggled out through her stiffened fingers. No more than a whisper.

"It is all right," said the shadow. "I will talk to him. It is over. Stay there."

BERG, THE EAST ANGLIAN, came back. He sat down in moonlight. It touched his cloak and glittered off his skin and the long pale weight of his hair.

Elene wanted to ask him what he had said to the boy. But she could not. She had behaved shamefully. She was mad, a marred creature of nightmare and disgust. This was the final proof, screaming in front of a frightened child.

"I do not know his name."

The brilliant head moved.

"I never asked," she said. "I did not get round to it. There was always something else to do, something more important. I should have asked."

"Chad."

"Chad? After the dead bishop of the Mercians? Humble, devout, zealous and an example to us all? A *saint?*"

"The same."

It was impossible to discern what went on in that mind. The rock-solid strength was too overpowering, masking everything. She could only see the pure side of his face. Perfection. She shivered.

The name, wildly inappropriate, pathetically touching, would have been the mother's choice.

"I should not have shouted at him."

It was as far as she could get. There was silence. Nothing but the moonlight and him.

He did not speak. The bulk of his body in the shadows was like a black wall, hewn out of stones, turned neither toward her nor away.

"He is just a child," she said for the thousandth time.

"No."

No. Chad, Mercian saint's namesake, was old enough to know about raiding and murder and rape and all the consequences. All the— She stared at the stars burning their way through the dusk. They were there in their appointed places, unchangeable by anything that happened on the earth. She tried to focus her thoughts on them, but the horror was there inside her, like a great blackness. It was people who changed.

"I meant to help him. I wanted his trust and then I—I frightened him and I pushed him away." The horror seemed like something living, stirring. "I pushed him away like his—" She stopped speaking.

He turned to her. "No. Not you. The boy has a mind of his own. Besides, you are going to pay for this tomorrow."

"I—"

"He will be waiting for you with a bowl of water and a hazel twig."

For cleaning his *teeth?* "Of course," she said. The summer stars hung motionless.

"Aye. You get to demonstrate the finer points. It is beyond me."

She saw his eyes. There were a thousand things to be read in their depths, even the danger, but the thread of humanity was there. All at once she was aware of the small details of her surroundings, of the screen of brushwood, the soft moss beneath her body, of Berg's closeness. Of the way his fingers laced loosely about one knee.

"Can you manage that?" The words were light, all the other depths hidden.

She tried to laugh, as though she were quite sane and she knew what a jest was. The sound choked on tears she had not known were gathering. The blackness inside her became edged with terror. She never wept, because that would have meant that she was not in control. She would make some reply to his jest, to show that she could, that the whole distasteful, petrifying subject could be dropped.

"How could his mother have left him?"

The question she had never meant to ask, not even in her mind, hung in the moonlit space between herself and Berg. The big softly laced hands stayed still.

"Sometimes people cannot do what they should, at the moment when they should. Or even what they wish. Life is too hard."

"But it was not his fault," she said softly.

His face was now fully turned toward her. She could glimpse the scars through the moon-silvered shadows.

"No."

It was not the reply she expected. People were brought up to seek revenge. It was a sacred duty, to warriors most of all. Particularly warriors who had suffered disfiguring damage, warriors who had lost their home.

"Why would you think such a thing?" Her question struck with the force of an arrow. It was born out of her madness. She had not asked why he would *say* such a thing, but why he would *think* it.

She did not want to know what he thought, what any man thought.

"Because I know it is so."

The conviction in his eyes was absolute. It blotted out

everything else, both seen and guessed at. It was like a layer of rock-solid certainty on which a person could rely. She could not accept that. Nothing in this world could be relied upon, certainly not from someone like him. She clenched her hands.

"Elene."

He leaned toward her and the certainty was like something tangible, some magic force that flowed through the night air, that came from *him*. He was so close, like a living sheet of power, like a bright-edged shadow of enchantment. Heat and brightness and shadow all at once. A man. With a man's eyes and a man's mind.

A man's strong body.

She thrust herself backward, the movement raw and uncontrolled, shamingly obvious in its intent and its desperation. She stopped.

He was watching her with the kind of intensity of someone who hunted.

"Elene." His hand moved.

"No." It was a whisper, but it could have been as desperate as the scream that had partially unleashed itself at the child. She forced rational words through the painful constriction of her throat.

"There is nothing more to say. Nothing more to do."

He got to his feet, lithe muscle and darkness, as heavy as Kraka. She watched.

"Stay there."

She waited in the moonlight and looked at the impenetrable blackness of the Andredesweald.

He came back, his arms filled with spare cloaks and a flask of ale.

"You can sleep here. Come, take the cloak. You are cold."

It was then that she realised she was curled up, bent double, with her arms folded over her belly. That she had been so since Chad the half-Viking boy had described his mother.

She straightened out.

"No. I am not cold."

Still, she took the cloak. Then she swallowed just a little of the ale as though everything were perfectly normal.

He drank the rest. She wrapped herself in layers of wool and lay down with the spare cloak pillowed under her head.

She stared at the thicket of unidentifiable undergrowth in front of her face.

He moved behind her. She heard him lie down.

She thought about how far it was to Winchester.

He did not touch her, even though she waited and waited. Perhaps he was tired. Perhaps he guessed that the scream was still lodged in her throat and threatened escape. She stared at the shadows.

She thought that she would fight him as she had never fought Kraka.

Nothing happened. But she knew he was there. She could feel him, so close.

She would not sleep.

The bulk of his body blocked the wind.

She would not close her eyes.

Nothing.

He must not want her, but neither would he let her go. Somehow, it was even more frightening.

She woke, out of a dreamless sleep, with dread crawling down her spine. The stifled sound that betrayed nightmares had come from her companion.

She did not turn her head. But in the jumbled, sleep-addled paths of her mind, she wondered what he dreamed of, what Berg, thane of Alfred, held so deep in his mind.

Who he was.

The thought was a trick of darkness and exhaustion. She knew what he was. A king's man, who fought in a struggle with the odds against him that was at best unequal, at worst suicidal. But that was what warriors did, fought. It encompassed all that he was.

But the question hovered in the air.

Who are you?

She would never ask it. She did not want an answer.

THE WOULD-BE SWINEHERD was inclined to be sullen, which probably meant he was wary. Elene could not blame him. But Chad arrived, dutifully clutching the necessary equipment.

"I got the hazel twig."

"So I see."

"And the water," he said, slopping half of it over the bracken.

"Perhaps if you put the bowl down and…and sit next to me." She held her breath. The boy sat without fuss beside the pooling linen of her borrowed skirts, but he kept his eyes on the twig. She had no idea whether it was because of the aftermath of last night or because he was nervous about the forthcoming operation.

"There is nothing to it. You just—"

Berg walked past. She could see his enormous boots.

"You just—"

The boots stopped.

"You just what?" said Chad.

She looked up the solid length of leg, farther, past a belt set with wolf shapes, adorned with heavy gold and precious fragments of blue glass, past a neckline that revealed tanned skin.

The face was outlined in sunlight. She was getting used to the scarred flesh. She did not even flinch. His eyes were steady, unreadable. Not the eyes of a man who understood nightmares.

"You just *what?*" demanded the boy.

"I am sure the lady will demonstrate."

His eyes were so calm, no trace of last night's emotions. But then they had only been *her* emotions.

Now Elene knew he was as utterly aware of her as she was of him. Aware of last night, of this moment in the cool early morning sun, of everything she said and everything she had done from the moment they'd met.

She sat with a matching hazel twig in her hand.

"Well?"

She could not bear such terrible awareness. She summoned a mocking smile.

"Are you not busy, lord? Do you not have a journey to arrange?" She took a deep breath. "Fresh orders to give to poor Wistan, perhaps?"

"Wistan?" His attention was sharp, redoubled. She thought of Kraka and the way he had wanted to possess everything she did. She could not take that from anyone ever again. She concentrated on the child.

"Like this."

The boy followed her movements.

"Ouch."

"Well, perhaps with a little less force."

She stood up. Chad followed. They walked after Berg.

Chad forgave her before the sun reached its zenith. Short memory. She recognised the survival trick. Only the moment existed, just the particular one to be lived through.

He talked. She was no good at chatter. She had accustomed herself to the loneliness of a single child born to older parents whose kin were scattered through the five kingdoms. She had kept company with her own thoughts, and the past year had made the subtle sense of isolation absolute. She had been alone, an alien in a Viking camp. She had learned enough Danish to get by, but that was all. She was out of the habit of talking for its own sake.

"Look at the size of that oak tree."

She had taken him to the stream to wash him while the evening meal was cooked. He was not enamoured of more water.

"Why do they use oak to make ships?"

Anything to create a diversion.

"Because the timber has a straight grain and you can use it to make planks. You choose the best wood for what you want and work it while it is still unseasoned and then you—" She stopped. She sounded like a Norse pirate.

"Then you *what?* This is cold!"

"Not so very cold. It is nearly summer. You are lucky if you can find water when you are travelling. Do your feet."

"Then you what? With the wood."

"Feet."

"What?"

He was impossible. She knew nothing about children. She swallowed panic.

"You cut the oak log to the right lengths and then start splitting it so that you get wedge shapes and then you—"

"What was it like in a Viking camp? Everyone says you were there."

Everyone says. Berg. But they—*he*—did not know she had shared Kraka's bed. Kraka, agent of Guthrum, Kraka who had once served Ivar, destroyer of East Anglia.

"Well?" The boy was not concerned about cold water at all, or the properties of trees. She sat back on her heels. What he wanted to know about was the kind of life his father would have led.

There was silence except for the rustling of the splittable oaks close around them and the sweet double notes of a thrush.

"You will not tell me."

He was looking at her with eyes full of belligerence. And guilt.

"No."

"He said you would not. He said I was not to ask you."

Berg. Berg with eyes that saw through things and understood nightmares. Perhaps.

Chad picked up a stone and threw it. It smacked off a tree trunk and then lost its power in damp ground.

"Can I go back now?"

"What did you want to know?"

The boy watched her. "What it is *like*."

Helletrega. The tortures of hell.

"Noisy," she said at random. "Always full of noise all night and all day. People everywhere." Every moment until you could scream with it.

"Was it like the fortress at home?"

"Aye. I suppose so. Much the same." No writing, no one trying to put a Latin inscription on the gateway. "No church. Places for Thor and Odin. It was very…dangerous."

"What were the people like?"

There was the question. What did she say to a child about his father? That he would have been a man like Kraka who…

"What is it like at the village at home? Lots of different people who think different things and do different things. That is how it was."

"Everyone says they are all monsters."

Yes.

No.

"They have their own thoughts and feelings. Ordinary. They are people. People sometimes do things that are right and sometimes they do things that are wrong." Appallingly wrong.

"Is that how it was?"

"That is how it was." She could not manage another word. She could not even think the things she was saying. She got up and took a step.

It was not a surprise that he was there, standing against the trees in silence. The sudden awareness of his presence startled her, but it was not a surprise. She sat back down again because her legs would not work. He came forward into the slanting sunlight, making the boy splash water, then stare at him with overlarge eyes.

As, perhaps, she did.

"Not teeth again?"

All those words that had been forced out of her. All those words he had heard.

"Feet, this time."

He sat. It was impossible to move.

CHAPTER 6

Berg forced stillness, a clear mind. Two sets of eyes stared at him.

"It is all right," said the woman called Elene. Her voice held the challenge that had been there from the first moment and the stone wall behind it that shut out everything. The wall that made it plain she neither needed nor wanted anything from him.

The bright orange glow on the water filled his sight.

That is how it was, she had said of Kraka and his Viking war band. *Ordinary. People with thoughts and feelings.*

Yet last night something in her had been close to breaking. Or so he had believed. That belief had forced a reaction out of him that no longer had any place, or any purpose. He heard the rustle of her movement. He knew nothing about her. Nothing… The lights on the water shifted. He narrowed his eyes against the glare. It was not the small stream in Wessex he saw, but the wide expanse of the fen waters reaching out past the horizon.

"I wish I had been brought up like you," blurted out the boy at his feet. "I wish I was rich and had parents and knew how to fight and nothing had ever gone wrong—" The belligerent voice stopped. "I am sorry," said Chad, curiously formal, like an adult. "Wistan said. About East Anglia."

Wistan was—young and unmarred. But Wistan should learn when to keep his mouth shut.

"There is naught—"

"What," began the child at the same time and then stopped again, nervous.

He would not have said a word about his home. He never did. He could not; he did not know how.

Then he turned his head and he saw that the woman, the girl, was looking at him. Elene.

"East Anglia is a world apart." He watched her as he spoke to the boy. "The land is mostly flat and the line where the earth meets the sky has no limit, whether it is over land or water."

"Fens," said Chad, fright forgotten. "And trackless marshes."

"Aye. And the clean sound of the wind and the paleness of the sky."

"What about the marshes?"

He could not look at the eager face of the boy, only at the woman.

"What about the marshes? Were they really trackless?"

"No. The paths were there."

"But—" It was the woman's voice. She stopped. Whatever she had wanted to say beyond that single word was lost. Yet her eyes stayed on his.

"But you had to know," he supplied. "Because the paths could shift with the flow of the water or the turning of the seasons. You were only safe if you knew."

The woman was silent.

"But you could still drown," said Chad. "If you did not know, you could be drowned, lose your footing and get sucked under and…" The boy made squishing sounds. "Everyone says that East Anglians have webbed fe—"

"Webbed what?"

Berg kept his face straight. Apparently Elene could not, not entirely. He caught her hidden smile. The smile touched her eyes, brighter than the sun's fire across the water.

"Oh, nothing. That is…"

Berg crossed one booted foot over the other. The woman clenched her hands and hid her smiling mouth. But not her eyes. They danced with light, infinitely blue. So that all he could see was a different child, a girl child, flawlessly fair. He thought his heart stopped.

"Nothing," said the boy hastily. "Marshes are good, though."

"Aye. Believe it or not, there was pastureland, too. Good for raising horses. In some places there are even hills."

"Horses? I like horses."

"So I noticed."

Her blue eyes held his and time seemed to stop.

"They are almost as good as pigs. So," said Chad, oblivious, "were you rich?"

Past and present collided.

"Yes." He could see his cousin dying. All the fineness and the dignity gone. Only the blood. And he himself was still alive. "I was so, once."

The woman stared at him. He could see the smile fade out of her eyes. She seemed to have no consciousness of who he was, had been. The possibility of a connection seemed fanciful, born out of his own imaginings.

"What was it like, being rich?"

"It was…a thing full of grace." Which was a damned stupid thing to say and inexplicable. Chad looked at him with his mouth hanging open. The woman looked away. It was like the breaking of a binding rope.

"What does that mean?"

It was a miracle no one had hanged the boy long before Berg had thrown away his chance.

"It means, pest, that you are given the chance to know how to read and calculate and have a church built and think."

"Oh." The disappointment was undisguisable.

The woman kept her gaze on the small Wessex stream, now quite dark. The head veil he had given her for decency and the half-concealed richness of her brilliant hair hid her face.

"I would not like reading," said Chad. "Everyone says letters are full of magic."

"So they are. But it is good magic. Magic enough for kings." He stood up. His cousin's bloodied corpse still in his mind, as it would be until he died. The girl did not look up.

"Come here." He held out his hand for the boy. His voice was quite steady.

"But what—"

"No more. It is near night." He forced his mind onto the present, on what was needed now.

"But you do get to have gold as well as magic letters? And—"

"Yes, you do, greedy urchin. And webbed feet if you keep them in the water so long."

"What?"

Berg swooped, catching the hopping child lightning fast. Chad shrieked, making Elene look round, her eyes wide.

"I did not mean—"

"Just as well." He swerved round, hoisting the small body in a wide arc. The second shriek was one of delight, but only after a small gasp of surprise. As though no one had ever thought to make sport with the child when he was smaller.

He carted the lad back and dumped him on the ground beside the fire with his men.

Wistan's face told him immediately.

"A scout?"

"Yes."

So soon. "Kraka's man." But it was not a question. He knew. *Too soon.*

"Lord."

"And?"

"The man will not be taking tales back to his master."

"Good." Then the other mission, the deception, was safe. Perhaps. Something was awry. He did not so much as glance at the baggage they had carried from the fort.

Even though there was only Wistan to see him. The men finished off the remains of the meal. The boy dropped into sleep already.

And the woman waited by the stream.

"Were there others?"

"Not that we could tell. No. I would stake my life on it."

He nodded. All their lives were staked on it; it was not necessary to say so. He touched Wistan's shoulder, briefly, and caught the flash of a grin. Unmarred youth. He went back into the shadows.

The woman sat where he had left her. He watched the supple line of her back and the tangled fall of her veil.

"Elene."

She turned, looking up, matching her gaze with his. He walked toward her and she watched him, every move, each harsh breath.

"So?" she said.

Her eyes were clear in the shadows, quite steady, blank as the stone wall inside her.

"Will we sleep here?" she asked.

Last night and the edge of desperation. Thoughts that were entirely mad. *We.* The long smooth line of her body and her softness, her woman's scent and her warmth. The rich hidden curves that fired his blood just from her nearness.

He controlled breath, the hard needs of lust, the other kind of madness that defied thought and all restraint and the very essence of being.

"We could," he said. He let his voice pause. "But—"

"But?"

The only word she had offered in the whole of his difficult exchange with the boy. The only word that could mean all. Or nothing.

"We are further from the fortress. It could be dangerous to sleep apart, here and alone. For you and I."

The clear eyes widened. They were as open and as clear as deep water. Perhaps.

"But they would not follow us, the Vikings? Surely? They were defeated. You defeated them."

"I defeated that part of the war band which attacked the fort. The leader was not there."

"But he will not come here. *They* will not."

She did not name the Viking leader. She doubtless believed he did not guess she was Kraka's mistress.

Kraka and Earl Guthrum. Kraka and King Ivar. Perhaps she would offer him another lesson in war tactics. Perhaps that was what she thought of, not the things he imagined. His mind burned.

He saw the stone wall form across the limpid gaze, even though she did not move her head or glance away.

"I have not the means to be so sure," he said.

He saw it then, the fright she tried so hard to hide. It flickered briefly, shockingly visible, and then it was gone.

Fear of what? Of him, or of the consequences of breaking her secret bond with Kraka?

He could not stomach the thought.

"Do you not wish to come back to the camp?"

"Of course." She got to her feet, as obedient as the most arrogant lord could have desired. Her back was straight, her face as calm as a summer sky.

When he took her hand, it was shaking.

There was no alternative. She would sleep with him.

THEY LAY TOGETHER. Elene pulled the cloak over her clothes. She did not complain. No point.

The weariness hit her as soon as she touched the ground. She did not give in to it, not yet. She lay still. Even though she had seen in his eyes, in the taut power of his body, all the things there was no disguise for. That power had hung round him like unbanked fire, all the time he had sat beside the brook, while he had spoken and made jokes with the boy. All the time that he had looked at her as though he would have her heart out.

Her body trembled.

She despised the thought of it being here and now, with the others so close, sleeping or not. Every move and every laboured breath to be laughed at or slavered over. Kraka had not cared when they had had to sleep with no privacy like this. If he had thought at all, it would have bolstered his pride.

Kraka. Who might be out there, somewhere, pursuing them, so the Englishman thought. But Kraka would not do that. He would go back east and north. There was nothing for him here after his brother's defeat, nothing he could want so much that it would make it worth the risk.

Except her.

She shut her eyes. She could not think such a thing. Kraka had always had others as well as her to see to his needs. He could get a hundred concubines, some willing. There were enough Danish women, and enough captives. Always. She was nothing special.

But she thought of what he had done, of the bargain they had struck, she and Kraka. The fact that he had agreed to it even though he had not needed to.

The look in his eyes.

Kraka did not give things up.

She moved, curled inward on herself. The back of her thigh touched heat, tensed muscle. She froze.

He did not move, even after that witless, terrifying brush of hot fully clothed flesh. He did not move against her, but neither did he move away. He could have been sleeping.

She knew he was not. She was so aware, as she had never been with Kraka. Her skin tingled with it and her breath shortened. She felt tight, stretched beyond endurance. Waiting.

He had made her so, just by looking at her beside the stream, and talking. Not even talking to her, but jokingly to a small boy and sometimes in all seriousness, like something out of the deepest part of his mind.

She hated that, the way he talked. The things he said and seemed to think, as though the world could be different from what it was. Her body tensed. She managed to stop herself from moving again, but the heightened tension was felt, not just by her but by him. She could sense not just his closeness but the urgency underneath like unslaked hunger, the tension like a mirror to her own.

She bit her lip.

She would go mad from this. It would slowly kill her. She did not know why things were so different with him, so deeply terrifying. She knew only that she could not bear the feelings he roused inside her. She had to end the feelings before they swamped her. It was best to face what there was no escaping. It was like a paradox. The only power of those who had none.

But she was so afraid.

She moved her hand.

She touched him. She knew what to do, after all. Kraka had taught her well. Her hand slid across his leg underneath the covering of the cloaks. She felt the tense flesh hidden by clothes, the dense muscular outline of his thigh, precisely sculpted despite his heaviness. Her fingers moved over the tight, scarcely yielding shape and it filled her hand. His warmth. Him.

She remained still, just for a moment. Her hand trembled. She tried to stop the shaking. But the awareness he had forced on her seemed to burst inside her head, inside her body. So that there was only him in the darkness and the moonlight with the breath of the moving trees all round them. His heat and the dark lines and planes of his body, its power latent and unexplored, frightening in its masculine difference, its strength. That sense of power was like a glimpse of the unknown depths that were in him. Spellbinding.

It was the potency of spellcraft that sent the same heat through her, filling her and binding her to him as though it were possible for two utterly different people to feel the

same witchery. As though something could be shared beyond the final soulless act.

The sour, hard-fought assertion of her own power
against him slid beyond her grasp. A small sound escaped
her throat in the moon-silvered dark. It might have been
her terror. It might have been a thousand unknown things
she could not give a name to.

She moved her hand, higher, across thickly tightened
flesh, trying to regain the weapon of her own bitter power,
but an arm made of steel closed over her, stopping movement, breath, all power of thought, with an abruptness
that cut resistance before it was born.

His movement was so uncontrolled, so utterly unlike
anything he had done before, that she lay under it in utter
shock. She felt the full heaviness of his arm crushing her
ribs, the powerful leg thrown over, trapping hers. There
was a split instant without breath, an incomprehensible
fragment of time, not even enough for the black fear that
was the Vikings' legacy to bloom inside her. And then he
drew back just slightly. She could breathe, think. Know
the unexpected danger of what she had done.

What depths were in him?

There was utter silence. She lay still. She could feel
him at her back, his harshened breathing, the moment
when his control was back in place. He gave her room, so
that they did not touch at every point. It made no difference. She had felt the savage struggle. She sensed what it
left—intensity, anger.

Elene did not pull away from him. She could not. He
did not move his arm.

Across the clearing, someone stirred in sleep, or in wakefulness. She stared out at the blind dark, tense.

Still they stayed, locked together in the dark like two lovers. Utterly sundered. Close as a breath. She held every muscle still until she was sure she felt him sleep. It took a long time.

She moved her arm cautiously, until her fingers found the sharp metal outline of the fine brooch pinned on the inside of her clothes. Her fingers closed round it. His hand brushed hers. In sleep, surely, not by intention.

After a while, she closed her eyes.

"DID YOU HEAR what they found yesterday?"

Berg watched the wench pick up the saddle while the boy darted round her and got in the way. Her reply was too soft to be heard.

"No," piped the boy, treading on a trailing girth strap. "I did not see it, but I heard them talking about it this morning. That is just as good."

She shook her head, moving the saddle aside. The boy jumped.

"There was a Viking scout and—" Chad hopped from one poorly shod foot to another. "Look out! You are dropping it."

Berg heard her swear.

He strode out of the trees. His fingers caught hers over the girth strap. He stopped her moving. She stared at him. His hand covered hers the way it had last night, flesh fused. He could see the rise of her breath.

"Do you need help with that?"

"No." Then, "What scout?" she said.

He was reminded anew of the ruthless intelligence that lay behind the smoke-blue eyes.

"The Vikings', as the child said."

She did not blink.

"Here, take that." He pulled the saddle out of her grip and tossed it to the boy. "Make yourself useful and get the lady's horse ready."

"Yes, lord."

Mayhap the creature was learning manners.

"Lord, there was a Viking, though, wasn't there? What did—"

"The horse."

"Oh. Yes."

The boy finally gave up his questioning. Berg led Elene away; he stopped walking when the oaks were so thick he could hardly see her face, just its paleness and the shadowed eyes.

"What happened?" she said.

She sounded as though she did not know.

"Tell me."

"What is it that you wish to know?" he answered.

"Whether…" Her fine lips moved over something soundless. "Whether the Vikings are following us."

She would not look at him.

"I thought you had decided last night that the Vikings would not pursue us," he said.

Last night they had slept in the protected circle of his men. Last night she had touched him as she must have touched Kraka, and his body had responded like the wild-

fire that consumed all in its path. Just as Kraka had doubtless responded to her.

She had chosen to do that, even though he had thus far
found nothing in her eyes beyond bitterness and defiance.

He still had hold of her arm. He should let her go. But
he could not.

"I know not what the Vikings would do," she said. "But
mayhap they might follow you after all."

"If I had something they wanted."

"Perhaps."

"And what would that be?"

He caught her face, tilting her head upward with one
hand, leaning over her so that their bodies touched and
she could not take a breath without his being aware of it.
She gasped, pulling back, away from him, until her spine
pressed against the gnarled oak wood. There was nowhere
to go. He did not draw back.

He had to know. Perhaps because he was mad.

She stared at him with the wide blue eyes.

"Perhaps he—they want me."

She did not say the man's name even then, even though
it hung between them like an unsheathed sword.

"Kraka?"

He felt her reaction as though it passed through each
sinew of his body where it touched hers. Her gaze wavered
and then fixed upon him, the way it had when she had
tightened her hand on the spear shaft in the instant he'd
first seen her, in the endless moment on the battlefield.

"Yes. I am what he wants."

She said it, straight out, and he could have sworn that

he had reached the certainty he sought. She had been Kraka's unwilling captive and she had fled from him. That was a truth whole and entire. He could make a decision on that basis and rely on it.

But the calculation based on sense and logic mattered nothing to him beside the fact that she was terrified. That fear lay in the depths of her eyes, behind the sheen of resolution like steel, and she could no longer disguise it. It lived in the soft press of her flesh against him and the rapid beating of her heart. He could scent it on her skin.

"I have told you the Danes will not catch us," he said. "It is true." He drew back from her even as he said the words, but to his shock she followed him. As though his touch were something sought, not forced on her.

"You do not make promises like that." Her hands reached for him, catching at the sleeves of his tunic, the short nails digging through the thin linen, down into his flesh. "Not about the Vikings. Not about—about Kraka."

The blue eyes that might hold his own memories sought his.

"This time I do." The words came out of the stillness of the forest air like magic; they seemed alien to him. Or so he might have believed, if he wished to deceive himself.

"Is that a promise?" Her gaze held his, the intensity searing.

"Aye. That is a promise."

The words had naught to do with the deep forest, spell-rich at the change of light. They had only to do with himself. With her. With the deeper layer of truth that lay behind the bitterness of her eyes.

Truth he had scarce yet touched on.

She looked at him as though she believed him. She did not move away. It was plain that she could have. She held his arms, her body almost touching him. Overhead, the trees were silent, breathless like himself.

Her hands moved, slender fingers white against the expensive dark blue dye of his tunic. Her palms flattened against him, exposing the shape of flesh underneath. Her touch was slow, light enough to deny sensation, strong enough to burn. It might have been a movement of wonder at something unknown. Or the action of skill, long taught. Both, perhaps, with her.

"Elene."

She responded to the name. Her nearness was fire in his veins. The sense of her closeness blocking out all else. *Elene.*

He could see nothing of her eyes, only the shadowed crescent of her lashes. Her gaze was locked on the movement of her hands across the solid mass of his arm. Touch. Shared.

But he could remember the taste of her fear. The sight of it and the sense of it would never leave his mind.

The muscles in his arms tensed under her fingers. Her gaze followed the swelling tightness he could not mask. She made the move. Her hands slid against his flesh, their touch no longer light but intense, as though filled with need.

"Stay."

CHAPTER 7

STAY. THAT WAS ALL she said. One word. No explanation. Whatever coursed between the two of them had no words.

Berg raised her chin, just as he had before. She moved toward him, the movement simple and direct, with no revulsion for his disfigurement, as though their connection had a power apart. This time his mouth came down on hers in a possession that was close to ungoverned.

The world receded. Nothing but the soft pliant touch of her against the burning ache of his body. The scorching heat of her under mouth and tongue and ragged breath.

Her mouth held his. The smooth line of her flesh yielded against every movement that he made, bringing them closer. The awareness of her was enough to drown sense, dragging him deeper, as though it would break restraint. As though something buried inside himself, brutally hidden for a long time, perhaps six blank winters, would shatter.

The richness of subtly rounded flesh filled his hands, the smooth dip of her waist, the curving fullness beneath. She was like a dream, the dream he wanted more than the bitter expanse of life.

She turned into the movement of his hand, to give him access to the erotic, fluid lines of her body. His arm brushed the curve of her breast. His breath roughened and stark desire beat through his blood. The need was limitless, harshly held back, tearing at hardened flesh. The power of it was a force beyond his disguising. Yet she accepted his touch.

Pliable as a reed.

When his lips slid from the burning touch of hers to find the fine skin at the neckline of her dress, she made no attempt to reclaim his mouth. She turned her neck to expose the long line of her throat. Lips and tongue took smooth, unresisting flesh. She stayed.

The silence of the forest closed over them. She let him touch her. He could have everything the urges of his body, the madness inside him, wanted.

He was suddenly aware of the coolness of the early morning air outside their heat.

He shifted position against aching flesh. She followed his movement. The silence grew, and with it the coldness. He lifted his head. She waited, while they stood so close, their hair entangled, skin one breath away from touching.

His body loomed over the open, vulnerable line of hers. She stayed motionless beneath him, waiting, her clothing disordered, her breath uneven. The fine erotic beauty of her spread out for him. Whatever he wished. *No man could want more.* The cold air shifted like their breath, finding its way inside him.

Only her gaze was hidden. He drew his fingers across their tangled hair, the warmth of her skin. Pushed his hand downward to the laces that fastened the neck of her tunic. The movement was no longer so light or so smooth, not something she could so plainly resist if she wished.

Nothing in her changed.

His fingers tangled in the lacing.

She turned her shoulders toward him. The peak of her breast brushed against him. Her left hand moved from the tight muscle of his arm, down the line of chest and belly, skilful. There was no hesitation.

She leaned closer. Her hand slid forward across his hip, downward, fingers splayed across his flesh. Deft.

She touched him.

She moved to the stark, hard urging of his body. She turned to his will. The force in him was elemental. Stronger than his reckoning. Strong enough to take. If he had known nothing. If the madness of need that scored through body and mind had stopped him seeing. If he had not known, nay guessed, so much about her.

The movement of her body showed no reserve, even then. Even though she saw the power and all the mad traces of need in him, all that pressed inside him with a force that would be impossible to hold back.

He pulled back, before the force killed something inside him, catching the sudden flailing drift of her hand, trapping it. She gasped, every small muscle of her body rigid. The bones of her hand felt so fine they would break just from the touch of his fingers. He had always been aware of his strength in relation to others, but never so much as in this moment.

He dropped her hand, turned away, blind. Because there was nothing to say. Nothing that could be done. The cold took him like a thing that would maim.

He moved away. But her right hand, like something long forgotten was tangled in his sleeve. It stayed there, a small white patch of desperation, just as it had held him in the first moment. Through all that brutal passage between them, she had never moved it.

He stopped. The silence was as deadening as the cold. All he could hear through it was his own painful breath. Hers like the breath of fear.

What in holy God's name could he say to her?

She made a small formless sound.

"It is all right. It matters not." His words were inane, beyond the power of meaning, drowned under the frozen air.

"I did not mean…" she began. "I would have—"

"Aye. You would." He cut off the words, all the impossible feelings behind them. She would have sensed his anger. It scored through him. He felt the fine trembling in her hand. He fought the anger. It dragged at him like a crippling force.

He had to get through it.

"Elene." The other name, *Elgiva*, took shape in his head.

"I do not understand," she said.

"Truly? Which part is it that you do not understand?

That I might not wish to force myself on someone who is unwilling? That I do not want to take a bout of one-sided pleasure like Kraka? Did you think I would want pretense? That you still had to offer me payment despite my word?"

He had been given a voice that could terrify. He watched its effect. The shock blossomed in her eyes, blossomed and then faded before a thousand things he could not name.

A thousand things he never wanted to see.

"Yes," she said. Her eyes held his, burning with intensity, fierce with the terrible things the Viking had taught her. What he had compounded.

"The fault was mine. I should not have touched you." And yet he had. Because the need inside him had surged beyond expectation, beyond his controlling. The mad desire that had taken hold from the first moment. Yet not just that. "I thought—" He caught breath. *What? That things could be different? All the black power of the past changed into what should have been?*

His anger grew, mixed with the terrible rage that had taken hold six winters ago and had never died. Never would because the cause could never be wiped out. What was lost could not be restored, and only destruction was left.

"It is my fault," she said.

"*Your* fault—" The anger gathered, balanced on a knife edge. She was not looking at him. He fought the urge to touch her again.

"I will not take from you anything you do not wish to give. Can you not understand that much?"

"Nay. I do not understand. I cannot understand. That is how I am. Nothing can now be different."

The rage found its shape.

"Yes it can!" The words he did not believe burst out of his lips.

"No." Her thick brown hair, now veilless, coiled over her face and her neck. "Some losses are beyond restoring." Her hand tightened on his flesh. "You must know that, East Anglian."

The breath seared his lungs and he could see the destruction all over again. The blood. Soaking the trapped, writhing figure five paces away from him. The blood filling his own mouth, so that he could have drowned in it, and the pain had begun to darken sight. But not enough. Because he had still been able to see. He shut out the image.

"That is how things are," she said. "No one can get back what is lost."

He straightened, controlling dangerously tightened muscle.

No one can give me back what is gone. It might have been himself speaking the first day he had arrived in Wessex with Wistan and six others, a *wrœcca,* an exile, with no option but to take service in an unconquered kingdom. He had been there at Alfred's crowning and he had offered his oath.

It had not been a fair oath. It had been made for the sake of vengeance. Yet it must have been the kind a desperate king would take, because Alfred had accepted it.

"We cannot go back," Berg said into the silent air of the Andredesweald. "But we can make something new out of what is." They could have been the new king's words, spoken over his brother's grave, beside the bones of saints. Alfred had seen a future.

He watched the woman's bent head.

"Elene."

She looked up, so that he saw the deep blue eyes that to him meant the limitless skies of home. He did not know who she truly was, whether she was what he believed, what he had long dreamed. He would find out. But either way, he knew he would follow the same course.

"It is possible to make a future." His words struck through the dawn air.

She said naught. Neither of what she believed nor what she did not. But it was impossible not to touch her.

She came into his arms easily and without fuss. It might have been something meant. Or it might have been the compliance without will that he did not wish. She lay against him. He could feel the soft curves that had created spellcraft and disaster.

"It can be done."

His words hung with the same power as a king's oath. Yet she had no reason to believe them. And there was nothing he could explain. He was not gifted with silver-tongued speech like some men and he could hold her no longer, because he did not know if it was by her will or not. She felt fragile under his hands, infinitely breakable.

The truth was there. She did not touch him by her will. He was not some wreaker of magic. No more than a *wræcca*, with a face to turn the strongest stomach, a face that he sometimes forgot about. A man clumsy with too much strength and the anger still there under his skin.

She would sense that. He released her and she turned away the instant he let her go. Whatever her future was, it was not something they shared.

The light had changed, the summer dawn already bright. There was so much to be done. Somewhere to the north along the ridgeway was Kraka. Mayhap. Ahead lay the forest and, beyond it, the cleared land round Eashing.

What he carried on the journey was more than the worth of his life and the lives of all the men with him.

No turning back.

THEY WERE TOO AFRAID to tell him.

He watched the craven faces of his own men. His hand still stung from the blows he had dealt.

"Where are they?"

Silence.

"Speak!"

What kind of a return was this? He had come back from Jarl Guthrum's base in Cambridge to find disaster. He kicked out at the body hunched at his feet. But the man could hardly get the words out through a bloodied mouth. Kraka turned to the next.

"Tell me."

He got a stare of sullen silence. But he could break that. He could break anything. There was not a man living who could match him for power of muscle or quickness. It was a quality to be used. More than that, he had fought alongside Ivar and he had learned.

"Where are my brothers?" He flexed bruising knuckles and dropped his hand, not to the sword, but to the gold-wired hilt of the short single-bladed *seax*. So much quicker.

"Tell me the rest," said Kraka. His voice was soft, so quiet every one of the men sent to confront him would have to strain to hear it. Five warriors of no account and the high-ranking *hersir* he had beaten. It was one of the ordinary warriors who began to speak.

"The Saxons took the cargo out, not through the forest but by the ridgeway. We sent scouts to find what they did."

"They moved the cargo out?" It was not possible. Not unless the gods would kill him. The breaking of his orders, the ill-fated raid on the fort that had depleted his force by so many men and cost most of his plunder, were nothing compared to that.

"You let them? You allowed a handful of peasants and white-livered thralls to beat you and then escape with such wealth under your noses? What are you? Warriors or—"

"We fought. It would have been our glory." It was the *hersir* he had struck, mouthing through blood.

Glory. That was what they had wanted, why they had defied him and would not wait. All of them, the fool he had struck down, most of all.

"But?"

"The numbers favoured the Saxons." The lie was there, in the faint shifting of the swollen eyes.

"Numbers?"

The bruised eyes came back to his. "And they had king's men with them, one of Alfred's own who led them."

"Alfred's man." Kraka spat. "Alfred of Wessex will share the same fate as the King of East Anglia." The young king would have been another screaming sacrifice to Odin by now if Ivar had still been here.

But it was not Ivar who commanded the south now. It was Guthrum, waiting in East Anglia. And it was Jarl Guthrum whom Kraka would have to answer to, whom they would all have to answer to. His hand tightened on the knife hilt but the man was still speaking, crawling at his feet like an eager dog.

"The lord Horik your brother is pursuing the Saxons. They will be slow, hampered by the wagons and the pack mules. He will catch them. He may have reached them already."

Then not all was lost. At least his older brother had done something right. But it would have been his younger brother's idea. The brutal tension in his shoulders relaxed slightly at the thought of Toke, youngest and yet wisest. Favoured by them all.

"Horik and Toke will catch them." It was said to himself as much as to the watching group of his men, but the effect was like fire. He stared at the fear-sick faces, the nervous movement of hands and feet suddenly shifting and as suddenly stilled; and he knew. He could feel the string of fate tighten.

"No." He dragged the *hersir* to his feet. "Tell me." His hands tightened on flesh, the quickly stifled sound it brought something to be heard by all his men. "Tell me." The battered face was like stone, but he could smell the fear in the man's sweat.

"Tell me my youngest brother is not dead through your stupidity."

"The lord Toke fell in the battle. We tried—"

"You fools!" He roared at all of them. "You were all arrogant enough to break my orders. It is your blood-guilt."

"Lord, your brother fell in battle. It was a warrior's fate."

"Fate?" He could not accept that, even though the air beside the trackway stank with it, as it stank with fear. "It was your fault." His hands twisted in the *hersir's* flesh and the rage that would come to him out of the air, like a burning mist, took mind and heart. Such black rage. It would not be stopped. "You were the leader. You will pay."

The force inside him was so great he had no consciousness of moving the blade. There was only the startled gasp of sound, the look of total shock that had only one ending. He read it, just as he had done once before with the Saxon girl's father and mother who had cheated him. Just as it had happened all through his life when he did not control the rage.

His hand slackened on cooling flesh. This killing had been for his brother's memory. It was not dishonour. His mind set even as the dying man's eyes stared into his.

"I have my vengeance." It was over. Done. No going back. Ever.

But the battered lips of the dead man moved.

"You do not. You cannot." He could scarcely make out the words. "It was not me who caused Toke's death. It was his fate. Fate and the king's man. He brought your brother down on the battlefield so that his life was lost. He has taken everything from you, the cargo you wanted, even your Saxon slut. He will keep all if you cannot take it back…Berg."

The last word drowned in blood.

"I LIKE BEING IN THE FOREST. Did you see them? I did."

"See what?"

"The wild pigs. I like—"

"Pigs," finished Elene.

The boy laughed out of a grubby face.

"You should have seen them. There was a boar with tusks. That long. The tusks can rip—"

"I am sure they can."

"I wanted to follow them," offered Chad. "But Berg said not."

Berg. Who was a creation in equal parts of magic and terror.

"Berg said—"

"Look out. You are going to spill that."

There was a small pause while a leather bottle was righted. "I had a stain on my tunic anyway."

"So you did. An entire collection."

There was a further pause while the contents of the bottle were consumed. Elene looked at the fire and drew her cloak tighter in the darkness. Even though the weather had warmed.

"Do people have to have clean clothes all the time?"

"I suppose there are exceptions for travelling." There was no stream tonight. No freshly hunted food. Only what they carried, and a sense of urgency that had been muted until now.

She stared into the carefully banked embers that gave heat but little smoke. No pleasant glade outside the circle of light where she could suggest sleeping apart with the creation of magic. Just because she had a point to prove. That she was the equal of anything life could give her and afraid of no one. No *man*. For no other reason and for a thousand of them.

She shut her eyes. But she was holding him again. Her hands round his arms. The touch of his flesh under hers, the heat and the fine lines of it, the thickness of curving muscle against her palms. The intimate shape of the body hidden beneath linen revealed under her fingers. The body she had seen in the firelit darkness.

"Are you cold?"

"No."

"You are hugging your cloak."

She opened her eyes against the memory of the kiss, she had been lost in the heat of that. Lost as he had been. The banked fire flickered. But what had happened after…

I will not take from you anything you do not wish to give.

She could feel the long-trapped bitterness inside her as if it were poison. She could feel the worst thing of all, the thing she had never admitted in one moment with Kraka. The thing that had been present all the time. Fear. That was the shame she could not bear. She had never admitted it. Dared not.

She stood up.

"The bottle is empty. Do you think…" began Chad.

He was standing two paces from her. Berg. He was

speaking to Wistan, one hand resting on the other man's shoulder, head bent even though Wistan was tall.

"I said, do you think that—"

The light glowed and wavered. She could see his shadow. She could see the full damage to his face. He would turn. She took a step, even though something was tugging at the hem of her skirt.

"I *said*—"

Berg turned round and her heart contracted.

"I was *saying*," insisted the boy, "do you think they would give me unwatered alc?"

"No."

It was not she who spoke. It was the fire and shadow. He was laughing, the danger held lightly just for that fugitive moment, the stark intensity inside him muted. Beside him, Wistan rolled his eyes, and after a moment, walked away.

The shadow creature moved toward her. She took a step back. Her skirts caught.

"Why not?" the boy persisted.

Berg sat down beside Chad.

"I am old enough." The sticklike hand dragged at her hem.

"A good warrior never gets *over-drunken* in enemy territory," said Berg. "Not until the victory feast."

Go to the victory feast, make a speech… Get drunk.

But she did not think there had been much *symbelgal*, much wantonness of feasting, even then.

"Oh," said Chad. "Only then?"

The man did not move. The firelight made shadows out

of his heaviness, glinted on the polished metal fittings of sword and *seax*. Chad's wild boar with tusks. All she could think about was what was hidden in his mind. Why he should be so unhappy deep inside that it was like a spear wound that allowed no healing, a bale that killed joy.

"But you can get drunk then?" asked Chad.

She could not know that he was unhappy. She had no way to know.

"Aye."

She thought of East Anglia and the fields of horses all taken by King Ivar the murderer—Ivar, whom Kraka had once served. Stolen riches.

"Really drunk?"

Fire shine glinted off the small throwing axe looped through his belt, off the solid muscular line of his side. He had power. Even if Earl Guthrum could never be defeated, a man like Berg could still gain riches enough out of battle spoils. He was doing that. He had the strength. Like Kraka.

"Really, really drunk so that you—"

"Fall off the mead bench and cast up your drinking again? Preferably not."

Not riches. Grace.

She looked away.

"I would get that drunk," declared the sainted bishop's namesake. "I would."

"Ah, but you would get nothing out of it but a sore head and the ridicule of mere maidens. Would he not, lady?"

She started. He had not addressed her directly through all of his exchange with the boy. He had not so much as looked at her after that first turning with the gloss of laughter in his eyes. *Lady.*

He could feel nothing but anger for her and disgust after what had happened between them. There could be naught else. Only resentment.

"Lady?"

The laughter in the deep voice caught on something forgotten. It suits him, she thought, that is how he should be, *was*.... But the strange thought escaped her, evaporated under the heat of his eyes. The laughter was still there, bound in by a thread because of the boy.

She did not want such laughter. She no longer knew how to respond to it. But it held her.

"Is that not the way of it?" demanded Berg.

"Aye."

Then she said, "But there is nothing *mere* about maidens." Her heart pounded. The fire burned brighter.

"But it is manly," argued Chad. "I would not bother about what girls thought. Besides, why should they care how much a man drinks?"

The laughter shimmered, out of reach, but visible to her.

"They might have reason."

The flames touched her across the empty air. He was still looking at her, not the boy. She could feel the heat. But the laughter lingered, alive.

"Might they not?" The deep voice choked on the laughter.

The heat was inside her, under her skin, the way it had been at the very start when he had kissed her. Before disaster had come.

She had a sudden remembrance of Kraka slack-bodied and over-drunken, cursing and fumbling about because for once he could not... It had been something out of a nightmare and yet now there was a strange sensation in her throat, like something that wanted to escape and would do it. She made a small sound between laughter and suppressed tears.

She thought of Kraka being helpless.

"I suppose a maid might be disappointed," she said. "Or, then again—" the mingled sound escaped her lips, louder "—she might be relieved." She choked.

"Well, that was wounding." The man's brilliant grey eyes watched her, but in her mind she could see only Kraka. She put her hand over her mouth and sat down. She found she was shaking.

"Why?" piped the boy.

"A maiden's scorn. I told you." He moved. The child, as always, disregarded finality.

"But what—" The question was lost as Berg picked him up one-handed.

"Why would a maiden be disappointed if a man drank too much?" said Chad in a voice the entire camp could hear.

"Bed," replied Berg with spectacular double meaning. They disappeared into the deepening shadows. The boy, now dangling upside down and giggling, was still asking questions. She lowered her head onto her upraised knees.

She could hear the muted sounds of the camp settling for the night. She felt his nearness when he came back. She looked up.

He had brought a flask from their precious supply of mead.

She straightened her spine.

"I do not need that."

"Well, I am afraid to drink it now. So you had better."

"Idiot," she said before she had time to think about it. He sat. He was weary beyond reckoning. She recognised the bonds of fatigue, though the core of primitive virile strength in him was unbreakable. The sense of heat and male power radiated out from him in waves, frightening power laced with a deeply sexual edge after the things they had almost shared.

She pulled the loosened cloak tighter. It was darker, now, the night deepening. The fire burned lower into the heated embers. She took the flask out of his hand. She was careful not to touch skin. She allowed one small swallow.

The smooth liquid burned.

"I had forgotten about laughter," she said.

"Aye."

That was it. One word to describe the cataclysmic effect of a dubious jest, of accidental words. She stared at the bulky shoulders, the pale-gleaming hair. The half-hidden axe.

A person could easily think that here was a mere warrior of plain wits.

"Did you ever wed?" Elene asked suddenly.

"Did I...?"

Of course, he had reason for that tone of voice. The question was mad. Not what she had intended to say at all. It followed on from nothing, only her own mad thoughts, and she did not want to know.

But he was not a Viking who would take as many wives as he chose.

"Nay." He turned his head, and her question now seemed not crazed at all. The air tingled, froze. "I was betrothed."

"'Was'?"

His eyes held hers and the night air touched her skin like something alive with hidden knowledge. Broken vows. As familiar to her as her own skin.

"The arrangement did not go ahead?"

"No."

Her hands were tight round the neck of the mead flask.

"I see. It is always easy for people to escape from promises they regret. If that is what they will." She put the bottle down.

Hurt and bewilderment were tight inside her, as though they had happened yesterday. The pain was absurdly fresh, like something renewed, as though it struck her again, now, here under the trees of Kent beside the powerful stranger.

There was no reason to think of her own betrothal. It had been part of another life. The match had been made years ago, as a matter of course, a practical arrangement made for mutual benefit like any other. It would have increased her social standing, her kindred's.

But practicality and all the advantages so precisely calculated by a careful father had ceased to exist the moment she had set eyes on her betrothed. She had been eight winters old and in love with dreams. One meeting and she had created an entirely new world in her mind. It had sustained her for years, only growing with the gentle passage of time.

And then her suitor had changed his mind.

She balled her fists. "A word of honour is such an easy thing to break."

"I would not give blame," said the heavy shadow with its highly charged power.

"Would you not? Then you are a fool. If there is no honour, there is no point to life."

Yet she still lived, beyond the bounds of honour, one man's captive and now another's. She watched the firelight on the axe blade, the gilded hilt of the sword. But all she could think about was the way he had almost made her laugh.

"How could you have broken such a promise?" she said, as though she were a child again and he were not Berg the warrior, but the brilliant fourteen-year-old prince of East Anglia, the handsome boy who had filled her with enchantment.

"Sometimes such things seem better."

"Better. You mean more convenient and more…honourable." Her mouth twisted on the sound made by that last word.

"Aye."

Light glinted off the axe blade as though he had moved.

"That cannot be." Her voice was a grating thread of sound.

"It might. The family of a young girl of wealth and respectable position might make a bargain for her with the kindred of a person who could offer advantage. Such a bargain might be fair and made in all honour. But it is not in me to imagine that the girl grown into a woman should have to tie herself to the same bargain when circumstances alter. When the man is an exile who can offer none of the things promised, neither wealth, nor lands, nor position. When he has become not so much a man, as a maimed creature who would turn her disgust."

"She? *She* broke the promise?"

"I have said that there is no blame."

Elene watched the shadowed body, the face outlined by moonlight and firelight that he made not the slightest attempt to hide. She had almost screamed when she had first seen him and he knew that. He would see it in every place and every day.

"She should not have done it."

"Nay. She was right. I have naught that I once had. I came here with nothing except this armour. There is only what fate may bring now on the battlefield. And that may be death. I will not turn away from what I do. I cannot. But it is not right to expect someone to share a life that is not fit."

Not fit. That was, indeed, why her own marriage arrangement had never taken place. Her father's fortune had waned. He was not precisely a nobleman and her prince, emerging from the disaster of East Anglia, had needed more money, more influence than marriage to her had been able to provide. It had been a shaming blow.

Of course, it was laughable compared to what had followed for her.

The short, harsh sound she made might have been laughter. But it was a thousand leagues removed from the bubbling outpouring of warmth she had felt before. A warmth that could not last. Not now, because she was so changed.

"Elene—"

"What was she like?"

"Fine." He looked away. Away from her in her borrowed clothes, another man's castoff. "Summer," he said. "Like the sun in the sky. That is how she is to me."

CHAPTER 8

ELENE HAD MOVED her resting place, very gradually, farther away from the dark silent shapes of the sleeping Saxon warriors, into the blackness. There was no one to stop her, no captor to sleep with her.

Moving meant that she lost the heat of the fire, but she did not care about that. She had slept on cold ground before. She had become used to physical hardships, but the frightening tiredness dogged her, out of all proportion to anything she had ever known. Sleep dragged at her mind.

She lay in the dark, behind the screening of lush early summer growth and low bushes. She did not want anyone to see her.

Berg was gone. He had left after speaking of the woman who was like summer and the sun in the sky. He had not told her where he was going. There had only been a low-voiced conversation with Wistan across the sleeping form of the boy and then he had vanished into the shadows.

The only word she had caught had been a name, Macsen. It was a British name. Not Viking.

But the disjointed thoughts in her head did not turn to Kraka, either powerful with menace or drunk and slack-bodied.

Laughter.

Laughter that welled up as naturally as springwater. Laughter that had no place in this world.

It could not be as strong as the sorrow.

Did you wed?

How could she have asked that? Broken promises.

Summer…that is how she was to me.

No, not *was, is.* He had said *is* and then he had turned away from the sight of her.

Of course, that was what she wished. She thought of the warmth of his kiss and the fierce strength of his body when he had held her under the trees in the dawn's light. She did not want that.

Summer.

It coiled out inside her head, heated and alive, her own summer of ten years ago, gold and filled with magic, with promise. It was buried so deeply in her senses that she could taste its honeyed warmth.

She stirred against the makeshift bed of leaves and bracken but she did not feel the cold ground of Wessex. She stood on the flatlands of East Anglia with the wind off the water whipping through her hair and her clothes. The sun beat down and the tall grasses and the red poppies and the yellow-rattle flowers bent and danced, but she saw nothing of that. Only a bright figure with pale gold hair, a strong body, fine and straightly held, imbued even then with a heady sense of power still to come, a boy at the moment where childhood ended and manhood began. Fourteen.

It had been a fine age to a maiden of no more than eight winters with a head full of fancies. It had seemed an age of magic, somehow grown up without being adult, perfect, like every still-developing line of the flawless face and the body that was half child, half man.

Perfect.

Her mind floated out of waking and sleeping, the movement of her thoughts formless, impossible to control because she was so tired. The cold and the growing dark of the Andredesweald lapped at her. She lay curled up under the heavy cloaks that belonged to the stranger, Berg.

But in her mind she was running, her hand clasped in the boy's because, miracle of miracles, it belonged there. He was her betrothed. One day she would marry him and he would be wholly hers and she his. Her mother had explained. Her father had arranged it and while the adults of two differing kindreds discussed such things as money and property, they had fled into the open air, she and the boy who was her betrothed.

He was a prince, an atheling, a king's kinsman.

Bought from his family, the unassailable glamour of his position and his lands would be given in exchange for her father's money.

Neither of them had thought of that, not the ecstatic

eight-year-old maid, nor even the half-grown-up golden boy. He had never mentioned such mundane things. Perhaps princes did not, not directly. The gifts they would speak of would be those of honour, won by brave deeds from a grateful king.

He had shown such unexpected kindness to a young and insignificant girl. Nothing else had mattered. She had followed him and she had been swept up in the blinding quality that defined him, an uncomplicated joy in whatever gifts life would offer.

What fools they had been.

She moved aching limbs on the crushed bracken and the hard ground. But the dream seemed more real than the Wessex forest, the colours and the taste and the intensity of the memories brighter than they had ever been, more compelling.

She ran with the boy, clinging to the warmth of his roughened hand, his wrist already nearly as thick as a man's. Her dress with the silk ribbons that she had thought so grown-up caught at her childish feet. She had been worried about her fine blue tunic and her underdress of embroidered linen because she wanted him to think she was fine, and perhaps pretty. But then there had been sudden silence, only the sigh of the wind across the grass.

"Come here. Watch."

She had dropped down, oblivious of earth stains. The boy, always so noisy and impatient, had been so still, finely poised like a wild animal himself. She had seen the skylark's nest in the sedge grass and the miracle had happened. The bird had burst up into the waiting air, so close she felt the rush of its flight on her heated skin. The mad beat of wings cutting the wind had taken her heart. The unrestrained intensity of it had the same quality as the boy himself had—joy.

The trees of the Andredesweald rustled. Her fingers were closed round the small piece of metal sewn into the hem of her shift. She had no consciousness of having moved, no consciousness of anything but the power of the dream. The coldness of the Andred Forest was there outside the edges of thought, its darkness wrapped round her. But this time she did not want darkness. She wanted the dream.

She had hardly ever let herself feel it for more than two years, not since she had reached sixteen winters and an age full-ripe to marry. Not since her betrothal had been broken. The dream was so powerful. Sometimes after Kraka had taken her, she had let herself feel its magic, had let herself think it could make her safe. But only rarely.

Dreams were dangerous, false, misleading. She courted the emptiness. That was the path of survival. Yet the dream had still been there inside her head. She had not realised. So strong. She had kept it over all the years of her life, building and embroidering it, letting it grow as she grew. She had used its bright power to make her feel cherished.

Safe.

In her mind, the boy was holding something out to her. She moved to take it but the heavy, cloying bands of exhaustion held her limbs, a woman's exhaustion, deep and frightening and complete. She could not reach his hand.

"Look. Take this," said the boy. "I have broken your father's coin. But see how the two halves match?"

She watched the hammer-beaten, die-stamped silver join and pull apart in the young fingers.

She tried to reach out.

"It will be a token," he said. "I will keep my half. Will you keep yours?"

Yes. Always. The words were there, locked inside her head. She did not know whether they made sound, whether the suddenly distant figure of the boy could hear them. She stirred restlessly on the piled bracken. In her mind, she spoke the words, but they were lost. They had no power, no sound to touch the brilliant figure with its hand extended toward her in an invitation that was so simple, so utterly beyond her reach.

She had to touch him.

She had to make him know what she felt, otherwise their tie might break and she would lose him. She would not be able to bear that. She would be alone in a way that mind and soul could not comprehend.

Elene wanted to follow him into the sunlight and the bright moving air but she could not. It was not possible. She knew such things, evil and blackened things. She knew that all that lay ahead was the emptiness she had created in her own mind. She had created it to be her refuge, but it was as strong as a prison. There would never be anything else in her life. She had lost the chance forever. She moved. She could feel fear at a level beyond imagination. Terror.

She touched him. He was there. His hand closed over hers. She felt its warmth, the heavy fingers and the solid wrist. That was all she wanted. She clung to the hand and her body relaxed almost instantly, floating. Warmth seeped through her, deep and heady and blissful. Strong. The strength held comfort. She craved that. There had been no comfort for so long. She wanted its touch.

She thought the exhaustion made her dive under into sleep, but she still felt the warmth holding her, all of her. The bliss of it seeped through her bones. Unreal. She moved. The dreamlike awareness of her senses, at once diffuse and oddly heightened, told her of the shape of the other body. She touched it, felt its outline, huge and engulfing and night-dark, close behind her. Still. A creation of power, of spellcraft.

The hand covering hers was no longer that of the sunlit boy. It belonged to the witching dream a girl had created as she'd turned into a woman. It was the hand of her dream-lover, the enchanted shape the lonely girl-woman had imagined out of longing and magic.

Her soul's *fetch*, a male counterpart, match of a Valkyrie spirit.

She turned into its embrace. There was no fear because he was hers, made of memory and wishes, part of her self. She floated in his arms.

In the distance was the black bulk of the Wessex forest and the scent of night air full of trees growing and decaying and breathing, the faint tang from the distant campfire. In his arms she found light and the heat of midsummer, shared memories, because a *fetch* was a holder of past thoughts and actions, attached to the spirit for the duration of life.

Her fingers played over the magic hand that had held

the coin. It was such a heavy hand. She traced its warmth, its solidness, the flesh surprisingly thick across the bones. She smiled with the memory of the fleeting joy he had shown her.

She smiled because really, it was a great clumsy hand that she held. Though sometimes it was not clumsy at all, but very deft. It had been taught skill. She avoided the healing bruise down the side that had come from fighting. She knew it without thought.

His hand turned in hers, gliding across it in a movement that was both smooth and fluid. The strong fingers parted hers, sliding between in a caress that penetrated deep inside her, that was private, intensely intimate. Her hand touched his, joined. Her sleep-softened flesh grazed the hard, unyielding surface of wrought metal. Not a halved coin—a ring, the shape of an eagle holding a fish in its claws. A symbol that encompassed past grief and new life.

Berg.

It was his living warmth that she touched, his hand she held. Her heart should have stopped. Her breath should have caught in her throat with fear and the driving urge of rejection. But the *memory-fetch* was still there, the dream-lover. All of that lived in his silence and the smooth, slow touch of his hand, in the heat. Summer sun.

Her senses swam in the exhaustion that was unreal and the dreams came back in coloured fragments, bright and hot and rich with life. Not like the nightmares that belonged to now, filled with darkness and despair. She stirred restlessly, but the heavy warmth moved with her, drugging and complete, holding her in thrall, like someone spellbound.

That was what magical beings did, fire-and-shadow creatures from other realms, strong and uncanny and desirable beyond mortal power to resist. Not just *memory-fetches*, but other creatures, *ylfe,* bright fierce elves. This was the maddening witchery of the male spirit that could seduce a woman in sleep, in the dark hours of the night, an incubus.

She lay still, caught in the gap between sleeping and waking, the gap between middle earth and the other worlds that surrounded it. Dreams. She shifted. But that only let her feel his shape, powerful and warm, full muscle and intensely carved lines, fineness beyond mortal sense.

The touch of the heavy hand soothed her, gentle in its touching, sense-stealing. Immortal seduction, potent, impossible to resist. Attraction and longing bound her like the darkest bewitchment.

She fell back against him, solid warmth and power, dream-lover. Beneath her cloak-wrapped body, the bracken of the Andredesweald rustled and the night air stirred. She heard the soft catch in his breath. She thought of the healing bruises.

Berg.

Dreams. He had spoken of them from the first moment and the dreams were so strong inside her, filling a mind loose and floating with exhaustion, perilously vulnerable and light. She thought she felt the same exhaustion of mind and body in him, impossible to combat, frighteningly deep and dangerously complete.

She did not know how long he had been away this night, what he had done. So little true rest, even from that first day at the fortress. She knew the marks of the battle were still there.

Her body lay still, angled only obliquely against his because she was afraid of touching bruising.

But he only pulled her closer and her body moved to the smooth, dreamlike urging of his, the dark mysterious touch of him whole and entire and a thing of magic. The closeness overwhelmed her and she was falling, into heated darkness, into him.

They did not face. She did not want to see him and he would not want to see her. Dream-lover. His hand caressed her, the touch rhythmic and darkly warm, full of the binding spellcraft. Her body responded to it in a way she did not understand, could not think of. It was a primitive instinct, a strong force beyond her will. Or sprung from a wanting so deep it bypassed will.

A sweet ache uncoiled deep in her lower belly, something buried inside her that wanted to take flight, a need that responded to the touch of his hand. She lay against him, her back pressed lightly to the solid wall of his chest. The full curve of her hips rested against him, thighs touching. It was the way they settled for the night, the way he kept her close in sleep. A familiar closeness. Highly charged with awareness.

She had lain so with him in silent intimacy, but he had never touched her like this.

The heat and the powerful strength held her from behind, his hand caressed her body and the closeness pen-

etrated through clothing and flesh and blood. The unac-
customed feelings he aroused, the vulnerability to him,
deepened. As the feelings increased, so did the intensity
of his touch, as though he knew, as though he could sense
what she felt without reserve, through the touch of minds.
Memory-fetch.

But it could not be so. He could not belong to her, nor
she to him. It must be someone else he held, another
being who had a warmly yielding body, soft and supine,
voluptuous with unspoken desires. Not her. She did not
respond so.

Her thoughts floated, dreamlike and at the same time
full of awareness, burning, burning all the time he touched
her. Her body rolled back against his heat, pressing closer.
Her clothes were loosened for sleep, disordered and tangled round her limbs, her hips. His hand touched skin.

The magically heightened awareness had slipped beyond the grasp of thought. Her senses, mind and body,
were attuned only to her lover's touch, to the shivering
slide of heat-moistened skin, to silence and closeness, a
heartbeat, shared warmth. She was lost in the dark world
of enchantment, in her *dream-fetch* and his magic, in his
human closeness.

The sweet ache in her blood intensified; the rhythmic
touch of his hand both assuaged and incited it, a melting
pleasure that grew and released with the movement of his
fingers. She stirred against him. She felt the flesh of the
body behind her tighten. But he did not speak. There was
only the quiet laced with intensity. Nothing to shatter the
dream, every movement slowed to an aching languor.

Her body twisted for him as he touched, the turning of her limbs luxurious and outside the bounds of time. Nothing known except the rhythmic insistent pressure of his broad heavy palm against the curving flesh at her hip. The slow urging of that movement made the ache deep in her belly intensify, so that she pressed harder against his hand, mindless, seeking release.

His fingers slipped round the curved fullness of her thigh and he touched her.

An erotic lover's touch.

Her senses swam. The intimate sensitive folds of her woman's skin were moist and softened and tight-feeling under his fingertips. She held motionless, poised on the edge of another world, a world that did not belong to her. She had never taken her private, intimate world so far, even in dreams. It was beyond her power, beyond who she was.

She could not move, unable to press against him even though the burning ache built, unable to do anything but lie in his embrace, the shadow-prince, a creature born of loneliness and pain and longing and memory.

More. A real person. Berg. Sharing the cold ground with her under the stars in the Andredesweald, the same night, the same touch, the same warmth and exhaustion and stifled pain. She could not think of that. Because if she did, she would be her real self, frightened, ruined, useless. A Viking's whore.

Elene.

It was not Elene the dream lover held in his arms. It was not Elene to whom he gave warmth and life and the luxury of sharing. It was another self, another body that warmed and flowered and responded to such close intimate touching as he gave.

Not her.

She heard the black exhaustion in his breath. The woman who was not her moved, into the heated curve of his body, the touch of his hand. She slipped into some other realm. The dream-lover's hand caressed softened flesh, fingers slipping over desire-damp skin, seeking the source of the moisture inside her body, the unexpected slickness only increasing the open eroticism of his touch. The heavy palm cupped the heat of her sex, the broad fingertip, slickened and smooth with moist heat, touched— She knew not.

The touch was so light, so full of power.

She twisted in response. The small movement changed everything. Her feelings caught and centred in a dizzying rush, so darkly sweet, melting and spilling over into the greater darkness until it enveloped her. She could not keep consciousness, the intensity and now the dizziness and the weariness held back and released, folded over her in waves.

She wanted to touch his hand, to keep the connection she had sought. But his fingers lay against hotly aching flesh, his arm across her inner thigh. She could feel the weight, like a lover's, warm and heavy and male.

It was too intimate, too real. She was afraid of such sharing. No one truly divided their soul with a *fetch*.

She held on to the vague sense of his warmth, then nothing. The darkness closed over her head.

HE WAS GONE WHEN ELENE WOKE, as though he had never existed, as though she had not spent the hours of darkness in concourse with the other half of her soul.

Berg. East Anglian warrior.

It was not possible.

She had been dreaming, the dazzling dream she had spent her nights embroidering with vivid colours, the way she had once spent her days embroidering white linen with dyed threads of silk.

But her dream had never been so intense, so full of dark erotic magic. Heat...

She put her hand to her lips. Her fingers were cold, stiff, blistered and aching. That was reality, the journey through Wessex, the journey to Winchester where she might find her parents. The flight from Kraka.

The carrion crow.

She did not lie willing and heated in a man's arms, fainting and burning with desire. Seeking magic. Finding a soul mate.

It had been a dream, the madness of unquiet sleep. Such things had no reality. They were bitter, mind-destroying illusions. She had set her face against that, everything that remained of herself and the strength of her will.

She did not deal in magic or pursue lust; she knew too well its bitter pain. She would never seek carnal pleasure from a man or expect it. She would never want to share...

People did not share, not in that way.

Beyond the edge of the leafy brushwood someone cursed. She heard the irritated whinnying of a reluctant horse, the sounds of an armed camp preparing to move with the first dawn light. That was what she was used to.

The rest, heated thoughts and the warmth of comfort and intimate pleasure, were a dream.

"Lady."

The voice called to her across the screen of summer growth. She sat up, forcing movement through the aching heaviness of her limbs, stretching her stiff neck. The familiar wall of fatigue hit her. She could scarce move a muscle. The raw feeling was like a terrible weight, harder to lift each day.

She choked back the fear that brought and raised her head. The light was changing reluctantly. The air felt oppressive, warmer, as though it held the day's heat already. She fastened the looted brooch with the white crystals and the pretty red and green glass. Then she picked up her bedroll and walked back into the camp.

The forms of Berg's men moved through it, blurred and indistinct. The boy, shirt still untied, hopped between them, tripping over saddlebags and under impatient feet.

"See. She is awake. Look. I told you so. When are we going?"

Berg was not there.

It was Wistan who brought her food. Dried fruit and small strips of meat. The men were in a hurry.

She began packing her saddlebags. There was no huge figure with heavy tread to roar orders. Still, everything moved very swiftly. She loaded the horse.

The sense of urgency was palpable. The hopping boy was sworn at.

Berg did not come. He had left before the night had truly fallen, after he had spoken to her of his lost betrothed. He was not here. He was not part of her dreams.

No one seemed surprised by his absence. She tried to concentrate her exhausted thoughts on what was happening, on what was real. Chad upset somebody's quiver of arrows and tripped two people in the ensuing confusion. One of the victims stood on three arrow shafts at once. There were snapping sounds followed by more cursing. Things became heated. If Berg had been there, he would have sorted it out. Perhaps he would have laughed the way he had yesterday when—

"That Viking's brat…"

The boy plunged off.

What was real…

She let go of the recalcitrant buckle, the saddlebag still in her hand. She followed.

She found Chad beside the spare horses hiding in a pool of shadow. She coaxed him out.

"It was not my fault."

"No?"

"It was not me who trod on the arrow shafts."

"Who knocked them over in the first place and then banged into two people?"

"But—"

"They told you to stay out of the way." She regarded Chad's bent head. Her heart clenched. The child leaned on the nearest horse, fingers picking at the fastening of the thick saddlebag.

"I suppose so."

"Well, then. Come back and—"

"I am *not* a Viking. I am not disloyal."

Her heart seemed so tightly bound she could not breathe, or swallow or find words. The bony fingers stabbed at leather.

"I know."

"But it is what they think."

"No. They do not. Not really. They were in a hurry and not in the best of temper. People will say anything when they are vexed, whether it is what they really believe or not."

She watched the lost miserable boy. How did she know it was not what those men really thought? They lost their comrades to the Danes each time they had to fight. Sometimes they lost all they had. There was no place for half-measures and fine distinctions. Or pity. She kept her voice even.

"People always feel cross first thing in the morning and it must anger a warrior to lose valuable weapons. Particularly when he cannot immediately replace them."

"I bet they can. They have loads of spare gear. Look at all the extra horses."

Coldness touched her neck despite the sultry closeness of the air under the trees. One packhorse could carry enough supplies for two or three men, four at a stretch. Berg had far more. She had been so wrapped in her own concerns she had not thought about it. Just assumed it was plunder from the battle, extra supplies.

But they ate and drank sparingly and they travelled fast.

Chad punched the abused saddlebag. The horse snorted its protest.

"Careful—"

"I asked Wistan. He said it was extra weapons and things for the journey and—"

She caught the reins before the irritated horse could trample its tormentor. Her arm banged the saddlebag. Something fell out, glinting in the light, so small as to be unregarded.

"Lady? Is something wrong? Was there something you needed?" The new voice cut the closeness. The reins were snatched from her hands. The horse quieted in an instant and she was standing in an unobstructed space with the boy.

"Lady?"

One could forget how strong Wistan was because of the youthful fairness of his face and his quiet manner. He was nearly as big as Berg.

"Nothing is wrong. Thank you. Chad was just recovering from his upset. I think he would like to make his peace."

Wistan nodded, hand still on the horse's reins. The saints be praised, for once in his short life, Chad chose not to argue. She turned. The leather strap of her own saddlebag was still in her hand. It slipped.

She stooped to retrieve it, quicker even than the boneless speed of the boy. But she let him pick up the bag. She had what she wanted. It rested in her palm, a shape so familiar it belonged there.

She could not look at it more closely in sight of Wistan and the boy, but she did not need to. The coin warmed against her flesh. On one side a man's face, a hastily executed profile crowned with laurel like a Roman emperor, the die-stamped image that stood in for the brilliant features of the king of Wessex, round it the letters *Ælfred Rex*. On the reverse another name, Bernfr.mo.

It stood for Bernfrith, moneyer and minter of new coins.

The boy trotted beside her.

"Do I really have to say sorry?"

"It would help."

There was silence and the heaviness of the air, prickling over her skin, waiting, no breath of wind under the shadows of the trees.

"Do we have to tell Berg what I did?"

"Perhaps not. Besides, he is not here just now."

"No. He has gone hunting Vikings."

"Hunting—" Her voice stopped of its own accord. Her chest tightened.

"Wistan said it was just scouting and the Danes might not even be there. But Wistan always says things like that. I bet they are there. Hiding in the trees. Ready to pounce." The boy chopped his right arm through the air as though he held slashing steel.

The tightness closed round her ribs, the taint of fear in the expectant air familiar. No, not familiar. Startlingly new.

Berg the East Anglian.

The boy bounced at her side.

"I saw him take his spear."

THERE WAS NO ONE. He could swear nothing moved in the narrow band of the forest that lay between the position of his men and the open country rising to the ridgeway across the Downs.

Berg urged his horse up the rise, the cramped muscles over healing bruises in his thigh protesting. He pulled rein, scanning the empty expanse of the land, holding the restive horse still in the shadows. There was no breeze, nothing to carry sound or scent. Sweat coated his skin.

Overhead the thunderclouds hung, cutting the light, blocking the air and the heat until there was nothing to breathe. The closeness choked him, like an opponent's hands. Like expectation. He wanted to smash it. To send his mount plunging over the rough slope, out of the shadows and into the open country and the blue bulk of the Downs. So that he could break the weight of waiting. So that he could— What? Fight? But why?

The fight was not his. The plans had been confirmed last night. All he had done this day was to make sure the danger lay north, across the slashing line of the ridgeway. For someone else to face.

He turned the horse, the restless animal responding to the urging of his body as though it were the call to battle he could not give.

There was nothing more he could do. It was the hardest truth it was possible to accept.

He still had not learned.

He urged the horse back into the trees, toward where Wistan and the rest of the men would be. And the hidden cargo and the small boy.

Back to the frightened woman who in the dead hours of the night had created a closeness that was unreal.

Even now the thought of her warmth and the fine contours of her body heated his blood. The desire for her was bone-deep.

She had responded, turned to him, burned with the same desire for his touch. Like the banked heat of a long-held dream, a connection that ignored time.

But he knew what was real, what still lived inside her head. He had seen it in the unsparing light of day, in the shadowed depth of her eyes watching him in the dawn light beneath the trees. Bitterness and fear and the sharp edge of despair.

Perhaps there was a trace of hate.

Kraka's mistress.

The shadows cut off the view of the Downs, the ridgeway, the setting for the fight that was not his.

Not yet.

He tried to keep his mind on the future, on the promise he had made to the woman.

He would not break that.

Yet the reckoning pressed at his back, the shades of the dead, of loss, of killing that knew no end, the demands of the duty owed by what had once been an atheling. The demands of a new oath given to a king who was in bitter need. The reckoning that would come with the Viking. With Ivar's man. With Kraka.

The anger built.

BERG CAUGHT UP with the train of horses just as the first heavy drops of rain fell and the lightning split the sky. The thunder followed quickly, sending the boy wide-eyed. The men steadied the horses, cursing.

But it was orderly. They were used to this, the hardship surmountable enough, even for the boy, if handled with care.

The pest of a child hung back, but Elene came toward him, which he had not expected. His heart caught. After last night, after dreams and shared heat, after...nothing that seemed real.

He watched her, the way he would assess the weakest member of a troop. The horse bore her well, living up to the high price of its worth. She was a fair rider. Skilfully taught.

"You took your time," she observed.

All that was to be seen was the calculated challenge she used against the world, against him. Her face was pale, her skin white against the growing shadows round her eyes.

"I had enough to do."

Her gaze followed his slightest movement, as though she could not look away.

"Just as well we tarried for you then," she said. "You were slow."

Her mount bent its sweat-streaked, rain-streaked neck. The next decision came.

"Another two hours' ride," said Wistan, appearing at Berg's shoulder. "Perhaps more with this rain."

Two hours at least to the standing stone, the way hidden and unused because it led toward the world of spirits. Perfect concealment.

But little shelter to be found, even when they reached their destination. The thunder made Elene's well-mannered horse shift. She controlled it. The fatigue of her limbs was well disguised. She mastered it, as she must have mastered the fatigues of a dozen journeys, a dozen storms like this, trailing between one Viking camp and another, from Repton in Mercia to Cambridge in what had once been East Anglia. Courage.

"Only two hours?" The soaking linen of her veil framed her face. She used the smile that left her eyes untouched. It made the delicate skin outline the fine bones beneath. The depth of her fatigue seemed unnatural. There was something hidden she did not show or speak of, not to him.

"No," he said to Wistan. "We find somewhere closer to shelter tonight."

"Closer? Lord—" But Wistan was a perfect second in command, always had been. He shouldered his horse through the rain.

CHAPTER 9

THE PRIOR WAS AFRAID to let them in. Elene looked at the loose straggle of buildings inside the wooden stockade that made up the small house of religion—shelter. The need for it was primitive, life or death. The intensity of it shocked her.

But she sat the horse and waited. *Never count on anything in journeys.*

She watched Berg talk the man into it. Perhaps it was the size of him, or the dripping sword hilt. Or perhaps it was the money. He carried enough of it.

She buried her head briefly against the neck of her patient mount. Silver coins. That was the reality that had the power to decide life or death.

The boy dripped silently at her side, even his spirits drowning in the downpour, or from the guilt of his misdemeanours, or from fear of the storm.

They were shown inside. She ate hot food in her chamber. Then the brothers brought heated water. She stared at it for a while in case it might disappear before her eyes. The steam wrapped round her. She could smell its humid warmth.

She took off her clothes. Before Berg could repent of his decision to stay here, before the rush of an entire Viking army striking through the forest to reach them, there would be this.

The water was bitingly hot over her chilled skin. She sank into it, over every aching limb, her wet hair spread out like pond weed. She buried her head and closed her shaking hands over her face.

It was a long time before she left the bath. But there was no sign of him. She should be glad. Perhaps this was her chamber alone. It was a house of religion after all. She tested the notion of being by herself. She walked round the bower. An empty bower. Possibly hers. She had not been alone at night for over a year.

She stretched out her arms and felt space. She could get into a bed made up with fresh linen and sleep. The tiredness that never stopped washed over her warmed skin in waves.

A fire burned steadily in the hearth. The rain drummed on the thatch. The flames hissed.

She lay down. A small hard lump touched her leg. She had put on her old shift since the new one she had changed into this morning was now drying before the fire. She moved her leg. A familiar shape brushed her skin. Half a coin. With a different king's image. A different moneyer's name.

She rolled over.

Sackfuls of coins. *Ælfred Rex. Bernfr.mo.*

She sat up. The silence enfolded her. No man would intrude on her in a monastery guesthouse, not even one who owned her. No Christian man at any rate.

Not even the dark shade of the dream-lover.

In her mind, she could see his hand and the ring with the eagle holding the fish, life out of death. She would never comprehend new life the way he did.

There was no connection between them, neither in the insubstantial realm of shadow thoughts, nor in the brutal truth of reality.

She wrapped her spare cloak over the thin, patched linen. She let herself out of the chamber. The prickly rushes scratched at the soles of her feet, then the blank coldness of flagged stones struck skin.

He was there.

The chapel lamps showed the fresh, dark green linen stretched tight across his shoulders, the fall of damp hair still darkened from the rain, or perhaps from the boon of heated water like hers.

He knelt, unmoving. Like the figures carved in stone on the walls. So still. He might have been dead.

Except she could see the tension in the solid muscles, harsher than the sleepless weariness. He was like someone waiting for something to happen, all his thoughts bent on it. A man who hated to wait for anything without taking action. It must be something terrible.

Silver…

She crossed herself, walking down the aisle into the circle of light beside the altar. The coin, Alfred's coin, pressed against her palm.

"Why did you stop here this night?"

He raised his head. The darkened hair slid down his back.

"Why?" His hand moved in the sign of the cross, like hers, like someone well schooled. He turned his head. "Why do you ask me, Elene?"

Waiting…

The walls of the chapel seemed to close in. She stood her ground and opened her palm. The rich glow from the decorated brass lamps caught the whiteness of silver.

"Hurriedly made," she said. "The lettering is unevenly spaced and the decoration above the head. But the metal is quite pure. I could not break it."

He looked away. So fast she could not guess what lay behind the shadows of his eyes. It must be shock that she had found him out. His huge fist clenched. Anger. That was what lay behind the tension. She took one step back.

"My decision is made." His voice echoed off the walls. "I will not change it."

She sat down on the wooden bench. Her legs were shaking. She did not know whether it was from fear or from her own store of hidden rage.

"Do you not realise the danger of what you do?" she spat.

He turned his head. "Do you mean to explain it to me?"

His eyes burned. She could see what had not been

shown before or what the physical strength had blinded her to. The lines and the shadows etched into his face, on the fair as well as scarred flesh, lines of thought and determination. Lines of strain. Her anger boiled over.

"What should I explain? What is so obvious for me to work out in my head? That the mint at Canterbury must still be working behind the city walls? That the coins have to be brought out? Some perhaps left at the fort to pay for what must be bought above those dues owed to the king? That the rest is taken westward for the king's use by a group of armed men too few for the task? I do not think I have to explain any of that. You know it. My guess is right, is it not?"

His eyes watched, measuring. The stillness of his body was complete. Yet under it was something feral. The lash of awareness that struck between them told her beyond the possibility of disguise.

But she kept speaking, words she should not say because they were more deadly than barbed arrows. Words that desecrated the chapel. They spewed out of her mouth, unstoppable.

"What you do not understand is what *this* means." She thrust the coin at the beautiful, ruined face. "You think like a noble king's messenger. You do not understand what this means to a Viking who came to this land for gain."

Her hand was shaking. She tried to stop it, but she would not lower the silver coin from before his skin.

"What do you imagine this much treasure means to a Dane? To a fractious group of adventurers who must survive in a hostile land? King Ivar has taken the northern half of England and he will share it out with his companions. What is left for a latecomer like Earl Guthrum in the south? Mercia has already been plundered. East Anglia is a kingdom dead."

She saw his eyes. She could read them. All the dark bitter agony and the unslaked rage. Still she went on.

"East Anglia is accessible to Denmark, an easy target now that it has been defeated. Not only Guthrum abides there. Its lands have become crowded with newcomers. Vikings." She watched his eyes, even though she no longer wanted to. She could not look away. "It is full of those greedy for gain. They will fight to get what they want. They will even fight each other. Or they will set their eyes on Wessex. Wessex still has wealth that can be taken. Wealth like this."

The hard die-stamped metal of the coin dug into her fingers.

"Those who can gain this kind of wealth also gain power, over their enemies and over their fellows. Kraka is a man who likes power, over people and over things. He has an ambitious master to serve in Earl Guthrum, a clever and dangerous one. More than that, he has his own position to make. I know what is in his mind. There were no secrets between Kraka and me. I was his mistress." The hideous, dangerous truth defiled the air. Kraka the Viking, Earl Guthrum's man, Kraka who had been in East Anglia when it had fallen.

"When we lay together in the straw, close—" She choked on the word. *Closeness. The heat and the closeness of dreams.*

Dreams were deadly, untrue. She had known that. She

should never have allowed the power of them into her mind. The truth spilled out.

"When he and I came together in the straw, rutting like animals, sometimes he would tell me things that he planned, what he wanted, all that he expected to gain. Things that were in his head."

She could see nothing in the stormcloud eyes now but the anger, and the feral edge that had always been kept hidden. He could not hide it any longer. She was used to the sight of such force. Besides, she could see everything about him. He stood up. She did not stop talking.

"Kraka gives up nothing that he considers his." She did not step back, but she had to lower her hand because it was shaking so much. She thought there was some noise behind her. She did not look round. Nothing could break the power of her gaze on his. "Kraka will not give up the treasure he covets, nor the vengeance he must take for the defeat of his brother."

The noise got louder.

"Neither will he give up his whore."

"Lord—"

It was Wistan. Berg had neither sensed his presence nor turned his gaze from hers. For one splintered instant, he was as stunned as she, as blinded by intensity. But then he moved, taking her arm, turning her not toward Wistan and the main aisle, but back toward himself.

"Go back to your chamber."

Sanity returned, coldness crawling down her spine like ice flakes. With it, came the awareness of where she was, standing before an altar, and of what she had said. To someone who had lost his own country, whose rage was boundless, all the more potent because it was hidden.

"Lord." Wistan's voice came nearer.

"Get out." The words were not for Wistan, but for her, breathed against her skin with lethal softness. "Now."

There was a side door she could use. She could see it. She would not have to turn and face Wistan's questioning eyes. Or the altar.

Or the man she had tormented with loss.

She paused in the blackness, but she could not hear what they said, only see the way Berg strode away and Wistan followed, the swirl of his wet cloak making the candles flutter. Berg made the sign of the cross.

HE CAME TO HER.

She could feign sleep if she wished. She could have taken her chance and fled from the walls of the monastery into the storm. Mayhap.

She could keep silence. She should have kept silence.

She watched Berg drop the heavy oak bar into place across the door, pick up the unlit lamp, walk across the floor.

"Do not make light." She could not bear for him to see her shame. All that she could no longer hide.

He stopped beside the fire. Then he set down the dead lamp and came toward her, black shadow against the banked flames.

He stretched out on the bed. She could feel the solid wall of his closeness. She could hear his breathing. She could feel a thousand things she had sensed about him in the chapel, banked down like the flames.

She did not know why she had gone to warn him, why she had finished by taunting him with loss. She reminded herself of the greater truth, that in the end she was still a captive. He held the power and that was the sum total of what he meant to her, of what he was. Her goal did not lie with him. She had to get to Winchester to find her parents, to know that they were indeed safe, even if she could never go back to them. Her fingers brushed the brooch pinned inside her cloak, the brooch that had been looted from Kraka's men after the battle at the fortress. Kraka and looting.

"What did Wistan say?"

"Naught that cannot wait, now."

She thought of the way Berg had moved and of the fluttering candles. Berg, who had been waiting in such furious tension. Berg with the stark, exhausted face.

"He had news." Her heart stuttered on the fear of it. The new fear for— She glanced away from the breathing human shape beside her.

"The Vikings." She said the word. "Kraka."

"Kraka is not here." She heard the finality of Berg's living breath. "There is only us."

Us. The small word shivered in the dark air. *Us.* She looked at the solid shadow beside her, felt his presence. Heat. She thought of the way he had first touched her. How that had felt, despite the bitterness of fury and despair. Despite a death wish. The longing for it hit her like a rush of flame.

She wanted to touch him again, not in imagination and dreams, but now and in reality. She did not move.

"No. Kraka is here. He will always be here." She held so still. "I lived as his mistress. What can change that?"

"The future," said Berg, in the darkness.

She thought of his strength and the measure of it. She thought of her fears. The old fears and the ones that were quite new.

"The future." She watched his uptilted face, gaze apparently fixed on the smoky thatch above their heads. "Do you believe in it? Can you?"

He did not speak. Not for a minute, and she thought it was because he could not. Pretense was no longer possible. She had felt all that he had felt in the chapel, the anger and the pain.

"Yes, I do."

Her heart seemed to catch, but then it went on beating. Nothing changed. Nothing could. "You cannot believe that."

"I have given my word to it." He turned, the movement of his body slow. Power held back. She could see the gleam of his stormcloud eyes in the dark. "I did not realise at the time what I did. But it is so and there is no going back."

The rough power of his voice, the heat of it, split the dark. Like something that would take her soul.

He could not take her soul because she no longer had one to give. "No future is possible. You do not understand." Elene thought of all that Kraka had taken from her. "You do not know what it was like."

"Then tell me, now and in truth."

His words hung in the air, so softly said. Yet she knew that all the burning power she had sensed in the chapel lay beneath them, all the pain and loss. And the anger, bright and unappeased. He would hate her if she told him. All it would take would be one more word.

"It was my…" The word hovered at the back of her mind and then she said it. "My choice." She cleared her throat. "I made a bargain. I got what I wanted and so did Kraka."

After a moment, she shut her eyes. But the awareness of the man beside her was a thing beyond mere sense. Almost inside her skin.

"What did you want so much?" he said.

The picture of her mother's face swam behind her closed lids. She could see the horror in her mother's stretched eyes, in her father's face. Fear. Such fear. And then there had only been Kraka, his men behind him destroying all that they could not take. All that was of no use.

Kraka and she, quite alone, and somewhere back in the captured hall, her parents.

Why should I spare a man too weak to fetch a slave's price and an old woman? What could you give me for that?

I will make you a bargain. She could hear the bravado in her voice, pushing out the terrible words that had stuck in her throat. Her heart had raced and her skin had turned clammy with fear. Yet she had believed she could accomplish it. She had believed that she could do so much. Even preserve honour.

Honour. The idea no longer existed. She opened her

eyes. She stared at the thatch in the unknown bower the way the man beside her had.

"Kraka's men came raiding, for killing and for plunder." She moistened her lips. "But they did not kill me. I am still here, am I not?"

She shrugged her naked shoulders. The bedclothes pulled against the solid weight beside her. She knew what she said. The East Anglian would know—

"Elene." Her name, the intimate one her parents had always used.

The East Anglian knew nothing.

"Did you think it was something else? It was a bargain."

"A forced bargain."

She thought about not saying the rest. There was no reason to say it. A victim owed her captor nothing. She had been Kraka's captive.

"Kraka did not have to make such a bargain. No one could have stopped him or his men from taking what they wished. He could have killed me. Killed—" She stopped. What did she say? *I made a bargain to save my family, to honour rightness.*

She did not look at the living shape beside her.

"I made my decision. I gave myself to Kraka and I was his. But he kept the bargain. He was not without his own honour. He kept his word."

"There is no honour in what he did." He was no longer looking at her but she felt the flick of the hidden anger, as raw and hot as flame, as raw as her own unhealed rage. He still spoke.

"There can be no honour where—"

"No!" She screamed it. The spectre she could not face took shape with his words, the bitterness of it like a poison unending.

"There was no honour." Her voice shouted the truth. She might have taken the first step for honour's sake, but afterward she had not been able to hold so much as the idea of it in her head. "There is no honour and there can never be. It will not come again." Her insides tightened. Her body wanted to writhe with the pain. She fought the urge to drag her arm protectively over her belly. She knew he was not looking at her but he would sense anything she did, were she as silent as a spirit. She fought for stillness.

Perhaps he would go. He did not want a compliant *hórkona* like Kraka. He had said so. There was no survival for dreams. What a man like Berg truly wanted was something different from her. A lady. Someone pure.

Fine, he had said. *Like the sun in the sky.*

His weight shifted and her heart stopped, the pain choking round it.

"There is honour for you, Elene. It is only that you have stopped believing it."

The bitterness cut. Despite her will, her body clenched, curled in on itself.

He was looking at her.

She did not know when he had turned, the movement of his shadowed head a thing missed in the fierce inward focus of her body. His gaze touched her, the thing she had most wanted to avoid. The light and shadow of his eyes held.

"There is still honour and a future."

"No." She forced her limbs to straighten out. "Not so."

The sound of her voice beat at his gaze. "You do not know. You are a warrior who has always had power. You do not know anything." She choked, and the clearness of his eyes in the shadows was like an abyss she would fall into with one more breath. All that she had never wanted to see, all the qualities in him that had no right to exist, were shown in the face that was turned toward her. Everything that had forced her to speak for his sake in the chapel. All that she had wanted at the same time to destroy because she could no longer bear to look on it.

"No," she said. "A person should have power over their deeds." They were the words she said, over and over, to herself. What she believed. It was certainly what a warrior believed.

"Not always."

There was no ground under her feet. The abyss had opened wide and she was falling.

She flailed out. The anger and the despair took her and she was so base, so desperate, she would have struck him. His hand caught hers, the force of the combined movement so strong, it hurt. She was glad of the pain. Their hands tangled, less than an inch from his face. He did not let her go. Their fingers were meshed. The terrible force was so great and her heart was so full that she no longer knew whether she struck out to save herself or whether she clung to him against the fall.

She made a small sound, raw and ugly in its desperation. The grip on her hand lessened. But that made no difference because she could not have moved away from him.

"You would have touched scars."

The muscles in her arm were stiff, aching.

"Shall I light the lamp after all and show you?"

"*No*. Do not make light."

Their hands held. "It makes no difference. You do not need to see, only feel."

His fingers tightened, drawing hers down, closing the last fraction of space between them. She touched flesh. No, not flesh, the ridged indentations of severed muscle and twisted scarring, thickened and distorted. Dead.

He felt warm. She could sense his breath. Hear the soft rustle of his head on the pillow and feel the whisper of the trailing strands of his hair. The rich guard of his hand held hers, guiding her fingers, letting them move, all the strength of his body held still.

Not dead ruin. Living skin and flesh and bone. He would feel every nuance of her touch, even through the damage. Damage that could never be repaired. The shell of rage inside her shattered. The shards of it struck her and there was no defense for what lay beneath. Her throat was hot. The weight pressing against it was unshed tears. They pressed against her lips. She could not let them go.

A wordless sound escaped her mouth, thin and wrenching in the dark.

He let her hand go, and she wanted to speak, to find the words to tell him that it was not revulsion and disgust that shook her. That she would have touched him so a thousand times if things had been different. If Kraka had not existed. If such impossibilities as honour and a future could find their place. But the unshed tears stopped the words.

"Shall I tell you how this happened?" said Berg.

CHAPTER 10

ELENE TRIED TO FORM an answer. But the damage filled her mind and only the choking wordlessness came out. She forced her voice to conquer it.

"Battle," she said. "Battle scars. It could be naught else." *Battle against someone like Kraka.* "I have seen you fight."

The memory of it, of following him down a sunlit slope into bloody strife, filled her mind. Her muscles tensed. The same tension was in him. Shared images. But he was a warrior and that was what she had touched. She remembered how he had looked, fighting. The power of it invincible.

"No, it was not battle. There were no great deeds. No glory. No *herespell,* no brilliant tale to sing of round the hearth fire afterward. It happened to a prisoner."

"A *captive?*"

"You said in the chapel that East Anglia was dead. I was

one of the ones who let it die. There was nothing but disaster and defeat and all that happens afterward. Powerlessness. It has a particular taste."

She buried her face in the coarse linen of a bed meant for strangers in an unknown priory. Emptiness. Except it was not empty. Beside her, she heard him breathe.

"The loss was total. The army was broken, the dead lying in heaps. But some were still alive."

"You."

"Aye. I thought there was some point to it. Because my cousin, to whom I owed my faith, still breathed and I believed something could be saved. I believed I could do it. I was twenty winters old. I believed—all sorts of things."

If I do this, those I love will be safe. I can do it. I know how and I am strong. Invincible.

"I could do naught. They took my cousin's life from him. But not mine. I saw what—I saw how he died and yet I lived. I had no strength to stop anything they did. They showed me that. You touched the proof."

"I did not know…." Her voice came out like a whisper in the darkness. Something he could not hear. *I am sorry.*

"It took not much more than one blow and a piece of rope to tie my hands. I can describe the axe blow. But what I cannot describe is how it felt to be helpless."

"No." It was not a thing one could see, *only feel.*

He knew. The knowledge burst in her mind. The connection they shared was not only that fleeting moment of high-heartedness on the battlefield, it was something far stronger. She thought he moved. She felt the warmth of him in the shadows as deeply as she had felt the pain.

She said it, the truth and the dark things she had never said to anyone.

"I hated what he did. Kraka." Her breath scored the quietness. "I hated every moment of what happened. And there was nothing I could do."

The words she had never uttered took their place in the dark. She felt the warmth and the solidness of the man beside her. Her hand reached out, touched his shattered face of her own will and her words found their home.

"I did not want to go through with such a bargain. I had set myself a task. My choice. I thought I could survive it. I thought I could keep my honour in my heart because I had done what was right. But in the end I did not care about what was right. There was only living."

"And sometimes you did not want even that because death seemed an easier thing to bear."

The warmth of his breath touched her skin. She rested her head beside his. "Yes." Their breath mingled. "You know how that is." Their mouths were so close, as though they kissed.

She crept nearer, so that their bodies touched and the dark shadow of him was real. Living flesh like his face.

"Elene..."

"I kept on living." She had to say it quickly, before her courage failed. Before he left her and this moment in the darkness was gone. "I went through every day and I did all that was required, but..." She felt his tenseness, through every strong muscle she touched, the hidden core of his anger unassuaged. She tried to marshal her words, to keep to the barest things she must explain. Not to tell him how she had lain with Kraka. *Rutting in the straw,* she had said.

Not that.

"I could tell myself because I kept alive that I was brave. That my decision was noble and I could maintain it. But I was afraid. Most of the time. In different ways. He made me so." The words choked. "He had that much power and he knew it and he used it." She had said too much. The jarring tension in the strength she touched brought back the other fear, the new one as yet unexplored.

I have seen you fight.

Kraka and an English warrior were destined enemies, with or without her existence. Kraka, with his deadliness. Kraka who had quite probably been at that last fatal battle for East Anglia, when Berg had fought and been maimed. Did he know that? He could not. He would not lie in the same bed with her, talk to her with understanding. *Touch* her.

Berg would hate all that a raider like Kraka stood for, hate *him.* And so he would need what every warrior needed, vengeance.

Her body tightened like the echo to his. *Please.* The unexplored fear began to claim its shape. If Kraka brought harm to this man… If it were through her fault…

She tried to order her spiralling thoughts, to find the words. She could not let the bitter spirit of Kraka touch him. Not him.

"It was a bargain, you must remember that. He kept his side." The worst came out. What was truly the worst thing, beyond the shame of her fear or the desolation of captivity.

"He was a harsh man and of high temper. Sometimes he could not hold it in check. Sometimes people cannot control such feelings." What was she saying? How did she excuse what she had hated most? "He did not intend to make me fear. He—" She sought the words, acceptable words, how to explain what she herself could not understand.

"He tried to be kind to me."

Hot muscle contracted under her touch. She concentrated on what she had to say so that he knew there was no honour payment for her, no proper vengeance. She was not worth it.

"Sometimes I was grateful to him for that."

She felt his reaction through the heated muscle, through the hidden fire that lived inside him. Frightening power. She recognised what must be its source, the anger that even his understanding could not conquer.

"I lived as Kraka's mistress for a little over a year. I lived with a Viking. I should have hated him for what he was, for all that he did. I did hate him." The pitch of her voice rose. She got it under control. "But at the same time I saw what he did not do, all the things that would have made my captivity so much worse. Unbearable. It was like part of our bargain. I had to acknowledge it, and so I did."

And yet he wanted far more of a return for that. Things I could not give.

"He did not harm me."

Only once.

One single time had she experienced that wild rage. She could feel the pain striking through her head, through the hands she had flung up to defend herself. But then one of the Danish women had come in, shouting, and Kraka's terrifying eyes had cleared. His heavy body had collapsed across hers, shaking like a child's and he had begged her. Begged and shouted and threatened for all those things she could not give. While the other woman had watched, stone-faced and bitter.

She lay against the tight, anger-filled body and closed her eyes. The familiar emptiness inside her was her only defense. But the dark behind her eyes was no longer empty, even though she wanted it. She felt the warmth in Berg's body, greater than the anger. Her skin felt the uneven heated touch of his breath, as he must feel hers. A bond. Like something that belonged and always had. Match and counterpart. But Berg was not hers. Never. She was not worth this fierce, angry stranger with the high heart and the belief in things unseen.

"I was not my own person." She tried to say it clearly, so that there could be no mistake. Her breath tangled with his. "I belonged to Kraka, for whatever he wanted." She kept the clearness, despite the heat and the impossible closeness of him. "And now I will never be my own person. I will never be free again." Living warmth and deep shadows. Deeper mind. "What happened cannot be erased."

She felt him draw breath. She knew the anger was there. Its strength matched the appalling, unresolved feelings inside her, feelings that knew no release. "That is how things are."

"Like scars," he said. His hand moved to cover hers where it lay across his face. She felt his warmth, the aliveness.

"Elene." His anger was suppressed. He would not give it rein. Her breath caught and hot chills began to course across her skin, frightening and unstoppable. Her throat was tight, all of her body, so that one touch could shatter it. The hand covering hers tightened.

Her whole body was trembling. Burning. She wanted his aliveness, the touch of it, the vital power that was his. The longing for it was so intense it brought shivering heat through the pores of her skin.

The scars moved against her hand. "The future is what you make." That was what he chose to say. The depth of his voice touched her and the power of his body thrummed with life in the darkness. She felt it. She felt the power of the mind that animated it. Such power. Yet it was not enough. Could not be.

But the heat burned between them and he moved, his heavy flesh sliding against hers. She heard the rustle of the bedclothes under him and the bright intensity coursed across her skin.

The dark bulk of his body leaned across her in the blackness. Intimately familiar. She felt the rich fall of his hair on her bare throat.

Alive.

She could smell the golden scent of his skin, the fresh tang of soap, the warmth.

His hand slid down her bare arm. The sensation intensified, so that he must have felt how her skin shivered. His fingers brushed her neck, sought the thin hollow at the base of her throat. She caught her breath, stifling the sound that would have escaped.

She wanted to pull away, but she could not. His fingers were roughened, battle-hardened, strong, but it was not that which held her.

His touch sought for gentleness, despite all the rage locked away in his heart, despite the harsh strength he hardly knew what to do with. *Dream-lover.* Her heart stopped.

But this was real, as real as the unspoken feelings locked inside his head, the feelings inside her.

She felt his hand move lower. She gasped and this time the sound split the black air. His hand stilled, but it did not leave her. He was gentle. For her sake. So that she wanted to requite that. Her blood sang. She did not move.

"Elene." The word was spoken against her skin, the vibration of his voice part of her, like something that belonged neither to the impossible future he had spoken of nor to Kraka's bitter mistress. Its shape was both new and immeasurably familiar, like something long remembered. From the time before all the disasters of her life, when everything had been possible.

"Elene. You are alive beyond the power of the past. Living. Do you not feel that?" The beat of her heart pushed against his hand, so fast. She was caught, in the snare of his aliveness and his strength and his utter sureness. "Can you not feel life?"

The damaged flesh under her shaking fingers moved with his words, with his breath. Scars that could never be healed. He let her feel that as he let her feel the strength of his life. That was what he wanted her to know. That both were together. As inseparable as the two sides of one of her uncle's coins, as one of her father's. A coin split in half. Dreams.

"Elene…" Such a rich accent. The scent of summer and the glow of the sun and the blue-grey horizon stretching to infinity. Memories that were pure, sparkling with life. Somehow they were inside the dark chamber in Wessex with the storm closed in and beating against the window shutters. The endless horizon of a different land. A lost land. Beauty and ruin like him. The horizon and the possibilities, past and future, were in him. All the compass of her life was described by him; it stretched no farther.

Their lips touched, melding over words and breath. She caught the dark richness of his mouth, all the burning heat that was held back, waiting like a pledge. She felt the suppressed passion. What if she failed him?

"Suppose I cannot?" All the nameless things that burned between men and women, all the things Kraka had tried to take by force and terror—what if she could not give them, things that were desired, deserved? Even though this time she longed to respond. Berg had turned from her once before because she had not been able to give those things. Kraka had hated her for that lack. She had killed that part of herself. Kraka had killed it. If she could not bring it back…

There were no words for such intangible things of the spirit. His body covered hers, fiercely hot and intimately alive. She feared that she could only give him deadness in exchange. "What if I cannot give you all that you wish?" *All that I want to.*

His mouth took the words, as the feel and the heat of him took her breath.

"Then we will sleep together, as we always do."

Always. She tasted the word against the heat of his lips and his tongue. *Always.* It seemed as though that existed when he was with her. She had slept with him beside her, as an unknown stranger, and then as a man achingly, burningly familiar so that the intimacy of it had been like a bastion against the dark. She had shared his touch in dreams.

"But if I cannot be what you wish…"

"Or if I am not what you wish, or what you can bear with…" His hand pressed hers across the scarred flesh. She thought of the moment of shock when she had first seen his face, the recoil from something marred that was as instinctive as being human. Beyond rational thought or fairness or control. She remembered every look and action. She could still see the patience in his eyes.

Her fingers touched his skin. "I would not wish to draw away from you." Her heart beat and her fingers were shaking. He would feel that.

"Elene—"

Her mouth caught his. This time she took the words, the breath, all the beating force of emotion. She held it, felt his body move over hers, come down and cover it with the age-old power of stark need. It blinded sense in its hunger and its deepness, like something that had waited long, and was as raw as the pain and the anger that burned his fierce spirit. She thought for a moment that there might be a despair that was the equal of hers.

But she was blind.

She lay still under his weight. She could feel the driving desire in every harsh line of muscle, in the full tight hardness of male flesh through the barrier of his clothes. She did not pull away. She never had. She closed her eyes.

But her hands clung to him. She became aware, like a drowning creature rising out of the water, that her fingers were buried in his flesh, biting through the thin linen with a force that must have stung him. She had said that she would not draw back. She kept her word. But the power of her hands went beyond that.

She did not want to let him go. Her mind still fought to understand that when he moved. She choked against the heat of his lips, clinging harder. But he did not abandon her. He took her with the rolling movement of his body so that she lay close beside him, much as she did when she slept in the awareness of his warmth. Dreaming. Real. They faced. She could see his eyes.

What if I cannot give you all that you wish?

Then we will sleep together, as we always do.

She craved that closeness with him. It was what she wanted. She pushed thought aside; there was only now, this moment. All she would ever have.

She moved in the circle of his arms, and his hands moved over her, skimming her body through the thinness of the worn shift. She watched the slow glide of his fingers. His touch was light, filled with the gentleness he had shown from the first moment. Her flesh tingled. His mouth found the bared skin at the base of her throat. Stark heat. And every line of his body tight with the driving need.

It would cost him, the gentleness with which he touched her. She could feel the restraint. And if that restraint broke? She knew his natural impatience. She knew what happened when... Her muscles tensed. Only a slight movement, but the careful flow of his touch stopped.

She looked at the size of his hand where it lay against the curve of her waist.

"Elene?"

"It is nothing."

The rustle of his hair against the bolster. The coldness against her skin where the heat of his mouth had been.

"It is all right," said Berg. "You can tell me what you wish."

What I wish. Wholeness. New life. To be free like the skylark soaring through the heavens. But I am earthbound now, my future unchangeable.

"If it is not me that you wish, you can say that."

She watched his hand against her flesh. She fancied she could see the shadows of fading bruises from the terrible battlefield they had briefly shared, from digging ditches for a fortress that should not have survived and had. Because he would not give it up.

The darkness and the glow of the banked fire danced.

She had met no one like him. Or perhaps she had. Her *fetch*, the stuff of dreams. Nay. This man was real. He felt and he thought and sometimes he made compromises. Just as she did.

"I want you, Berg."

"Elene..." he said. She followed the sound of his voice

fading into the darkness and in her head she heard the other name, *Elgiva*... She felt it whisper through the air, because her chaotic thoughts still ran half on dreams, the dreams that included her true name. But that was something that belonged to the time before disaster, to a girl who had existed in a limitless world. Berg did not know it. Could not, because he was a stranger... She lost the thought because his hand moved.

"Come here," said Berg the stranger. The dream thread was there in his East Anglian voice—the limitless horizon, the heat of summer.

"Come here..." Summer and the tall sedge grass. The joyous beat of a skylark's wings.

"Come." The man's voice penetrated her mind and the hot touch of his body drew her closer. The firelit dark of the Wessex chamber wrapped round them. His hand slid across her flesh.

Heat burned against the thinness of the linen covering her skin. Such heat. Her hand reached out like a white blur in the shadows, touched his flesh, held there. Her hand followed the sliding movement of his, was part of it. Sensation washed through her, so strong that she gasped.

But he did not pause this time. She watched their joined hands move higher across the shape of her body, the slow gliding touch achingly intense, daring, and at the same time the most sensual sight she had ever seen. His fingertips brushed the underside of her breast, burning the sensitive skin. His palm curved beneath her hand to mold the fullness of her flesh, the movement felt from without and within, through the press of his hand against hers and the heated flesh that filled his palm.

The heat struck through, it burned inside her like wonder. She felt the touch of his lips and the movement of his hand and the sensation spread out across her skin like something alive.

You are living. Do you not feel...

Her mouth sought his and her body moved under his touch and the life in her veins sang. She took his kiss and nothing was as she expected, not the feel of his mouth on her skin, nor the fiercely held restraint of his touch. The restraint never broke, even when her body moved against the tight hardness of his in a way she could neither check nor control.

It was like dicing with fire, but she could not stop. She could not think. Her thoughts would overwhelm her and the moment with him would be lost. *She* would be lost, and there would be no way out because there was no one like him.

She gripped his arms. Her fingers slid over hardened muscle, felt it bunch and release, then tighten again. He was so close. The moist heat of his lips followed where his hand had touched. The fierce sensation jolted through her. Her breast thrust against his open mouth. She tried to hold back but there was only the wet heat of his mouth and the flick of his tongue.

She cried out. Her hands tightened over the dense muscle of his back. His lips drew her inside his heat, lightly, teasing sensation out of the exquisitely sensitive peak of her breast. Shock passed through her skin. Her body writhed in response, tangling with his. It was like her dream and yet not so. It was imbued with power, dangerous. She had to draw back. Would do so.

She gasped. The sensation inside her wound tighter, because of the clever movement of his mouth. She clung to him, her hands moving lower across the curve at the base of his back. She was frightened. But the driving force held her.

Berg…

She did not know whether she spoke his name aloud into the fire-gilded air, or whether it was just in her mind. Her mind was seething, mad. As mad as her inflamed body.

Her hands framed the tight line of his hips, strong bones and heavy power.

Berg…

He raised his head as her hands still clung to him, and the power of that intimate holding scorched her palms. He moved under her touch.

"Berg." This time she spoke it. She tried to hold him. Her hands tightened across taut globes of muscle then slid round toward the hot swollen hardness of him.

He moved back, breaking her hold. She had thought she had guessed the measure of the strength she touched, that the shared touching had incited. Her heart beat faster. She wanted him to stop. She wanted to hold on to him and never let him go. She wanted the completion that must come. She was afraid her courage would fail.

"Berg…"

"Wait."

"No." Her body burned. He had made it burn. She was

still afraid. She watched the dark figure with its disordered clothes, heavy muscle and black shadow. The sharp line of quick breath.

"I cannot stop." If she let the fear stop her, she would not be able to live. She could find no way to explain to that dark shape with its harshly controlled strength and the feral power underneath. But perhaps he understood because he leaned toward her.

She reached out a hand. "Why would I wait?" she said into that instant of time. "What would I wait for?"

"For what I would give."

He touched her hand. She had one glimpse of what lived in his eyes before his head bent.

She could not move, not even when he pushed aside the inadequate tangled cover of her shift. His hand caught the ragged hem, sewn and resewn to repair the ravages of much use. To hide the half coin. The thin metal shape encased in linen brushed against his great thick fingers. She breathed. She watched how his fingers moved. The shape of the coin was small, the weight light. He might not feel it. His hands were so big.

She watched his fingers hesitate. She felt his heat, and the air in the close bower vibrated. Time ran back, circled. She watched the grown man's hand, adult, filled with power. Past and present collided.

She wanted to say his name, but her mind would not form it. It was filled with the other name that belonged to the dream-past and the coin. Edmund, prince and king's kinsman, the brilliant boy on the brink of manhood. Edmund and the bright horizon at the beginning of life. Edmund who had given promises and then betrayed them.

"What token is this?" said the man who touched her. Her breath choked, the sound helpless, childlike in a woman's body that burned with need. "Why do you keep it?" The soft rolling accent, rich and filled with beauty. The kind of beauty that had first stirred an unformed heart with yearning. *"Take this," said the boy, "I have broken your father's coin. But see how the two halves match. I will keep mine."* The split coin was in her hand. *"Will you—"*

"Will you not tell me of it?" A man's voice, deep and intense with power. But it could still make her believe.

"No."

She looked at him, darkness and shadow and harsh breath, the realness of his flesh touching hers.

"It belongs to the past."

The past had the power to kill, both the dreams of happiness and the nightmare of Kraka. Her anger at that would never stop. It was anger she felt, not despair and lost dreams. Anger.

"I will not tell you of that. It has no meaning any more, nothing beyond bitterness and sorrow. I will never go back." She fought the constriction in her throat. "It would kill me."

His hands on her skin were tight. It must be the terrifying hunger of the desire they had created that burned him. They shared that much, she and the scarred warrior. She watched his hands and his face. No beauty there. No false promise. She could not read his eyes because of the darkness in the Wessex room. Or else because the dangerous, banked tears in her own eyes blocked her sight.

But there would be nothing to read in his eyes beyond a brief connection of vulnerability, a moment outside time, only the heated desire, surely. Even though the shadows between them and the very air that they breathed seemed densely charged, volatile and dangerous. As tight as rope that bound, alive in a way her frightened, overloaded mind could not understand. She pushed the fear into the background with the last of her strength. She could not think on it.

"Wipe out the past for me. Give me—give me that much." *Take my burdens, just for this moment.* It was not fair, but she was too maimed and desperate to do otherwise. She felt the tension in his skin, the fierce burning breath like those who died of battle wounds.

"Berg…" She pushed everything out of her mind. Her hand caught his. She said the only thing left to her, the only thing that she could do for him—that she would not mar his future with the impossibility of hers. Never. Her fingers closed over his. "I want nothing more from you."

The tension in the air exploded.

CHAPTER 11

THE COIN JARRED against their joined flesh. Elene's hand closed over it underneath his hand, instinctively. She wanted to hide it, thrust it aside. But Berg's hand moved first.

His hand dragged away, taking the coin out of her tensed fingers, jerking the threadbare linen tight against her body. The movement was uncontrolled. The hidden power inside him slipped its hard restraint, the way it had in battle. The gossamer-thin material and the resewn seam ripped. The half coin spun out and was swallowed by the dark. Lost.

She gasped. The mind trained by Kraka screamed warning, but her heart disregarded it. She caught the black shadow in her arms. She felt his heat and the harsh breath and the edge of madness that could have been her own.

He stopped, the movement and the impulse and the wildness locked down.

"Elene? I have frightened you."

The stone-hard body held still in her arms.

"I am sorry."

"No." Her face touched his. Scarred skin. "No." Her lips met his the way they had before, held him, forced him on. There was no going back.

He was gentle to her, despite the guarded tension and the edge of shared madness. He stayed with her and there was nothing but his mouth skimming her skin, his hands, the dark heat of him. Somewhere beyond that was the wild power on the rim of perception, but the gentleness was all he showed. She knew with absolute certainty that he would never let her see more than she wished. It was a gift, something won with pain she did not yet fully understand. So rich she would never be able to put a price on it.

His hands caressed her and it became a matter for intense desire, shared and…pleasuring. She was already half-accustomed to him and her body responded to his touch on bare skin and hidden curves. The patched, torn shift could no longer conceal anything, so that mouth and palm and fingertips found the bared swell of her breast. And this time the stab of feeling inside her was deeper, more intense, something learned in one brief teaching and now craved. She moved against the insistence of his mouth, as she had before, and she thought she understood. But it was something new.

The moist heat moved and the sound ripped from her mouth was low-pitched and thwarted, something outside herself. It was tinged with the threads of madness that had been called forth in both of them, frantic and carnal. Beyond her experience. She bit her lip on the edge of old fears. He would not hurt her.

She forced stillness. His mouth touched her skin. Lower. Her whole body tensed. He kept moving. Her hand reached out instinctively to shield the soft roundness of her belly from him. But all the time, her skin responded to his touch and her body would no longer be still but turned, seeking the burning heat of his lips, inciting it.

She tried to stop but she could not and her body moved for him. The futile shield of her hand was pushed aside. His mouth found the faintly rounded flesh, lingered there as though that was what he wished. As though he could understand all her longing and her fear and her desire. As though he knew…other things, and those things made no difference. Not to him. Not to Berg who held magic inside his heart.

It was impossible. Beyond dream or reality. She shut her eyes and the blackness came and she did not see when he moved again. She only sensed it, through the luxury of his mouth and the erotic slide of his long fire-gilded hair against her skin. Her body moved for him, molding into the heated touch of lips and tongue and hands. The longing built. Need and fear and bright excitement. Until he held her as she had tried to hold him in her ignorance.

His hands framed her hips, moved, drew dancing, tingling sensations across the swell of buttock and thigh, teasing her skin. The fierce low sound escaped her lips again. Her heart beat. Beyond the newness of the excitement, the old fear clawed at the edges of her mind. She waited for what he would do. For his body to cover hers.

The heat burned. She wanted to move, with him or away, she did not know. But she could not. He held her imprisoned, not just by the power of his hands at her hips but by something far stronger. The dark unknown thread that coiled through her. His breath brushed her skin, just that and nothing else, and the excitement gripped.

She remembered what she had seen in his eyes.

What I would give...

He touched her. His mouth sought the most intimate part of her body, his lips and tongue on her secret flesh. Finding her swollen and heated with the fierce pounding of her blood. The subtle folds were densely moist, the way they had been in her dream. Her skin was unbearably sensitive to the shocking, uncivilised touch of his mouth.

The instinct to draw back was not there. There was only desire. The dark thread pulled tight, linking them and drawing her tumbling over into the newness. Into the bright-edged fire. Into him. The desire scored through her. Her body sought the maddening heat of his mouth, the touch of it on sensitised skin, even as her mind dizzied with the shock and the strangeness of what he did.

But the urgency held her, overwhelming, goaded by the hot sensations he unleashed. Clear.

Her body moved, aching flesh turning against his heat and the depthless desire with which he touched her. She could sense the unappeased hunger in him, as great as her own.

The hunger drove them both, like something shared, yet she did not know what he wanted from her. She had never pleased Kraka. Never. She had felt only bitterness and now she was maimed by it. Nothing could change.

He touched her and she moved for him. She moved because of her own frightening desire, because of its deepness. His hands caressed the hot tenseness of her skin, lightly, as though he guessed her fragility, the danger of it. His mouth softened further, like a whisper of sensation, so light that the only fear was of losing his touch.

But he would not let her go.

Even if she failed in this, they would sleep together this night. This night was hers and she would not look further. This night, this man. Not Kraka. That was what she truly wanted. Him and only him. Her body turned into his heat and the touch of hands and mouth and tongue. The longing inside her caught fire, limitless and elemental. Heat and passion for a man, like the heart of a flame.

The flames shivered across her skin, coursed deep inside, consuming. So that she cared for nothing, only that, only Berg. Her body writhed, twisting against him, with him, sharing his heat until the longing shattered, the power of it soaring, not earth-bound, wrapped in pleasure and pure desire. Mad as the flight of birds' wings. Complete.

SHE LOOKED SO VULNERABLE, breakable. Berg stared at her glowing skin, sheened by the aftermath of passion so that the reflection of the fire's glow touched it. Yet, as always with her, the glow seemed to come from within. A flame that had never died even through torment.

He would kill Kraka. His breath choked on it. Duty, the

power of his oath to the king, the hidden depth of his own need, gave him the truth. Every action the creature had taken demanded it. Kraka would be stopped. There was only one way and only one payment possible. It was mad to talk of bargains, of gratitude.

He watched Elene's ragged breathing. Her skin looked translucent, as thin as Rhineland glass that would break under his hand. What Kraka had done…

He thought of the creature outside the walls this night, on the black, mud-slickened line of the ridgeway, seeking more death in pursuit of what he wanted. He thought of the small troop of men led by Macsen who had to challenge Kraka. Their faces swam before his eyes as they had in the chapel. The prayer he had said lived in his thoughts, but the moment of transcendency he had felt before the altar seemed impossible to hold on to.

The destructive sense of powerlessness lapped at his mind. There was nothing he could do to change the destiny of any of them and the helplessness built on the old anger.

His gaze was fixed on Elene. She was so close, and the helplessness bit deeper. One movement of tense muscle still strained with stark hunger, and their bodies would be joined. Her shining, desire-damp flesh would touch his. The hunger tore at him.

Elgiva…

Wipe out the past for me…I want nothing more from you.

What had he wanted?

What had he wanted to give?

"Elene." Her taste was still on his mouth. The sight of

her body drove the hunger and the madness through him like flame. What he wanted tore away everything, all that he was.

She turned her head. Her gaze fixed on his mangled face and he tried to read her eyes in the half dark. If the fear and the pain were still there, he had to know. But her gaze met his, straight on. It held a kind of wonder, and threaded through that, the erotic aftermath of heat.

The reaction in muscle and sinew and harshened breath stole sense, clawed at the control that had broken like the split coin lost in the dark. A need strong beyond bearing. The drive inside himself was as strong as the power that fought through battles. He knew it.

He forced himself to see what was real. All of it, not just what he wanted. He gauged the sharpness of the black shadows round her eyes, her thinness, the translucent skin stretched tight over delicate bones. The delicacy frightened him. It seemed to grow, to deepen with each mile of a journey that was too hard for her, a journey he could not shorten by one step.

He shifted in the intimate heat of the bed.

He could not show all the hidden things that were in him now, the black need for vengeance that would lay the demons of the past, his and hers, the terrible anger. So much had to be done before the future could find its place, if it could even exist.

She turned toward him. The heat was still in her skin. He could feel it because of her closeness. The heat of him. The heat of their joined touching.

He wanted her with a desire that was consuming, was

in some measure the other face of the anger he could not speak. As though unleashing that desire could wipe away the corrosive sense of failure. But the failure was his, not a further burden to place on her.

She held out her hand, the way she must have done a hundred times to Kraka. The drive and the edge of pain were so strong that he might have taken it. But then there would be no difference between him and the Viking who had forced from her what she had not wanted to give, who had shattered her life.

Kraka had taken.

He clasped her hand.

His strength drew her down to lie with him in the flesh-warmed disorder of the bed. Their bodies fitted, like something matched. She lay against him, as he had accustomed her to do each night since he had found her. She gave warmth and an impossible sense of closeness, the way she did in dreams. Her body flexed against his, pliant with the fatigue of the journey and the exhaustion of what she had just experienced.

"Berg." She said his name with the same acceptance, the way she had said it moments ago when he had touched her skin and felt the hidden desperation of her blood.

He could take that, and all the fear would come back. He would have given nothing. What mattered was the compass of what Elene needed.

"Sleep," he said. He felt the small shock of disbelief. The uncontrolled movement cut through his skin.

"But—" Her voice was faint with exhaustion. His own harsher voice cut across it.

"That was part of my promise," he said. "One half you have had and now you understand." He paused and the breath scorched at his lungs. "You do not need to fear."

It was impossible to find words that encompassed all that was in his head. He could not frame what was there even to himself and he did not know the way through the morass that held them. The fatigue clawed at him now, and the burdens of past and future that had no ending. He closed his mind to it. To anger that matched too closely on despair. To the questions that had no answer and might never have.

All that had to be done was to see that she survived.

"Take the other half of the promise," he said into the fire-edged blackness. "Share sleep with me." He did not know whether she heard. The exhaustion claimed her, claimed everything. Past and future. There was only the dark and the reckoning still to come. He waited until he was very sure that she slept.

THE SAWDUST RAN THROUGH his fingers, spilling out of the torn saddlebags, out of the sacks that had been loaded in the cart. It swelled in the rain, mixing with the mud that covered his hands. The mud plastered his clothes, filled his mouth with foulness where he had fallen in the mad pursuit.

Fruitless pursuit.

"They are devils."

Kraka saw his elder brother's hand make the sign to ward off evil. The whites of his eyes showed clearly in the rain-filled dark.

"How could they have done this? I swear they did not have time to arrange it. I caught up with their trail soon after the battle. There was not time—"

"Fool." Kraka took a step forward, his sodden boots tangling with slashed leather, all that remained of the saddlebags that had been carried by the mule train and the carts from the Saxon fort across the ridgeway. Horik took a step back.

"I thought they carried the coin hoard. I swear to you—"

"Swear what? That you are witless? That the Saxons knew it and sent a lightly guarded convoy across an open road to fool you? A convoy that you would not have taken even this night if I had not caught up with you and forced your hand!"

His brother moved like a blur in the sheeting rain, as though he would turn from Kraka before this was finished. No one did that to him, least of all his own kin. Somewhere at the back of his mind the burning rage began to spread, taking all, relentless.

"You would have done nothing if I had not come. Because you would not move for fear of a storm and the dark." His brother kept trying to back away. The rage burst. Mud and the remains of the sawdust slipped under his hand, grinding into wet flesh.

"I could not have known it was a ruse. There was no way I could have known!"

"Is that what I am to tell Jarl Guthrum who needs this English silver?"

The thin scream sounded only at the edge of his hearing, like something far distant, not impinging on the force of the rage.

"Kraka! Stop—leave it." The yelling got louder, like something he should listen to, but he could not focus because of his blinding rage and the intolerable sense of failure that had to be erased. He lashed out to prove his power. "Kraka—"

The slippery flesh gave under his hand, the helpless weight dragging off balance, slamming against him. It made his feet slide in the muck. The fall knocked the breath out of his lungs. He choked. The cold rain lashed him. It was that brief moment of shock that let him hear the words, such damning words and the terrible sound of pain "Would you slay your own kin and have the gods curse you?"

Cursed. He was cursed by what he did. By his anger. By the deeds of his own hand. He let go, frozen inside.

"Horik."

His own kin. His own brother retching for breath in the filth of the English hillside. He had attacked him.

Horik.

It was like the fog lifting, the red mist that obscured sight and sense wreathing away like evil spirits. He saw what he had done and it was his aching fingers that made the sign against evil. His hands that lifted Horik's face out of the dirt.

"I did not mean…" He stopped. There was nothing to say afterward. Not ever. Nothing that explained what happened in the raw impatience of his mind, the demons that tormented him.

He had meant it, meant every act of mind and hand. Only the chance fall had stopped him, something so random. *Cursed.*

"Horik…"

He knelt in the mud, scratched fingers closing on his brother's flesh, dragging him upright.

He had only once ever tried to explain it. To ask the forgiveness he had never sought from anyone. He had begged for it like a beast crawling on the ground. And she— He could still see the shock in her eyes and the livid bruise on her dead-white skin. Put there by him.

She had said nothing.

She had simply despised him.

"Horik—" The useless sound scraped at his throat, leading nowhere, pointless. His brother was speaking, cutting across his voice, the sounds raw and scarcely distinguishable.

"It was not my fault." The reddened throat worked. "It was the Saxons. This should not have happened. They are devils, not men."

The Saxons. *Devils.* The rage took its rightful direction in his brain.

"No. They are not devils. This was a man's work. Just a man like any other." He understood now. His hands moved over his brother's mud-soaked arms, soothing. He had always been the one to command their kindred. The one to avenge their hurts.

"This was planned. Even before the battle at the Saxon fortress. It must have been." He considered the sequence, his mind working again as it should.

"You were meant to think as you did, to pursue a false trail. They knew you would come and so they had a false cargo. They were prepared and they broke away without defending, and we could not catch them. Three men down and not one Saxon carcass to show for our trouble."

The rage found its true focus, waited in his mind. His hands rubbed the warmth of life into chilled flesh. Horik was shaking. But Kraka knew how to take care of him, of everything that was his.

"It matters not. I know where the coin hoard is, who holds it, who holds everything that is rightfully mine." *My Saxon mistress. Elene.* "The Wessex king's sworn man."

Berg.

The name rang in his head, spoken in the bitter voice of the *hersir* he had killed.

Berg.

"I will take back what is mine."

"But… But it is too late. You cannot. They will be the other side of the forest now. You cannot mean to go so deep into Wessex. The garrison at Eashing is too strong—"

"I told you. It matters not. I will get everything back."

Even Elene. He would take her. She would need to seek his forgiveness. This time it was she who had done wrong, who had broken her word. She would have to beg and he might not allow her back to the favour she had once had.

But he knew he would, even though the Saxon would have had her a dozen times over by now. Whatever she had done, he would take her back. But it would be the end of her disdainful pride, the one thing he had never been able to break.

"Come. We must get moving." He slid a hand under his brother's arm.

"You are mad."

Mad.

He released Horik abruptly. "I will have what is mine."

"Kraka—"

"I will have revenge for our brother's death at that Saxon fortress." His voice split the night. There was no other way to regain their honour, to let Toke rest in peace. "Do you not want that?"

Silence. The hissing of the rain. He stood up. Alone. He knew what had to be done.

"As for this king's man, he is already dead." Death was palpable in the chilled air, pulling at the fate strings.

"You will not be able to catch him." Horik stared at him on hands and knees in the dirt, eyes sullen, angry, overlain with something else. Growing horror. "No one can do it. Not now."

Kraka turned away. Horik's voice followed him, echoing like his own thoughts.

"No one sane."

ELENE WOKE ALONE.

The room was cold. The fire had died down to ashes. Clear light stole round the edges of the closed shutters and through the small gap in the thatched roof over the hearth.

She should get up and rekindle the fire. That was what

she did every dawn. She was used to the task, and it was not so very cold in the chamber. It was only her, chilled to the bone.

She gathered herself ready beneath the bedcovers. The movement of her limbs felt strange, different, as though her body had changed out of all recognition and was a stranger's. She bit her lip. He had done that. Berg. He had made magic, the sort of magic that lived in dreams, but it was stronger because it was real. He had created it out of nothing where she had not believed it existed. Nay, not out of nothing. Out of himself. Out of scars and beauty, out of sorrow and intensity and the unexpected wild-breathed madness of joy.

He had given her that.

Her hands fisted in the woollen covers of the empty bed and the tears leaked out of her eyes. The passion and the madness of joy echoed beyond her mind, unattainable, like something she still could not realise. What she could remember so clearly was the giving, despite everything she was and everything she had done. She knew there was a cost to that for a man like him.

She moved. Not toward the grey ashes in the hearth but across the bed. She fancied she could feel the imprint of where his heavy weight had lain on the mattress, smell the tang of herbs from his hair, the hot male scent of his clean skin.

She could not expect him to be there. She had given him nothing in return for his gift.

She remembered the bright, frightening fire of his touch. The care. Her limbs shook. She smoothed her own hands over her skin, as though she could recapture the slightest touch of that magic. But in the morning light, she felt naught but cold flesh over bones. Like something dead without him.

Berg.

Her fingers brushed too-sharp ribs, the slight swell of her belly.

She had to get up.

The fire took sullen light under her hands and she dressed quickly, in the good clothes he had given her. They kept out the chill. She began to pack. She rolled up the thin shift she had worn last night. There was a small tear in the hem. She could not find the coin.

She was still frantically searching when something thudded against the door and then erupted through it with scarcely a pause.

"Lady! They keep *pigs*."

She stood up.

Chad, the hell-fiend, danced from one bare foot to the other, spilling what might be her breakfast.

"A whole herd of swine. I am not jesting—"

She took the gently steaming food out of his hands. It was hot, fragrant and rich. Food such as she had never had prepared for her since—

"Oh. Did I spill it? Well, not really." One grubby foot smeared telltale traces of gravy into the rushes covering the floor.

She shook her head.

"I hope you like it," said Chad doubtfully. "Wistan said he left orders that you have to eat it all."

He.

"Well, it is you who are spilling it now."

She tightened her fingers on the bowl. Chad scrubbed obligingly at the floor with his other foot.

"Anyway, this herd of swine. I came to tell you. They fatten them up in the forest and they eat beech mast and acorns in the autumn. Pigs will eat acorns even while they are still green, and the abbey swine are the fattest for miles. There is this one with a black patch on its snout and the monks let me— Are you going to eat it or not?"

She sat down.

"Anyway, this one with the patch, it is a sow and she— It does not taste *that* bad." She heard the first note of uncertainty in his voice. "Lady?"

She watched the wooden bowl.

"You are not going to eat it. You will not and I will have to tell him so when we get to the standing stone. He went ahead on his own in the middle of the night when it was still raining, so Wistan said."

She looked up.

"You are ill." The boy was frightened.

That was when she realised she was still crying.

THE STONE ROSE OUT of the predawn shadows like an accusing finger stabbing at heaven.

Macsen was not there. The impatience and the raw frustration that always came with the inability to control events bit through him. Berg stood still in the blackness, every sense stretched. The silence around the standing stone was so thick it was palpable. The rain had long since ceased. No breath of wind stirred the full-leafed trees. No animal moved.

He waited until the sky began to lighten. He thought of prayer and death and things destroyed. *Elene*. He banished the image from his mind. He could not think it, not now. Even though the warmth of her skin still touched him and her haunted eyes filled memory and her voice spoke to him in the silence.

Death. His grip tightened on the gold-leafed hilt under his hand. The sword whispered as though it had life, and he saw. The shadow was already there, as though summoned out of the earth itself by that cold breath. The shadow never moved. It stood beside the stone, closer than a prudent man would. He rammed the sword back into its sheath.

"Bastard," observed Berg. "I thought you were dead after all."

He caught the gleam of white teeth in the shadow, then nothing beyond darkness.

"Nay, it is not I who hangs by a Northman's fate thread."

Berg gave that the attention it deserved. He strode forward, toward the sentinel shape of the stone. Its sides were chipped, covered with lichen. It had stood in this place long before his people had come to this land from Angeln, no one knew how long.

Berg had no fear of such a meeting place or of the power of the stone. Not for the same reasons as Macsen who was uncanny, but because he did not live in the half world of spirits. Only in this one. It held enough tribulation and it was supposed to end in heaven. It was all he wished to know.

"So?"

He could not even cope with dreams.

"Success," said Macsen. He did not sound or move as though he had been wounded. Part of the hard-leashed impatience dissipated in the cold breath of the air. "If you can call it that. We fled. Rapidly and in very poor order. I fear no one will be singing our praises in the mead hall."

"Trust a Briton to think only of boasting."

"We took lessons from Saxons. Not to mention Angles." But the grin of long understanding vanished, just as quickly as it had before. "Your Viking friend attacked in the storm."

"I know."

"You never know how to leave well alone."

"Wistan scouted for me and—"

"You would have wished to come to our aid if things had gone ill for us."

What was the point of denial? If anyone guessed the extent of that particular weakness of his it was Macsen. Or King Alfred who saw through walls. It was probably why he had ended up with this part of the job.

Macsen said nothing. No need. Berg knew as well as he that it was part of their pact that the mission came first, not the fate of those who undertook it. It was the part he had most trouble with.

You would have wished to come to our aid… And yet he could not have done it if it would have meant the failure of his part of the mission. Berg shifted his weight. That kind of constraint was like some refined sort of torture because of the memories he carried in his head, the helplessness of watching something he could not stop.

Macsen had sufficient tact to keep his gaze squarely on the black bulk of the trees.

There was no place for the luxury of personal feelings. None.

Elene...

"We spent the night at a monastery a few miles away," he said. "Wistan and the others are following." He took a restless step. "Like you, I did not expect Kraka to attack yet, not in the storm."

Macsen shrugged against the gloom of the lightening sky. "The man is determined. He would have to be to risk what he did. It was harder for the attacking force in the blackness, despite Kraka's skill in fighting and even though we broke quickly enough. He lost three, maybe four. I could not tell for sure. There would have been more if we had not fled. That did not stop him."

"No. I do not suppose such a thing would."

Berg could sense the far-seeing black eyes suddenly fix on him.

"You have something he wants."

Macsen might have referred to the precious coin hoard that Alfred needed to stop the kingdom of Wessex from slowly bleeding to death, the money Guthrum needed to ensure his men's continued loyalty.

Or he might not.

Each chilled muscle in his body tightened, thick with the rage he had held back.

"Aye." It was all he said. There was nothing more.

"Then you realise quite how badly he wants it back."

It was hardly a question, but Macsen, descended in equal parts from vocal Celts and Roman orators, kept speaking.

"We captured one of the Vikings. The man talked before the battle wounds he had taken claimed him. He spoke freely, for no coercing of mine. He had no particular love of Kraka. It seems Kraka killed one of his comrades in a rage. Something about vengeance for his brother's death. But apparently it was you who caused this brother's death in the battle for the fortress."

The images filled his mind. The Viking leader behind the solid wall of his bodyguard rallying his men against the advantage Waerferth had lost for them. Elene. Elene with her spear and the Viking suddenly lunging for her. To kill her. Or to take her back?

"You know that Kraka is clever. He is not only ruthless in pursuit of what he wants, but reckless." The dark eyes that saw not only the present but sometimes the future, watched him. "You also know what has to be done."

"I know," Berg said again.

"But there is something you may not know of Kraka." The black gaze slipped beyond him, to somewhere over his shoulder where movement disturbed the jealous silence of the trees round the stone. "Do you realise the man is possessed?" The word reverberated through the disturbed air.

Berg turned round and saw Elene.

CHAPTER 12

ELENE WATCHED THE STRANGER who conversed with Berg beside the standing stone.

He was a living shadow, darkness and light. The fine skin of a Briton, the raven hair and night-black gaze of someone whose ancestors had lived here when the dark-eyed Romans had ruled the land.

He seemed to talk a lot. But he had stopped the instant he'd caught sight of her. His gaze fixed on her face. He was good-looking. She watched him.

She watched him and all she could think of was Berg. All the time that she stared at the stranger and he looked at her with eyes full of wariness and suspicion. His face was strikingly handsome. Without flaw. She knew that two minutes later she would not be able to remember it.

Berg shifted, the slightest movement against the changing light and she felt it as though it had happened in her own skin.

She did not look at him. This morning's tears had terrified her. She knew she would break.

But she sensed that he looked at her. She could not guess what he saw. She was utterly changed. She would not give back one moment of last night if she paid in blood for the rest of her life. Her hands were unsteady on the reins.

He took a step.

"Elene."

Her mind retold the whisper of his voice in the close night, the dark mysterious slide of his body over hers. It was as though she felt it now through her skin. Through dreams.

She looked. He stood close beside the other man, both of them so near the standing stone. Neither of them moved. Berg's face was a travesty beside the Briton's handsomeness. She turned toward him, ready to slide down from the horse's back.

Both men moved at the same time, with the same controlled grace and she recognised in that instant that they were firm friends, with the kind of bond that came only from shared fighting and shared dangers. Sometimes from shared thoughts.

She did not need help. She dismounted quickly, with the well-trained efficiency of long practice, disguising the frightening weariness. She walked toward them. The suspicion she had seen in the eyes of the Briton was like a stone wall.

She was still a Viking's whore.

Berg took her arm. Not just that, he held on to it. He truly did and then she saw behind his shoulder the dried mud on the dark cloak of his friend, the small telltale marks on his hand. Such marks were always there afterward. A man might wear gloves made with leather and be the world's expert with a linden-wood shield, but the bruises were always there.

"Kraka." The word choked her throat. "There has been fighting." *No.* But the last word made no sound in the chill of the air and it was the Briton's voice that replied.

"You are not surprised, lady."

She remembered the candles flaring in the wind and Berg making the sign of the cross. She straightened her aching spine.

"No." This time the word took voice.

"It is over," said Berg. "He is gone."

He kept hold of her arm and she could feel the solid shield of his closeness, the way she did when they slept. *Kraka is not here.* The rich voice in the lovers' dark of the firelit chamber, the strength and the warmth of it bright enough to send the power of life through her veins. Berg who believed in the future. And Kraka who fought and killed in his rage. Kraka who never gave up.

"Kraka is still here, somewhere in the forest. I know it."

The Briton's eyes flickered but her lover's eyes were utterly steady.

"We will get to Eashing."

"But—"

His grip on her arm tightened, steering her toward the

horse that was worth more than gold. His gift. A gift made before battle. Because he watched for death.

"Kraka—"

"We will reach Eashing before the light fades today."

Her free hand fastened on the solid edge of the saddle. "Yes, but—"

He caught her, lifting her and the breath left her lungs. Her body touched his, vibrant heat and fierce strength and then nothing. The cold air and the shadow of the stone. She clutched the reins.

"Can you ride so far? We will move quickly."

"Of course. Why should I not?" She watched his eyes and read things there that made her heart pound. Such things. Things that did not belong to her.

She found a smile from somewhere like a warrior reaching for his shield. "Do you think I would not be able to keep up?" *I am used to riding fast.*

She touched the mount's sides with her heels to encourage it away. His hands caught the reins, halting the horse without effort. It obeyed him. She could not breathe.

"You might not feel that you can." His hand slid down to hers as though the movement were natural. "If that is so, you will tell me." The steadiness in his gaze seemed as natural as his touch, rock solid, as though nothing could shake it, not even truth.

The thousands of tears as yet unshed pricked at her eyes. She gathered her courage. All that there was of it.

"There is nothing wrong with me." Her eyes held his. "I will not hold you back."

His gaze never faltered, as though the steadiness would last for ever.

It could not. She urged the horse forward and the contact broke.

"IT IS GRAND."

Elene nodded. It was the right word. She had forgotten. She and the budding swineherd hesitated on the threshold. It was still light. Berg had promised as much. She had not stopped him on the way, even though her back ached as it never had and her eyes burned as though she had fever. Or perhaps it was the pressing weight of her tears.

"Look. They have put strange colours on the wall pillars and there is a curtain thing at the back."

She looked at King Alfred's hall at Eashing. They had indeed put strange colours on the soaring columns that held up the massive roof. Her gaze took in a breathtaking and harmonious mix of blues and reds and greens, luxuriated in it. The sinuous, exquisite shapes of winged flame snakes and fabulous beasts clawed their way up the solid oak, carved by a master, their smooth intricate bodies flickering in the light.

She took a step. Riches.

The curtain thing at the back was an embroidered wall hanging. It showed a man, sword in hand, stepping ashore from a slender dragon-prowed ship. Elegant waves frothed at his feet. How had they done that?

She took another step. Fragrant meadowsweet whispered under her feet. Lying on the table was something

she had not seen for a year except to tear up and line shoes
with. It was a book. Not riches. Grace.

She stopped.

"Lady." A small wriggling weight dangled from her
sleeve. "I am afraid to go in."

She looked down at the swineherd's large eyes.

"So am I."

"Do you think we could wait for Berg to come?"

Sweet heaven. She wanted the balm of his presence so
much it hurt, more than she had wanted anything in her
life. The breach in her defense had been made. She did not
know how she would get over it, only that she must. She
had to move on to Winchester. Because she had to find
her parents. Because she did not belong here. Because she
did not belong to him.

She put a hand to the aching small of her back.

"No," she said. "We cannot wait for Berg. He has other
duties to see to. It would be unfair." *Unfair.*

She stood up straight. "Come on. It will be all right."

Elene turned to follow Wistan's broad shoulders, her
hand on the boy's arm. He would not move.

"Chad—"

"Suppose they find out I am nearly a Viking?"

Her heart stopped, then began to beat again as though it
would choke her. She would not be able to get through this.

"It will be all right. No one will harm you." She kept
one hand on the boy's wrist. "You will see."

She walked back into a Saxon hall. There was nothing
else she could do. Yet. The book on the table brushed her
hand. The bronze lamps flared in the fading daylight.

Their glow slid over the gleaming shapes carved into the smoke-warmed wood. It might have been her father's hall. He had loved colour. But even what he had built was not half as fine as this.

The hall was big. Men came and went with sure purpose. They talked. Sometimes she heard laughter. They might have been preparing for a feast. Except they were armed. She did not look at them.

The curtain thing fluttered against the wall in the evening breeze through the opened window. Her gaze assessed the design. Another armed man, yet not so. There was not the slightest doubt that the fair-haired man in the shadowed silver and gold of a chain mail *byrnie* was a warrior. But he did not hold a sword as she had first thought. His carefully worked hand brandished the mysterious symbol of kingship. It was a sceptre, gilded, wrought about with signs of unknown power and crested with a winged dragon.

"Look, Chad. It is Cerdic, first of the Saxon kings to reach these shores. Can you see? Watch the sceptre in his hand." The heavy cloth rippled in the air currents and the sceptre moved like something living.

"A dragon," said Chad, "and what is that below? It looks like faces."

"They are a symbol of Woden." The shape-shifting god. "Masks that cover what lies beneath like a hidden power. See how the shapes seem to alter? The changes confuse evil spirits. They are dangerous."

"Brilliant," said Chad, leaning closer, his face alight with the same ghoulish interest he showed in battles. "Danger."

The figure of the man reeked with it. But it was held back, contained despite the glowing force of his movement. The way Berg contained things. The hazardous figure paused, trapped forever in his moment of time between the sea and the land. He was stunning. And the waves... Her fingers itched. She stared at the threads.

"Like it?"

Awareness rippled over her skin in waves. She did not need to move her head.

"It is—" But there were no words.

Her gaze lifted from the trapped image to the man who was real. He stood still, heavy feet planted firmly in the hall as though he belonged, not like Cerdic endlessly caught between sea and shore, old home and new. Yet he was trapped the same way. He had made the gift of telling her so.

Lamplight glittered on the sword hilt and on the axe in his belt. "It is what?"

The steel links of his *byrnie* shimmered with the movement held back, the quick impatience that was his. Yet he waited for her answer, as though it held significance.

How could she say how the image made her feel? As though time could run backward and the threads of wool and silk could touch her own fingers again.

"It is—" Something jarred her in the ribs.

"Cerdic," hissed the swineherd, as though this were the answer to some test that would allow them to stay in the Saxon hall. He folded a sharp elbow away and glared at her. She was being slow.

"It is Cerdic," she said on a smile, but the child actually backed against her skirts. He looked impossibly young, nowhere near his claimed age. She put a hand on his shoulder as someone carried a bundle of spears past them. The smile died.

"It seems an unusually fine thing to have in a fortress," was all she could manage to say.

"Aye. It takes a while to get used to Alfred. People do not always understand why—"

"Then they should." *Ælfred Rex hanc fecit.* She thought of the Latin words in that other half-built fortress that had tipped her out of her senses. "I do."

The grey-flecked eyes narrowed, such intelligent eyes. Her heart beat fast. She saw him take the breath to speak. The silver links shimmered with the force of his breath. Someone brushed past with a painted shield. The edge of the wall hanging touched her skin. She caught it in her free hand before it could be damaged. Instinct.

"You can meet the woman who helped make that."

"I can?" The question escaped the fastenings of thought.

"I will show you."

Her heart tightened and the brilliance of the fabric clung to her fingers as though it had life. She smoothed the binding at the edge. Well-taught skill. And love.

Berg turned, the fabric in her hand rustled in a sound that was achingly familiar, but over it was the savage whisper of linked steel.

"Where are you going?"

"Out. Before the light fades altogether."

Before the light fades. Looking.

She let the sliding material go.

And will you come back?

She followed the broad swing of his shoulders, the bright sound as he walked. Her other hand tightened to guide the Viking child out of the hall. She tried to push back the terrible fatigue. She did not ask the question. There was no answer.

The woman was pregnant.

It was as plain as the sun at noonday. In midsummer.

Judith did not know how her brother could be so stupid, so—she thrust the more unseemly epithet aside—so thoroughly and culpably stupid.

She stared at the travel-stained woman. Her beauty was indecent, despite the conservative clothes. That was what had attracted her brother. Obviously. The child who was with her resembled nothing so much as an overgrown stick insect that had been dragged through a hedge backward. Perhaps the boy was hers, too, for all she seemed so young, although he was not, the saints be praised, Berg's.

"I have ordered a hot bath."

The boy's mouth fell open. Beneath the mud, Judith thought he looked green. He had very clean teeth. That was odd. But there was definitely a leaf in his hair. She cast more dried lavender heads on the brazier. The room filled with scent.

"Thank you."

That drew her attention back to the woman. Elene. How was that for an ill-omened name? The woman, girl really, inclined her head as though she were Queen El-swith accepting homage and Judith suddenly realised what Berg had truly seen in her. *Athelbert's bones.*

She directed the maid to fill the tub.

"*COMING HERE?*" Berg tied the horse beside the split oak tree. The rest had to be done on foot.

"Yes."

Berg bit the response back. A sworn man did not curse his sovereign lord. They went on.

"Tell me that was a jest."

Here they were, crawling up to the balls through clinging mud in the fading light looking for some mur-derous Dane, some *possessed* Dane, and the only free English king left was planning to ride right into the middle of it.

They slid round a drop that would have cost broken bones, holding on at a muscle-aching stretch.

"All right," he said into the silence. "Tell me when."

"Tomorrow by Tierce," said Macsen.

Before the morning was well advanced. Which must mean a bruising ride of many miles, surely. Damp seeped through his clothes, through skin. The trouble with a ruler like Alfred was not so much deciding whether to fol-low him as keeping up with him.

"How many with him?"

"The household troops. And Ashbeorn."

"Ashbeorn." At least that was something. Ashbeorn was useful in a fight. He sometimes had trouble remem-bering the rules, having learned them late in life. Ashbeorn was also good with forests. Better than Berg was. He avoided something nameless that seemed to consist entirely of spikes. More or less.

Ashbeorn had also had his own experience with Danes. Athelbert's bones.

"We have to find the Viking." He could not actually say the name out loud. It might rip something inside him and the dammed-up rage would come spilling out. If that happened, he would not be able to control it.

Macsen slogged through the filth beside him. Oathsworn to do what was right. They both were. As was Ashbeorn.

Ashbeorn now had a wife, and two dependents who were no blood relation.

"Do you remember the story of Waldere and Hildegund?" he said at the gathering dark. "Waldere could not marry because he lived a warrior's life and he would not have been able to fulfill his duty." The soft ground turned under his feet. Stupid question in the middle of a forest hunting Kraka. Macsen would—

"I thought Waldere's problem was not marriage itself but not wishing to give up his childhood betrothed. Besides, I understood he did marry his betrothed in the end after all that fighting, and then he wallowed around in bliss for another thirty years. Personally, I could not see the problem with marrying sooner rather than later, even if you are obliged to lead armies for Attila the Hun like Waldere." Macsen swung across a ditch. "But then I am not a Visigoth or a Frank, which must be uncomfortably close to being a Saxon. Or perhaps an East Angle."

Berg rolled his eyes. "Aye. Well, granted it was not a British story."

"No," said Macsen with irritating simplicity.

He caught his breath. The weight of the half dark seemed inside him.

"Over this rise," he said. "Has to be—"

"Got it," said Macsen on the same breath.

Berg saw it. The twig that had been snapped off so that the white broken end showed clearly, even in the twilight. Recent. So recent. High off the ground. Shoulder height.

They stopped speaking. No need to exchange so much as a glance. They kept walking, the silence complete, each step fluid because they had long since discarded the protection of chain mail, each movement aching through fatigued muscle. Lift the leg high to avoid snagging on growth. Keep the weight back. Place the foot toe first to feel out the ground before the body weight could shift forward.

They crawled the last section, hands and knees slipping in mud, the weight of their bodies dragged by willpower.

It was there.

No lights, only the black shadows against the dull light. They lay silent in the clinging mud, every fast laboured breath suppressed. They watched, assessing the position chosen for the Viking camp, the routes out, the number of men, the weapons, all that could be seen or guessed in the gathering dark. All the knowledge that Macsen could take back to Alfred before he rode into this.

They could not stay long. Kraka's scout who had broken the branch would be back.

They did not know when.

"HOW WAS THE BATH?"

"Beyond compare. I thought the mud must have become lodged in my veins."

"Aye." Judith was aware of a small spurt of fellow feeling. She watched as Berg's leman smoothed the folds of her borrowed gown. Her hands were slender, the fingers roughened and scratched.

"I am in your debt," said the leman.

But that was going too far.

"I think you are in my brother's *debt*."

She got that look again, the queen of ice, and behind it, the glimpse of fire. Oh, Berg...

She felt sorry for the woman. She could not help it. She thought this unacceptable lover had courage. Maybe more than that, but—

"You should retire to sleep, lady, like the child."

The strange boy had been washed and dispatched to rest. Elene had asked that he be given into the care of Berg's second in command.

"An interesting child," observed Judith. "Whatever must he have been like as a babe?"

The other woman smiled through bloodlessly pale lips. "Trouble I would imagine." It seemed genuine. Perhaps the boy was not hers then?

"I can only suppose—" the leman said and then she stopped. Judith saw her realise why the question had been asked. The pale mouth closed. That was it. No outrage and no denial. But Judith had seen truth. The boy was not hers. Even though they said the child's father was a Viking.

She stood up and walked to the window. It seemed impossible to contain what she felt.

There was no disputing that Berg's mistress was with child now. Athelbert's bones, what a mess. Did her brother even know? He had not mentioned it. How long had they been together? Suppose the babe was not even of his getting? They said the woman had been living with the Danes, rolling round in a bed with Kraka, Guthrum's man. Ivar's man. King Ivar who had—

Judith's fist hit the wall and all she could see was her brother's ruined face, the ruin that was on the inside that he never spoke of, just kept on fighting because he had to.

Behind her she heard the unknown woman get to her feet. Judith knew she would have shocked her, the way she shocked everyone when what was underneath Queen Elswith's lady in waiting broke through.

She turned stiffly. "I am sorry. I forgot myself."

"Maybe you just forgot the wall was there. Did that leave bruises? Or did it cave the planking in?"

Judith gave a laugh. It was either that or a sound of thwarted rage, she was not sure.

The woman was watching her, spine straight and as pliant as a sapling despite the desperate fatigue of the journey. And pregnancy. The fire leaked out of her eyes.

"What were you thinking?"

What was the point of pretending?

"I was thinking of all the things I would do if I could.

I wish I had been born a man. If I were a warrior…" But that was mad. Judith sought to command her breath. It was impossible.

"If that were so," said Berg's leman, "I can see there would be no wall of this fortress left standing. Or probably of any other between here and the western sea."

Judith's mouth twisted into a grin she did not expect. But the wryness of it still hurt. She said nothing and the blue eyes watched her out of the pale face. Then the veiled head bent. It was like acknowledgement, a trace of understanding. No lady of her acquaintance in Wessex had even attempted to understand.

"You are extraordinary," said Judith. "I think I guessed it—" *feared* it "—almost from the start, and it is so."

But the other woman shook her head. "No. It is not so. I am nothing." The blue eyes were like stone, the fire extinguished. Or buried. "What would you do if you were a warrior? Why do you want that so much?"

Judith hesitated to say it, but the words were pressing at the barrier of her lips. Truth she could not hold back.

"I would take vengeance. I would fulfill my proper duty. I would kill those who have harmed my country and my kin, those who still bring harm, so that no one else had to suffer what—" She balled her bruised fist. Memories. Her brother fighting pain and blood loss and the greedy claims of death. Losses beyond reckoning.

"Sometimes I think it is harder to forgive the hurts to those whom you love than the hurts to yourself. I would want to kill the men of King Ivar. All of them." She paused, but the words would not be contained. Impatience, Berg had always said, was the family sin.

"I would want to kill Kraka." She took breath and watched the Englishwoman who had slept with Kraka. "Would you?"

She watched the pale face turn like the death she had invoked. Her fists tightened and she wished she had not asked the question. Still she waited for the answer.

Elene turned away. Judith could no longer see her face. The answer she sought was hidden. She tried to stamp on the anger. This was Berg's choice after all, not hers. But the anger inside her was so old. It had had six winters to grow.

"Lady—"Judith fought for something conciliatory. She actually took a step back into the fire-warmed room. But the leman was turned away from her. The rather thin shoulders swayed, as though the weight on them were too much. She knew despair when she saw it. She cursed inside her head and she wanted to put her fist through the wall again. But that would not help. Nothing would.

She caught the swaying form in her arms, holding the fragile body, the small bones and the flesh that suddenly seemed frighteningly thin. She half expected resistance after what she had said and done. But it was not there.

Despair made strange allies. Sometimes.

No one said a word. No one pulled away. They clung to each other, complete strangers adrift in a sea of pain too strong for them. Two women who must bear the weight that would crush them. The mess closed over their heads.

"IT WAS STEM STITCH," explained the warrior woman with the bruised knuckles, Berg's sister. It was night. "I used that for the edge of the waves. I picked a darker colour and then I filled it out with lighter and thinner thread. Silk."

"Couch stitch?"

"Aye."

They were both lying in the same bed, Elene warm under the covers, the fistfighter stretched out on top, still wearing her shoes.

A rebel. Through and through.

"I liked doing the waves. I actually had more trouble with the feet. I am sure one turned out to be bigger than the other. As well for me that Queen Elswith did not notice. They would have thrown me back out of Wessex. Queen Elswith likes needlework, too. She did the face and the hair herself."

"Oh, that took skill."

"Aye." They contemplated the difficulties of skin tones in a silence that was almost companionable. Something that for a brief moment transcended the disaster both of them could see coming.

I will not stay here. I will not force on your brother a burden that is not his.

Elene wanted to say it. But they could talk of nothing but the embroidery. The night waxed but neither of them would sleep. Not until he came back and they knew he was alive.

"I like the sceptre."

"Aye. I met the woman who restored that. The real

sceptre I mean, after it was found again. She is so fine. One day—" Judith stopped. Perhaps because no one could look at the future. Not in these times. Whatever losses Berg had suffered, his kindred had, too.

"Cerdic's face is good."

"Aye. If you look on it carefully, you can see she modelled it on the king's face."

"He is handsome."

"Aye." The woman outside the covers suddenly shifted. "Judith?"

But the restless warrior sat up, seemingly impelled with the same impatience as her brother. "The queen loves her husband."

"I see. And the king loves her? Judith?"

"Aye."

Elene could scarce hear it. The piece of quicksilver was on her feet.

"He is coming."

Elene's heart clenched. She had not heard it. The drag of fatigue had been too great, even after the soothing balm of the water. Her whole body ached to the point of pain. She could have borne that. But not the true pain that was in her mind.

He is coming.

"Judith."

"I am glad you like embroidery."

"Judith?"

She was gone. Not toward the door and her brother's heavy footfalls, but across the ledge of the window, as lithe as the warrior she wished she was. Only the swish of her long skirts betrayed her. The shutter banged and Elene was alone again, watching in the dark, waiting.

CHAPTER 13

HE TOOK HIS BOOTS OFF in the darkness of the firelit bower.

Elene said nothing. What was there to say? *I have been lying here in your bed waiting to see whether the man who bedded me first had killed you. Or perhaps, I am going to leave you after this night because if I was ever foolish enough or selfish enough to think I could stay, one step inside the king's hall, one look at your sister's face showed me what was real.*

She wanted to move, but the heaviness of relaxed muscle, the warmth of the bed, the fatigue, would not let her.

He unbuckled the sword belt, set the sword aside carefully. Firelight gleamed on the axe head.

I believe I would have died if you had. That was what she wanted to say. This morning's tears were pooling in her eyes. She kept them wide open.

He moved into the fire's glow. He had shed the *byrnie* earlier. His clothes were caked in mud, all of him, even his hair. As though he had been crawling through it. On the ground. She blinked. Such a mistake. Wetness touched her face.

He removed his tunic. He dragged off everything he wore. She was reminded of the first time she had watched him do this from the shelter of his bed, the bright splash of water and the rapid fiery glitter of it across skin. She had feigned sleep then, because of the fear and the darkness in her heart. Yet she had not been able to look away from him. This was the same.

The water rippled into the brass bowl.

No, not the same. Nothing was the same as that. Not now. She had understood nothing then.

Mud stained the water that sluiced across his skin, his hair. Why so much? Why had so much earth soaked his clothes, as though he had been downed? If he was hurt—

"Berg." She sat up, thrusting the bedclothes back.

The dark head raised. She thought her heart stopped.

"Berg…" Their gazes met.

"I thought you slept."

"No." She got out of bed and walked toward him. Their gazes held, the grey-flecked eyes locked on hers. Her blood pounded.

"Why were you not sleeping?"

The glitter of firelight on the axe blade caught the edge of her sight. She kept walking.

"Did you find him? Was he there?" *He.* Nameless. Kraka…

The bright gaze snapped.

"Aye."

"And?" She stopped. Sweat touched her palms, seemed to gather at her scalp, along the line of her neck under the heavy swathe of her hair.

"Naught. Not this night. Not before the dawn breaks."

"And then?"

"Aye. Then."

She did not know when she had stopped looking at him. She was standing beside the sword belt. Her gaze was on the finely curved blade of the discarded axe, on the gold-leafed hilt of the sword lying beside it. *Then.* No need of a fuller answer.

No choices. Not now.

"Get back into the bed. It is late."

Choices...

"You told me that once before—that I might get back into the bed if I wanted to sleep."

His hand touched the water. She watched the ripples spread out from his fingers. The trail of mud.

"I do not want to sleep."

He picked up the cloth. "Sleep is what you need." He turned his head and the scarred face softened. Just for an instant. "Take the advice I gave you. I had no idea I could be so clever."

"Clever?" Her hand touched his over the cloth. "I would not want you getting an idea like that." The solid flesh under her palm went rigid. Her fingertips suddenly looked ridiculously small.

"It is late."

Late. So very late. Her own hand tightened against his. *Why did I not meet you before Kraka? Before any of this hap-*

pened? It was too late before I even met you. She moved her shaking fingers across wet skin, traces of mud. Power. *Yet I can still feel as though I have always known you and that time stretches out, not like a line but like a circle. Unbroken.*

I know it is not true.

His hand moved.

"Do not send me away." She watched his hand. "Do you remember that first night after the battle? When you came back? I was lying in the bed. In that room. You believed at first that I slept. But I did not. You came in. You washed yourself. Just like this. I watched you, but you did not know that. Not at first. I did not want to watch you. I wanted to look away. But I could not, not from you."

The hand jerked away. But she held it.

"Don't—" Her voice choked. She took a breath, trying to steady the rush of disjointed words, thoughts, pain. She swallowed. Longing. Longing for what was not hers.

"I had never seen or known anyone like you. Your presence held me as though it had always done so." She saw the sharp rise and fall of his chest, the glitter of dampened skin, mud-streaked, bathed in fire. "I wanted to touch you. Two strangers, as good as enemies, and I wanted to touch you, even then." Her fingers smoothed over the harsh bones of his hand.

"I wanted to touch you as I do now and I dared not." Her breath shivered. She tried to control it but she could not. She thought the edge of it must have brushed the bared skin of his arm.

"I did not approach you because I was afraid. You know why." *You understand that much. Oh, please understand the rest. All that I do not say to you and will never be able to say.* She saw the almost savage movement of muscle. Fire over shadow.

"Do not turn me away."

Her breath caught. From fear, from the hot-savage touch of his naked body and then from his mouth on hers. The blood came like a hot surge through her veins.

Only for now. She wanted to say it to him, to explain. *It is not for the future, only for now.* But her senses swam. The dizziness swept through her in waves.

He picked her up, carrying her across to the bed, and there was only him and the heat of him. She let it take her, the dark hard power of his body and the familiar taste of his mouth. Smooth touch. The core of kindness that mingled with all the fiercely full strength, his hands soothing her body, the softened touch of his mouth.

Gentleness, because he knew that was what she craved. But it was different this time. So different. Her arms closed round the naked skin of his back. It was like a dream. The fatigue and the fears, and the problems in her mind that were too big for her to contemplate or grapple with, made it so. The only comfort and the only salvation were in the moment. In him.

He moved against her, softly, and the touch of his mouth was more potent than wine. Infinitely richer. She glimpsed the straight shoulders, the broad back, the taut power of his hips, the sliding, full-muscled curve of his thigh. He was beautiful for all his size and his heavy weight, rough-smooth strength and tight lines. A dream-lover.

Her own body moved with his. So smoothly. Part of the

dream itself, the dream that had haunted her mind in shadows for so many years, though now its meaning was new.

He was her dream, yet at the same time, intensely real. The smoothness of his flesh, the cold drops of water from his soaking hair, the tingling friction of his skin against hers.

She writhed and the response was there in him, in the tightening of his mouth against the distended peak of her breast, the touch of his hands at her hips. She pushed against tautness and strong flexible lines, her swollen nipple buried deep in his mouth, the heated ache between her legs sliding against the fullness of his thigh.

Sensation scorched through mind and body, igniting fire, making her urgent for more. For him. He knew. His mouth released her, moved lower, brushed flesh so sensitised with desire and wanting that the lightest touch from him brought shivers racing across her skin.

Her breath tightened and her heart beat. She knew what he would do. He would touch her as he had last night, so intimately. She did not pull away. Her body slid round to accommodate his touch, the slow heady glide of his mouth. As though she were accustomed to him, as though the pounding excitement was hers to be taken. Shared. It must be how lovers were. Lovers who shared lives and hearts and bodies. *Always*. She cut off the thought. But the deep richness of his voice echoed in her head. *Always*.

His strength held her and she turned her body, opening to the urging of his lips, the intimacy of her lover's mouth on hot skin, swollen and wanting, the smooth glide of his tongue inside her body.

The release came, so strong, stronger than she had expected. Greater than the sharpened edge of desire that she thought she understood. The brightness burst through mind and aching flesh. The rolling waves of it knew only their own time, not bound by earth's reckoning. The winged joy.

ELENE LAY IN HIS ARMS and the aftermath ebbed through her flesh. Tears stained her cheeks, but she could not permit weeping. Not yet. Later, when she had lost him forever and she was alone. She brushed a hand across her face.

She moved closer, tighter.

He did not expect her to touch him. That much was clear. It was expected to be like last night when he had given her the gift and that was all. Because she could not take any more. But that was then.

This was now.

His skin burned. Fire in the darkness. So strong. She was struck again by the beauty she had been blinded to by fear, by the shock of his face. By her own weaknesses.

Hot muscle tightened under her hand like a sheet of power. She heard the sharp intake of his breath as she touched him.

"Elene."

He caught her hand. "Wait. There is no need. You must sleep now. It is too late." His words sounded like a death chant in her heart.

"No."

His hand circled her wrist, engulfed it so there was nothing to be seen under the broadness of his palm, the strong grip.

"No."

Her fingers rested on the flexible skin of his abdomen. "I do not wish to sleep. Not yet."

"You are exhausted. You are—" Tight breath, like someone who felt the sharpness of pain, not desire.

"Berg?"

She felt harsh breath. "You were crying."

"No." If that was all… "No, that does not matter." *Not now, not at this moment. I will not let it.*

"I am all right." Her words shivered across his naked skin. *Lies.* She tried to steady the wildness inside her. Behind the wildness lay pain, not just something physical, but the more terrible pain that lived in the mind. Loss.

No one understood maiming loss more than Berg. No one must feel it more deeply, even though he had a new life, the course of it mapped out with the Wessex king. He had the courage to take the future, the courage to start again out of nothing. She knew that. But she also knew the power of the pain.

She watched the fire-shadowed beauty of his skin. Her heart beat as though it would kill her. Wildness and longing. Nothing else she could give him. Nothing.

She moved her fingers, just fractionally because that was all she could manage in the power of his grip. She felt the tight skin under her fingertips respond.

"This is what I want." Her voice was hoarse with unwanted tears. She swallowed them.

"No." His grip on her tightened. She did not think he realised what he had done. A hand like his could break every bone in her wrist. She took a breath. Her eyes were

fixed on his in the dark. She was so close to him she felt
the uneven breath and the tension in each thickened
muscle.

"I know what I am doing."

"No. Elene, you do not." The grip loosened with an
abruptness that bordered on savage. "You are shaking."

She looked at her hand resting on thick flesh as though
it belonged to someone else, a thin blur of whiteness in
the dark. Small. Quite cold. Under it burning heat, pliable
muscle. A thin film of sweat.

"You are afraid."

The beat of her heart would stifle her. Their richly furnished bower at Eashing was silent, still, very full of shadows. On the small carved and painted table was the
outline of a book. Intangible grace.

Heat filled her hand. Now. Or not at all. She would
never have the chance to touch him again. She slid her
hand across the taut flesh, in a wide slow circle, touching the edge of his ribs, heavy bones, smooth skin, the
edge of one tight hip bone. She stopped and her heart
thundered.

"Let me touch you. I know— I can—" She stopped. But
it was there, pitilessly revealed. The curse of who she was.

*I know what to do. I have been taught exactly how to ful-
fill the need.*

Kraka.

The spectre of his malice seemed there in the blackness
at the edges of the warm room. Waiting. As lethal as a
death shadow.

She was touching Berg. She felt the fierceness of his reaction through the powerful flexible line of his body. A jolt of coldness shafted through her own lungs.

Her fingers tightened on the life under her hands, the strength and the power of it. She did not let go. She did not know whether it was courage or desperation. All she knew was that she could not let Kraka mar the strength she touched. Never. Neither could she let Kraka take this moment with her lover.

Her fingertips slid over the edge of heavy bone at his hip, brushed skin beside dark, sweat-damp hair, the blood-thickened shape of his male flesh. Her small, scratched, unsteady fingers waited one breath above burning skin. Black shadows and strength.

"Do not turn me away. Help me to know what to do."

His hand closed over hers.

HER THIN FINGERS TREMBLED under his touch. The bones of her hand were too slight for life. Too slight for him. Berg would have released her. Even then. But her hand turned, clutching at his bruised fingers. Her breath stirred the heavy hair at his neck. The soft weight of her body lay against his. So light.

He looked at her eyes. Forced his mind to read what was there, to look beyond the driving force of his hunger and the feral wildness in blood-thickened muscle, the darkness buried in his mind.

He saw the small traces of fear she could not hide. He had expected that. What he had not expected was the need, so strong, as depthless and still unslaked as his own.

Elgiva.

His body moved against hers, flesh on flesh, shared heat. Her response seemed so complete, unfettered. But he knew it was not and the rage stabbed through the bonds of his mind, unstoppable, as strong as the hunger, black and consuming. The only outlet lay in vengeance, in justice, or his soul would never be free. The shape of all that was unresolved burned between them. He thrust it aside. She would sense it, the blackness in him, and he would not have that touch her.

There was only now, Elene, and the need that was fathomless, despite the past and the future and all that had ever separated them. The need reflected in her eyes. He bent his head. This much first. He touched her lips, lightly, all the burning urgency inside him held back. Until she sought him, leaning closer, her skin warmed, hot with the scent of desire she scarcely understood.

He drew her hand down.

The first touch on his skin tore at control. The driving urgency pushed through him like madness. He held back, with the patience that was foreign to him, taught through the last six winters. But the need for Elene would take his mind.

He let her fingers wrap round his length, endured her sudden stillness, waited for her to get used to the feel of him. He controlled each aching muscle in the dark. The silence seemed filled with the harshness of his breath and the pounding of his own blood in his ears.

"Let me touch you." Her whisper cut into the blackness that was greater than the half light of the bower, the blackness behind his eyes. "Let me give that much to you. Pleasure," she said. "Joy."

Her hand moved. Her skin was hot against his. Her thin fingers and delicate palm traced the blood-engorged skin of his shaft. His body shifted, the sudden movement barbarous, beyond his controlling. She was so fragile. Damaged.

She was not a match for him, for all the burning need and the pain inside him. Yet the echo of that need had been there in her, like a reflection that had survived all the pain. And even as his body reacted to her touch, in wildness, beyond leashing, she moved with him. Seeking him as she had before.

He let her touch him until that was no longer possible and he moved, breaking her grip with the edge of savagery caused by loss, by the shameful blackness in his mind.

She did not draw away. That registered in some part of his brain and when he covered her, her body took him in, the soft flesh hot, moist with desire, welcoming. The need was still there.

Let it be so.

He had waited so long. Not just from the moment he had seen her at the fortress, desperate and poised like a war spirit. But even before that. Since memory lived.

He held back, the restraint forced, for one instant outside time. But then her body moved against him. He heard the sharp gasp of her breath. She had wanted the pleasure. And so he touched her, the tender flesh and the scorching heat.

His fingers slid to touch where they were joined, sought

the moist softness of her flesh where it stretched round him. Her body writhed. The pleasure. The only thing the Viking Kraka had not been able to touch. His fingertips quickened and she pushed against the movement of his hand, as though the gift that was only a bright shadow of all that lay behind it could be accepted. As though she wanted him. Despite everything, loss and disaster and separation and the fact that he had once left her, unknowing, to her fate.

Her body moved with his as though they were one, as though it was him she wanted, and she would not leave him again as she had chosen to before. As though loss did not exist.

She pushed against his hand, the sound of her cry harsh against his lips. One breath. One split soul, if such a thing were possible.

Then he was moving, restraint neither possible nor needed. Perhaps. But he could not think of it, his body so hard against hers, inside it. The need was too black, too long held back, buried under too many years of darkness. Her body moved with his, taking all he would have hidden, even the driving need and the edge of madness. Her heat engulfed him and there was nothing, only Elene and the wildness of his blood and the hot burst of his seed.

KRAKA AWOKE FROM NIGHTMARES, the kind of shapes of blackness that faded beyond recall at the instant of waking, but left their foul taste on damp skin. The women said such dreams came from Heimdall, the watchman, the god of secrets.

But Kraka was sworn to Odin.

"Lord."

"What now?" He stood. If it was more ill news— All had turned as sour as the night sweat on his skin since the moment he had laid hands on Horik.

Before that.

Since his brothers had led that disastrous attack on the fort at the other side of the Andredesweald against the king's man. He counted the disasters: a lost battle, three men dead on the roadside. Four. He could still see the face of the man he had killed himself. He moved, pacing the mud-slick ground, as though he could outpace his thoughts.

The journey had cost time and manpower and all the store of luck his men believed he had. And now they faced a far larger fortress, and no reason for the men inside it to come out.

"Well?"

He kept his face without expression. If it was ill news, he would deal with it. The anger waited deep inside his mind. He would deal with anything to get back what was his. For vengeance. For success. He never lost in the end.

Yet his hand touched the amulet at his neck. A spear. Odin's sign, not Heimdall's. Stronger. Yet they said Odin could turn, even on the Chosen.

He waited while the panting messenger got breath back.

"News, lord, from the scouts that—"

"The fortress?" He held still, night dreams forgotten, impatience surging through cramped muscles.

"Nay, from further afield." Guthrum. Ice touched his

veins. His failure would be laid bare and the consequences…

"From the west."

"The west?"

The man's eyes burned, eager. "One of the scouts you
sent out found the news from some travellers, by chance.
Without that he would not have—"

"What news?"

"The Saxon king comes here."

Here. Thin metal dug into his fingers. The spear. He had
forgotten he held it. His hand tightened.

"Here?"

"With only his household troops." The man's words fell
over each other, spilling into the damp English air. "He
comes down the ridgeway from the west. They think he
will be here before the sun is high. Lord…"

But he lost the rest. His head spun. The coin hoard, the
fortress, were nothing compared to this. The answer was
there, move and counter move, attack and defend. A game.

Take the king.

The chance was there. If he could take Alfred of the
West Saxons, the rest mattered less than dust.

His feet began to stride again across the torn ground.

What would Jarl Guthrum not give for that death? Or
for that life? That would be better. The mud churned
under his feet. Taken alive, Alfred would be worth more
than all the treasure of Wessex. Even if Guthrum chose
to restore him to his throne afterward, he would be no
more than a slave to Guthrum's wish, his power broken
forever.

And if dead... Alfred was the last of Athelwulf's sons, the last man of fit age to rule and with an undisputed claim to the throne. Without its king, Wessex would surely collapse. Guthrum could take it and *he*, Kraka, would have made it possible.

Dead. Dead was best. Another sacrifice to Odin like the East Anglian king. The scene was there again in his mind. The ritual death that was so necessary for a deposed king and the English watching, unable to do anything. His fingers ran over the spear. The luck had turned.

He was the one who was here. At the right time. Success out of disaster. Blinding success.

"Make ready." He could see Horik crowding with the others behind the messenger. He smiled at his brother's wide-eyed face. Everything would be right again. He would have made it right and his younger brother Toke's soul would rest.

"We move with the first light. Forget the fortress." The Saxons did not even know he was here. There would be time enough for the fortress afterward, for the silver, for the woman Elene and her lover. No king's man after tomorrow. Dead meat.

She would be glad enough to come back to Kraka because he would hold the power. The future.

"We move west."

"WHAT WOULD YOU WISH to do, lord?"

Ashbeorn, king's thane, watched his sovereign's face in the candlelight of the guest chamber hastily made available by the nervous local landowner. They were alone, which meant that Alfred could say exactly what he thought. It must be a boon for kings.

"I would want to drive Earl Guthrum back into the sea. But right now, I would settle for reaching Eashing." The king's gaze flicked to the doorway. "Or some ale."

Macsen kicked the door shut. "This is the best." He set the pitcher down on the table carefully covered with blue cloth. "If we stay more than one night, your host will be reduced to the verge of poverty."

Like the rest of Wessex. No one said it.

"You and Berg have my gratitude once more."

The precious hoard of newly minted silver. Ash watched only the guarded expression in Macsen's eyes. There was more. There always was. It was like an endless board game, the pieces moved here and there. *Hnefatafl,* perhaps. His wearied thoughts ran in Norse, the way they sometimes did. *Hnefatafl,* where all the opposing gaming pieces must try to take the king.

He watched Alfred's bent head.

The king was speaking to Macsen. "You say this man Kraka and his Danish war band are still there, so many miles within my realm."

"He wants the coin hoard, the woman prisoner. Vengeance for two defeats, I suppose. The man is obsessed."

"Obsessed enough to risk the lives of all of his men against Eashing?"

"Yes." Macsen put down the ale cup. "I believe he is."

"I see."

The king looked up. The steady eyes masked the next calculation that must be made in the game. Ash watched the limitless courage rise. It was like fire, as quick. As quick as the hidden thoughts.

"And what do you believe, Ashbeorn? What do you believe a Viking would do?"

The question would once have cut like a sword's thrust. Ash might have been born English, but he had been brought up with Vikings. His loyalty and his worth when he had returned to take his place among so many desperate Saxons had been a matter of open dispute. But the bitterness was gone. There was only the future the king saw. The future that hung by a thread.

"I know what I would do." His voice admitted no compromise. His mind was quite clear, his Danish past no longer a disaster, but the strength that supported the present.

"This is what I would see." He struggled to translate the thoughts into his acceptable, accentless, West Saxon. "I am a Viking in enemy territory. I have tasted defeat but that is only one of Odin's many faces. I still have my courage. In this case my determination seems as strong as an obsession."

He glanced at Macsen.

"I have the choice of withdrawing, of returning to the safety of Danish-held land. But that means I come before my earl's face empty-handed, disgraced." There probably were no West Saxon words for the next bit. "I know that my fate is not mine to rule," said Ash.

He paused. The three of them waited in the honourably furnished chamber, the almost-Dane, the Briton whose ancestors had moved across the sea to this land long before the Saxons had come. And the extraordinary king who held the vision that bound them all. Ash watched the fine wax candles brought out in Alfred's honour and said what had been obvious to him since the age of six winters. Words that belonged to the other world of the Norsemen, so similar to this world and yet utterly different.

"This is the way my mind works. My fate hangs by a thread which I know will break when the time is right. I can do nothing to strengthen that thread. All that matters is how I die, not when. Would I take a cow's death, in safety? Or would I fight, so that even if Odin seems to turn against me in this world, he will not in the next?"

He watched Alfred's eyes and now he could see the understanding that was sometimes hidden by the mask of those who ruled.

"If I were the Viking, Kraka, and I knew you were here, I would not touch the fort. I would see a greater prize, one that in death would give me the glory I craved and in life would give me my reputation and all the rewards I could desire."

The king's eyes never wavered.

"This would be my choice," said Ash. *Hnefatafl*. "I would take all of my men west across the ridgeway. I would do everything I could to take you—the king. Everything else would be there afterward, waiting for my pleasure."

CHAPTER 14

THE DARK SEEMED INTENSE, blinding. But Elene still touched him. Berg could sense her warmth and her fast breath. Her body brushed against his in the blackness. He wanted to reach out, pull her against his heat. He could not. He had shown too much of the darkness that drove him. He had taken too much. He expected her to draw away. But her body stayed where it touched him, lying against his, like a sign of trust.

He felt the dampness of her skin, the way her heart beat too fast. Because of the way he had loved her. She seemed so fragile. He fought for stillness in his own body. For control.

If she moved away, he would let her.

Elgiva.

They lay entwined. His heart felt as though it would burst, the control he sought beyond his reaching. There had been a primitive edge to what he had done, not just in the wild force of desire but in the need to possess. The knowledge of that burned his mind.

He had not withdrawn from her before the end; the possibility had not existed. He had taken the completeness. As though the act itself, the joining with her, the spilling of his seed could make her his beyond doubt.

The darkness clung to his skin, inescapable.

Perhaps that was something of what the Viking had felt.

He turned away. The darkness was no longer a separate force clinging at his skin. It was inside his soul.

"Berg?" She lay so close beside him. Perhaps the way she had lain beside Kraka. He sat up. But her small fingers clung to him, as though she would hold him back, as though that was what she wanted. He did not believe it could be. He could read what was in her voice and her touch. She was frightened.

He forced the only words he could say out of the rawness of his throat, the breath still ragged from sex. "I am sorry." He waited a heartbeat. "Elene—"

Her body became quite still, in a silence that would chill blood. He forced more words.

"I caused you more fear."

"No." Her voice nearly choked on it. "You did not. No…" Her fingers clutched at him again, scrabbling at his arm. But it was pointless. He knew she was lying.

"You are shaking."

The skin that had been so pliant before, so hot he had lost himself in the fire, was chilled, frighteningly vulnerable. He had not, at the end, been gentle with her.

He had not shown her what he had wished, what he had set out in his arrogance to do. He had not shown caring or healing, only the black depths of what was truly in his soul.

He moved away, and this time her slender body did not follow his. Only the very tips of her fingers rested against his arm. Like a sign of joining. Two halves of a coin.

He could not speak such things. Elene felt nothing but bitterness for the past. All she had wanted was for him to wipe it out. *Give me that much.* He had believed that he could do it. That he could make the future for her out of his own power. He had failed her with that, just as he had failed her once before.

Her fingers rested on his skin, quiet, as insubstantial as a spirit's and as far removed from anything he could grasp. Yet he could feel their touch, a human connection. The hidden truth hammered at his lips.

He turned. "Elene." He sought to keep the movement controlled, the size and weight of his body held back. Lamplight flickered at the edge of sight, disturbed by his movement. The restless glitter of flame caught the blade of the small inlaid throwing axe beside the lamp. The gleam of it drew her gaze away from his. Her fingers slid across his skin. He had to say the truth. Now.

"El—" But before he could form the completion of her name, her words cut across his.

"You will go out to find Kraka. You will leave as soon as it is light. You will meet him."

That was the other face of truth, and in the end, that was what came out of his mouth.

"Yes. I will find him."

"Because you must."

"Because I must. Because of what I have sworn to the king of Wessex. And to the king of East Anglia who is dead. Because the laws of honour demand vengeance and because I cannot let Kraka go on in search of plunder and conquest. That is my basic duty."

He could see from her eyes that she understood. But the more bitter truth was there, exposed by the way he had touched her. He gave it voice. "Because it is what I want."

Her body stiffened, the reaction felt, because they were so very close.

She moistened her lips. Her gaze flickered. From him to the sword and the axe blade. Back to him.

"Must you go? Kraka cannot attack Fashing. He will know how things stand and he will leave. He cannot do otherwise. He is not so…lost to all reason, so reckless."

He tried to control the bitterness, to give her words due weight. He thought of how Ashbeorn must have felt, moving from one world to another, from Viking to Saxon. So much never spoken.

But this was King Ivar's man, whatever face the Viking had tried to show to Elene. A murderer. She could not know to what extent. Even he did not know for certain. Yet.

"I must go. No other choice exists." But as he said the words, what filled his mind was not the duty of his oath, but the sight of her fragile skin and the dark shadows around her eyes.

Kraka.

The man was possessed. He would not let go.

Neither would Berg.

"What will happen?" Her gaze was fixed on him so that his skin quickened with the awareness of her, even now.

"I know not." But he did. The air was heavy with death. He could smell it. He was not attuned to other worlds like Macsen, or even Ashbeorn. But some things were clear even to thick-skulled creatures like him.

"You will be safe." It was the only certainty. His hand closed over hers. That much of the fragile connection between them must be allowed. They had just made love. She was frightened.

"You will be safe. I can promise you that much. The king will be here soon. He is a true *gold-giefa*, a gold-giver and a fair lord, the most generous friend I have known. He will give you protection as will I and my kin. I am no longer without riches."

He stilled the movement and the unquiet breath with which she would speak. It was hard enough to say what must be said to ease her mind as far as he could. Utterly impossible to say more. Even though the sight of her pale skin and her sleek disordered hair, the sense of her nearness, drove through him. Even though the need inside clawed like a caged beast.

His hand soothed her fingers.

"There are those who will help you, my sister who serves the queen, and there are others. There are—" He was almost afraid to touch her. "There are those who have sworn an oath to the king like me." His mind went back to Alfred's crowning and the stone chamber at Wimborne Abbey.

"It is a particular oath." Her hand curled under his. "It cannot be broken. Those who swear it are like brothers, more closely tied than that." *Ties that transcended time and place. Ties as tenacious as—* But he could not let his mind range further back. Not now. What use was the past if he could not offer a future?

"If I ask it of them, those people will help you. There is Macsen and many others." *Ashbeorn who was with the Vikings.* "They will find you and give you help. They are true."

Her hand tightened and the response in him was immediate, as shattering as pain. His arms closed round her and she came close against him. Her lips parted under his and there was no black shadow between them, only the heat. Their bodies melted under it. The rich softness of her mouth yielded to his and the kiss held everything that he had failed to show her at that last moment, all the tenderness that had no other expression. Everything he could not give was there in that moment that had no future— nothing he could do and no promise he could give that had not been broken before.

Too late. The light would change soon. Dawn.

He drew away.

JUDITH WOULD NOT LET BERG GO without her. Not this time.

She was clever enough to know not to wait for first light. Just like him. She sped across the courtyard in the cold dark, her booted feet splashing in unseen puddles. Some guardsman called out to her. She ignored him. His feet pounded along behind her. More mud. He would never catch her. She was very fast in breeches. He could take up his grievances with Berg.

So, she supposed, would she.

"Judith."

She did hesitate in the stable doorway and the heavy feet behind her slithered to an abrupt halt. Her brother's glance fixed somewhere over her left shoulder. *That* sort of look. It was usually followed by a great deal of unnecessary bellowing. The footsteps faded away. For half a moment, she wished she had followed in the hapless guardsman's wake.

Not that a woman of resource could ever be intimidated by a mere brother, but still. There was something about him since he had come back to Eashing, something she had never seen. Except perhaps in those first days in Wessex, after their cousin's murder, after... Her heart pounded with the memories.

"Let me ride out with you—" She had not meant to put it so abruptly like that. She had her reasoned speech all planned out, even her devious cajolements. But all of that fled under the familiar wrenching pain in her heart. Pain that would die only with vengeance.

Berg understood that.

He shook his head, but the look in his eyes, even in the torchlit dark, showed that edge of understanding. She pressed the advantage.

"How can you refuse me when you and only you know what is in my heart?"

"Because I must." There was pity beneath his understanding. It changed the pain to anger.

"I am not a fool! I will not burden you. I can fight."

"Aye, I have known that from the nursery. Little spitfire that you were—"

"Do not. Do not keep making light of me. I am not a child. I am full grown and hale, as strong as some of your men." That must be almost true. Her brother just did not realise the measure of her strength because he was such a mountain himself.

"No."

She watched his hands tighten the girth strap on the great black horse, saw the moment that his gaze and his attention left her, fixed on what would come. Without her. Her hands tightened into fists.

"Let me. Or I will ride out myself, with or without your leave."

He looked up. She almost took a step back. Almost. She stared into her brother's eyes that had seen more pain even than she. She could see the gathering of his anger. No, the anger had been there all through, hidden. Because he was one of those men who never found words for what they wanted to say. He fastened the buckle. The great black horse moved with the same impatience.

"I know he was Ivar's man," she burst out. "The Viking you are going to fight. I know who he is."

The cold air of early morning seemed stifling, something that would choke her lungs. "I have asked questions, too, here at Eashing. I know Kraka was there when—" She stopped. The torchlight flickered over hideous scars as the man in front of her moved. Even she could not say the rest, not through all the anger in her soul. Not to him, her only kin.

Yet something inside would not let her back off. She held her head high, neck stiff and almost trembling with the ugly tension.

"Please."

She had not said that since she was three. She thought the unexpectedness of it might swing things her way for once. He stood back, his hand resting on the horse's thick neck. There was silence and she thought, *Athelbert's bones. He has not slept in days.*

"No, Judith. Not this time. This is something for me. Something that only I can do."

He said that because of *her.* The Viking's mistress. The Viking who—

"…that is why I need you to stay here." Her brother's rough voice, still speaking. "I need you to look after Elene if I do not come back. She has no one. The others in the brotherhood will help you, and you are in the queen's favour and Alfred's."

Alfred. She stood against the wattle wall of the stables in her breeches and leather jerkin. The sword at her side clunked.

"If you will take on a task for the sake of what is right, do that."

A task for the sake of what is right. How much of the hopeless feelings in her heart did he guess? The anger came back, because it masked everything else. What she wanted to do was fight, like him. She wanted to prove by some great deed that her heart was as loyal and her courage as strong as any king's warrior. Not play nursemaid to a siren like Elene.

"Judith? Will you do that? She is alone and she has suffered. She still does."

Kraka's mistress. And now her own brother was going out to a fight with Ivar's murderous creature, who had already caused such damage. A fight he might not come back from. Because he was besotted with Elene and he was a fool for lost causes. *A fool.*

She could hear others in the courtyard. All the men ready. Leaving while she stayed. She watched her brother swing himself so easily into the saddle, despite weariness, despite whatever pain or fear or anger he felt. It was hidden, as always. Even from her.

He guided the horse past her, her agreement taken for granted. Because it was given, despite everything she felt, and he knew it.

"Elene has no one," said her brother. "She is ill. She needs…"

"My help." Not a question, just the acquiescence she had no choice but to give. He had done everything that a brother could do for her and she would always do the same for him. There were only the two of them left out of all their kin. She straightened up in her useless war gear and her men's breeches.

But the anger flicked her, so strong. It had to be to disguise what was underneath, all the pain and despair. Unbearable.

"Elene is not ill." She yelled the truth after the broad strong back in its sparkling mail. "She is pregnant."

"No, you will not," said Berg's sister. "There is not the least need for you to leave the chamber. I always get the news first. Even before the king when he is here, I should not wonder. I bribe his garrison."

Elene stared at the other woman. She was sprawled along the wall bench wearing trousers.

The floor seemed to tilt uneasily beneath Elene's feet. She felt as though she were seasick. She had had no consciousness of the moment Berg had left her. Only a black space, as though she had slept without knowing it. Just the sense of his warmth and the endless comfort of his strength, and then nothing. The nightmare had come with waking.

"Will you sit down, lady? I am supposed to be looking after you."

There are those who will help you, my sister…others.

And he had gone.

"Kraka will have to move back east," Elene said stubbornly. "He has no choice." *Let Berg not find him.*

Judith gave her a look that could scarcely disguise the volatile mix of anger and fear. Then she bolted off the wall bench, as fast as quicksilver, hauling open the door even as Elene first registered the hesitant sound.

A very young man stayed on the threshold. He gave one rapid glance at Judith's shapely form in trousers and flushed scarlet.

"Well?" demanded the Amazon.

"Good tidings, lady," he said, not looking at the trousers. "I heard that the Vikings have gone, left their camp and—"

"Gone? Gone," breathed Judith, her arm linked through Elene's.

Gone. The word beat through Elene's brain. She had guessed it must be so, wished it, *known*. Even Kraka had had no other choice. He was not so far steeped in recklessness. The relief made her head spin and she sat down, letting Judith bounce round the messenger.

"And when will my brother be back?" demanded the Amazon.

"I—I know not, lady."

"Well then it is only half the tidings. But still..." A silver coin was proffered but the young man refused it. If anything, he became a darker shade of red. Elene watched the reluctant closing of the door. The whirling sprite did not notice.

"A fine young man," said Elene. She could not imagine what it was like to feel young. "He admires you."

"What? No, I do not think so. He disapproves of trousers. They all do. I am going to have to do church penance." She grabbed a kirtle and threw it over her head. The long skirts billowed. "Besides," she said, her voice muffled through yards of female draperies, "even if he felt such a thing, I doubt he would dare to approach me for fear of Berg."

The blond head emerged from swathes of beautifully dyed blue. "If there is one thing you must have noticed about my brother, it is that he has difficulty letting go. Of anything."

There was a small silence where before there had been

a brief, heart-stopping moment of the rarest quality on earth—joy.

Elene moved to help the girl fasten the laces of her dress. Judith stood still for her. The complaisance was like all of their connection, half-sought, half-pushed-away. In another world, perhaps they could have been friends.

"He will not abandon you," said Judith softly. Elene's hands stilled, the ties unravelling under her fingers. "That is how he is. You do not have to fear." Elene looked at her unsteady hands. "He will do what is right for you. And for the babe. I—I know you did not wish to confide such a thing to me, but a woman can tell."

The silence, and all that lay behind it, choked her breath. She made no sound. Her fingers tied one very precise bow and then another.

"Done." She did not know whether she said the word aloud, whether her voice had any power.

Judith stepped away. "He must be back soon. Do you feel well enough to come out to the walls with me and wait?"

"No." The sound rasped on the thickened air. She swallowed. "No, I think not. But you go." The rush of blood in her head stopped sense. "I shall be quite well here. Go on ahead. I should prefer to wait here."

She gripped the hard edge of the table. There were bright patches of light at the edge of sight. They were mixing with darkness. *Go. Just go.* There was nothing more to be said. Nothing. No secrets left.

A woman can tell. Had she told her brother? Did Berg— No, he did not know. He would not have come near her bed last night, not even though she had pleaded. He would not have touched someone so unclean. He did not know. Yet. Judith just assumed he did and then—

She heard Berg's sister walk away, hesitate.

"I meant what I said. He will not abandon you. He understands what obligations are. We both do. We had a cousin who saw to that."

"Cousin," she said blankly. "He told me about his cousin's death."

"Aye. Well, everyone knows how King Edmund died, a sacrifice to Odin and now we Christians will make a saint of him."

Elene raised her head. "Your cousin? King Edmund of the East Angles?" But she could not see Judith the warrior spirit, Berg's sister. There was only blackness.

"Aye. King Edmund would have liked that, the conferring of sainthood. He was one of the few people who deserved it."

She heard another footstep, then the door latch.

"Are you sure you will not come?"

"Yes." *Quite sure.*

There was a pause. The door shut. She got up. There was sweat on her skin. The ache in her back took her breath. Stabbing pain.

Nothing to what was in her head.

She could not go out to meet the brother of Judith, the East Anglian prince, king's cousin and namesake. Berg.

Not Berg. Edmund the atheling.

Her betrothed.

How had she not seen who he was? She tried to overlay the picture of the blithe handsome boy across that of the full-grown man, the raw power, the deep mind, the ruined face.

It was wrong. Utterly wrong. Judith was wrong, pretending just the way she did when she dressed up in trousers, lying. Her feet paced the floor, scattering scented rushes. She stopped.

A strong and honourable maiden like Judith was not a liar. One had only to look at her eyes, so clear, grey as a horizonless sky, like—

She could see truth. Berg's grey eyes. Berg's East Anglian voice, deepened and roughened and changed, but unmistakable. She had seen all that, heard it, taken note of it inside her soul and understood it in the first moment of meeting him. Then she had used her mind to shut it out. She had not let one recognisable thought get through. Because of what she was, what she had become.

What she had become…

That was what mattered. Her feet resumed the restless pacing. Her muscles felt weak, burning. Just like her mind. She could not allow weakness, not now. She had to think. But it was so hard to think through the pain and fatigue caused because of the journey, because…

Because of the baby. She could think it now, say the words out loud. The truth was there, acknowledged. The acknowledgement of what she had tried to hide, even from herself, was such a relief. She could face it.

But Berg did not know. Just as he could not know who she was, or he would have said so.

She was Elene, Viking's mistress, not Elgiva the betrothed. If he thought of Elgiva at all, he thought she was a dream.

Summer…like the sun in the sky. That is how she is to me.
The betrothal was broken. It belonged to another life, not this one. Edmund the unattainable prince. In the last three years since their betrothal had been broken, she had thought of him with nothing but bitterness, as one who had abandoned her, a promise breaker.

But Berg. He did not break promises lightly. *Obligations.* She understood now. He would stick beside his promise to look after her, whether he knew who she was or not.

She paced the small comfortable room, willing the darkness away, the strength into her limbs. But the pain and the blackness were so strong. Her mind reeled with the shock. It was too much to take in after all that had happened with Kraka.

Kraka. The man who had fathered her child.

Instinct took over, the only thing that could force life into her body. She did not need to think. She already knew. She had made her decision long before. She had to leave him. She had known all along. She could not foist Kraka's child on any Englishman. To do that to an East Anglian prince who had watched his cousin die a martyr's death would be appalling. Kraka had been Ivar's man, Kraka who was dedicated to Odin.

She knew where she had to go—Winchester and then…
It mattered not where she went afterward. She would find somewhere safe for her and the child. *Viking's brat.* She thought of Chad. She knew he would be safe. She wished he could be happy.

Her hand fastened on the door latch. But the shock still

pulsed through body and mind like something physical. She forced breath. She could not think about what had happened. Later. She would shut it out of her mind, the way she had learned. She could cope with this. She had done worse things before. Worse things…

Now was the chance. There would never be another. Kraka had gone back east. Berg was returning here from that same road.

She could do it. Ride far down the ridgeway and disappear. She and the babe. She would look after the child. She would be safe.

She would travel west.

CHAPTER 15

"BEREN'S BONES! YOU BRAINLESS LACKWIT."

The West Saxon curse came clearly in the morning air. Berg dealt the man a buffet on the shoulder to remind him about silence. Dangerous idiot. A Viking war band hidden across the ridge and the king's men to ride down past them at any moment.

"Nay, but look at this, lord." The soldier from the Eashing garrison mouthed the words this time, then pointed. "Down on the road. She is going to ride straight through. Silly wench. Does she think she has all day?"

Berg crawled forward, keeping low, pushing from knee and elbow, moving up until he was close enough to see clearly over the edge of the outcrop.

"Comely," mouthed the man. "But slow. Maybe I should go down and show her the way. Lord? Do you see her? Benighted wench."

"I can see her."

"By all the saints, she must be ill. Did you see that? She will fall. Stupid woman. Can we do anything?"

"No. It is too late." *Too late.* Why had she done it? How could she have made a move so reckless? Did she want to go back to Kraka?

"Wistan—" He moved, concealment pointless now. He gave the orders. The sudden drumming of many hoofs on the roadway was as loud as his words. The king's troop. Then the yelling as Kraka broke cover. Too quickly. He had seen Elene. He must have. Something had thrown his timing, forced the mistake.

"Now." The savage roar moved his men. He was already remounted, pushing down the short slope, leaping the horse across the ditch and on to the ridgeway.

The plan unfolded. Both troops, his and the king's acting like a blacksmith's vise, one from each side squeezing shut on Kraka's men, what should have been an ambush turning back on the attacker.

The fight unleashed in a rain of steel and screaming. In the middle of it, as once before, was Elene. He could feel the same sickness inside that he had felt then, a thousand times stronger. She had turned the horse, instantly, making for the free space to the left. But she had no strength.

He pushed through. He could make out the king's standard held firm. Ashbeorn's boar helm. Macsen. The Viking Kraka had sent to take Elene. He had not come himself. Not yet.

Berg dug his heels into the sweating horse. He was still

so far away, the Viking closer, gaining. He saw the small *seax* blade in Elene's thin fingers.

His Valkyrie.

The throwing spear was already balanced in his hand. Impossible to get a clear shot. Someone blocked him, the shadow seen before the blow. He bent from the saddle, the movement instinct, faster than thought, twisting, striking out with the weapon in his hand. The other man's spear passed his shoulder as his own thrust home.

But the blade caught, too deeply embedded to remove, the man's body twisting on it as he fell. The other man's mount reared, one of the crashing hoofs glancing his shoulder. Berg fought for balance, to keep his seat. The pain was unfelt. He caught the reins, moving his own mount round the opposite way.

Kraka's Viking closed in on Elene. He shouldered the horse through the press of men, the war stallion a weapon as good as any fashioned of steel. The gap was there. It was all he needed.

The Viking dropped. Berg passed him, leaping the horse over the body. Then he had Elene.

He threw himself from the horse and held her. She was not hurt. It was the only thought in his brain.

She clung to him, boneless, her weight so slight. She was quiet, with the silence that sometimes came on people after horrors. Her eyes were black pools. She drew away, her gaze fixed on the battle. He kept the bulk of his body between her and the dead Viking. He did not want her to see the throwing axe buried in the dead man's neck.

She did not seem able to walk. He picked her up, running back toward the tree line. He set her down in the shadows. Two of his men followed at his shout, two men and Ashbeorn. He saw the boar helmet and the flash of chain mail. She would be safe. He turned away but her small fingers drew him back.

"Berg, I thought…"

"Why did you do it? Leave Eashing to come here?"

He had not meant the question, not now when she was so shocked, with the battle unfinished. But it was there, the force of his harsh voice yelling, uncontrolled. Her wide dark eyes locked with his.

"I could not stay with you. I could not—"

He pulled away. Her fingers could not hold him.

"I know who you are. Edmund of East Anglia. I know—"

Her words followed him. Then the battle closed over him.

It was possible to find his way through. The movement of his body and the surge of his blood could not be stopped. Nothing held him back. Nothing touched him. That was how it was when the battle luck was there. He knew nothing would check him. The pain and the weariness were gone. No feeling at all. Only the luck and the heated urging of his blood. Destiny held back. Or driving him onward until he found what it wanted him to. Kraka.

Ivar's man was oblivious, pursuing his prize. Held off by the impenetrable bodyguard near the king.

Berg cut him out, isolated him. That was how it should be. He pressed forward, fate still at his back. He never missed a stroke of swordplay until he had Kraka unhorsed, crawling on the ground, grovelling. He stopped with the point of the blade at the Viking's throat.

Ivar's creature. He looked into the pale blue eyes and the recognition struck through him, through Kraka.

"You…" The thick neck worked under the point of the rune blade. "You are King Alfred's man, the one who took what was mine." The words were English, struggled over, heavily accented. The stretched eyes narrowed, focused. "But it does not begin there. You are East Anglian. You were there. When we made a sacrifice of that pathetic king of the East Angles, you were there. You should have died then."

He was only aware that the blade had cut deeper by the hissing intake of breath and the thin trickle of blood. He drew it back.

Reaction registered in the narrowed eyes, surprise.

"You are going to kill me. How can you not? You know what I have done. It was me who helped to carry out Ivar's orders for the sacrifice of your king. Do you think I have regrets? I am glad I did it. How can you possibly hold back?"

"You want death?"

"What else would I get from you?"

Death. The air stank with it. It was all around them. This man had called it up by forcing battle and now it was so strong. Berg's hand controlled the weapon and the terrible power of death was in his head, in his mind, in every tensed blood-gorged muscle of his body.

"Not yet. Speak to me."

The pale eyes slitted. "What of? The treacherous

woman? The Saxon slut you now hold? Is that it—" The gasp of pain stopped the words.

Berg forced his hand back.

"The lady Elene. I want to know what happened when you took her. What became of her kin?"

"How should I know that?"

"Indeed it matters not. Someone will remember. Someone else will tell me. You will not be the only captive taken this day."

The narrow eyes flickered.

"The woman's kindred are dead, East Anglian. I killed them." The pale eyes locked on his. "Is that what you wish to tell her, the fair Saxon? That it was my hand that slew them both, the old man and his wife as well?"

The narrow eyes were sharp with defiance, with the edge of madness that had driven the man to this final disaster. With unease. The sudden awareness of it cut through the blood-mist that held sight and heart and tensed muscle. The consciousness snapped between them. Unlooked for vulnerability. The Viking did not want Elene to know.

"You took two lives," said Berg. "From a man who was too old to do you harm and from a woman."

The Viking's eyes gave nothing. "The moneyer had his chance. He should have given me what I wanted."

"What you wanted?"

"I needed the treasure, the coins he had hidden, buried." The throat worked beneath the sword point. "I had to have it." Berg caught what had so far not been visible, raw and painful and beyond disguising. Fear? The intent gaze flicked away from his, seeing not this moment, perhaps, but the past. Elene's parents.

"He goaded me, that pathetic old man who was nothing." *Elene's father.* "He goaded my temper. It was his doing and she, stupid old woman, tried to stop me, clinging like a worm that—" The flick of pain brought the gaze back to his. The defiance and the anger were strong, the fear not visible.

"So. Will you take vengeance on me because I killed them? Does the woman have you so besotted, even though she gave herself first to me?"

Berg's sword hilt burned. The blackness the Dane wanted to call out was there, primitive fire, mixed with the older feelings, the murderous rage that had been born of helplessness. But he was not helpless as he had been in his homeland. This time, the victory in battle was not with the Danes. It was his. The sword cleaved to his hand, the power to wipe out all that kept him from what he wanted, the release of vengeance.

Elene…

"She chose to give herself to me, Saxon. Did she tell you that? I had the power over her. It was mine, but I did not even have to use it. She offered herself to me. Can you say that?"

The long-broken promise was there in his mind. Elene's father returning the agreement, all the gifts that had been settled on Elene already, even the letters he had struggled to find the right words for, because she had not wished to keep them. All because of the other promised gifts that would never come, the losses caused by the Viking whose skin reddened now under his sword's point. Push the blade deeper and vengeance was there. A few inches. All it would take.

"She chose me." The pale gaze goaded him as it had once before over his lord's death agony and his own pain. "She did not have to, but she *chose* me."

My choice…Kraka did not have to make such a bargain.

The words formed in his memory, born from night in the dark bed, the touch of Elene's skin against his. *My choice…I was grateful to him.* And the hidden feeling for her captor, buried, unspoken, unexplained. But they had both known it was there. *He was not without his own honour… I made a bargain.*

His own voice asking, what did you want so much?

The truth existed, even through the blackness and the pain, if he could find it. If he would look.

"She gave herself to you to save her parents' lives." That was what a woman like Elgiva would have done. He looked at the face of King Edmund's murderer.

But Elgiva could not have understood, not fully. She did not understand yet.

"That was what her choice was," he said. "You made a bargain with her and she trusted you to keep it. You let her believe that you had kept your word."

The fugitive brightness flared in the pale eyes again. The fear he had glimpsed before. The blade under his hand vibrated. He could not yet steady it.

"When did you kill them? Before or after you struck your bargain with a woman who had no defence?"

He saw the hesitation in the eyes. The fear was uncanny.

It mixed strangely with the anger and the determination that would take death from him, with the courage. He was surprised when the man spoke.

"Afterward. After I spoke with her and— Their deaths were not intended." The strange brightness in the blue eyes grew. "It was not intended. I told you. They provoked me. I was angered. I…" The brightness of the eyes glazed.

The man is possessed.

The chill that had fallen on his skin beside the standing stone was there now, across all the burning heat of rage.

"Such anger. You understand that kind of anger, East Anglian. It is like madness. You have known it. When that arrogant king was sacrificed and there was nothing your defeated army could do, the madness still drove you. Otherwise you would not be here in Wessex, now, with only half a face. You understood the anger then and you understand it at this moment. You know nothing can stop it. We are the same in that much, you and I. You will use the sword."

He could. One harsh thrust and the souls of the dead would rest easier: the murdered king, Elene's parents, all those people lost in war and raiding. The past would be wiped out.

The hot blood of battle, the strength of it still coursed through muscle and bone. The Viking had no claim to life. Elene hated him. She must. She wanted Kraka dead just as he did. She had been a captive. What else could she wish? It would be over and the black bitterness would be appeased.

He drew the sword away from the damaged skin, held the blade back.

The cursing, the spit that flew from the man's mouth could have been thought of as inhuman. Rage. Such rage. He waited.

"Do you think I would take my life back from you? What do you want? What else would you do with me? Give me to your new king to be ransomed as a captive? So you can gain wealth."

"Treasure and silver coins? No."

The noise of the ranting stopped. Now it was Kraka who waited. The courage was there. No one could deny that.

The rise of breath in Kraka's chest scraped the slackened edge of the sword. "Expect nothing from me, not even the woman. You may think you have her but you do not. You never will. She gives nothing. She is not capable of it. It was me who gave." The glazed eyes watched him and yet did not, lost in whatever torment possessed his mind.

"I did everything for her. You do not believe it. You still want to kill me. You want to think she was only a captive. But I treated her well, better than I treated my wife, any of my women. I wanted to. It wiped out the debt, the killings. So that she belonged to me. And now she will always belong to me. I made sure of it, the way a man does with a woman. Do you know how things are? Did she tell you that even now her belly quickens with my getting? Did she confess that in your bed? Or did she think, once she had changed masters, to pass the child off as yours? She could have made you believe it, my woman. But now you know the truth. She knows she has my child. If you keep her you will watch the child grow."

The glazed, furious eyes suddenly sharpened. The intensity changed, human, tinged with the terrible unease.

"You knew that…. You *know* it."

Judith's word, not Elene's. It did not matter. It changed nothing. He could not let it.

"Get up." The battle was as good as over, finished. The heart had gone from it as soon as he had taken Kraka. There was only the pursuit of those remaining.

"What?"

He moved the sword.

"Get to your feet."

The movement was fast, skilled despite the madness of it, full of the uncontrollable fury. The weapon was only a jagged stone. The man had nothing else. The attack was what he had expected. He kicked. He could not use the sword because if he did, he would kill.

"Go now. Or it will be too late. The men of Wessex will take your life. You have tried to kill their king."

What looked back was an animal with a broken wrist. Perhaps he was wrong after all, and that was all there was, a beast, not a tormented man. He flexed his body, weight forward. His hand tightened on the hilt, so hard that the eagle-shaped ring dug into his flesh. But then the pale eyes cleared and he was not wrong.

He saw the fear and understood it. It was not fear of the blade or of death. It was fear of the kind of anger that possessed souls and did murder.

He grounded the rune blade.

"Go."

"Why would you do this for me?"

"Not for you. Or for me."

He thought he saw the acknowledgement there. The pale eyes were perfectly clear, sane. He was sure of that much. Kraka turned, running. The trees were only yards away and he thought it was over. But the strong figure swerved, darting back across the open space, toward the household troops. No hope of closing the distance. It was just one spear out of an anonymous hail that took him, the speed of what happened hard to follow. The blade caught him fair. Impossible to say who had thrown it. Kraka twisted, fell. He did not move again.

"What is happening?" Elene could make no sense of the swirling mass of men. Her head swam with dizziness and sharp pain. Fear.

"It is over, lady. Done with. Rest. The prince will come here."

Prince. The curiously formal turn of phrase struck coldness through her. The man was not Berg, but a royal prince, an *atheling,* even homeless and in exile. He was not hers. That was a dream, the way knowing him from childhood had been a dream. Something unattainable. More than unattainable. Broken.

She clenched her fists. He was out there in the fight, facing the Viking who wanted to kill him. Over disgrace and loss and failure. And her. He would face the man who had held her captive, whose child she carried.

She got up. The man who had spoken would want to stop her. He was strong, very fine, but with a look that was untamed. Dangerous. She had to evade him, but the pain stabbed at her, taking her balance. She nearly fell. He caught her arm. She tried to shake him off. She had to see. Someone blocked her view. Another shadow out of those that already crowded her.

She had to reach Berg, find out what had happened. Someone had to help him. No one else understood.

"Kraka." She tried to get the words out of the dizziness in her head, but they would not form. No reasoning. No thoughts save one.

"Let go of me," she said to the man who wanted to hold her back. "Let me pass," she said to the shadow that blocked her way. "Kraka—"

"Elgiva."

She looked up. It was him. He had said her real name.

He had taken off his helm. His hair was streaked with sweat. His face looked blank, dead, as though the life had been taken out of it. There was blood soaking his sleeve. She could see a rent in the chain mail, crushed steel rings.

Berg.

"What happened? What happened with—"

"Kraka?"

She nodded, unable to get another word out of the pain and the sickness and the dizziness in her head. It was as though she were feverish. Ill.

He held out his right hand, undamaged, she thought, apart from scratches and a bruise. He stayed still, just offering his hand, the way he had once before because he had known she'd been afraid. She had held back then. She had not understood, or only dimly. Now she did. There was choice.

She could put her hand in his as though everything were all right.

The pain deep in her belly clenched, driving straight through her. She stepped backward, away from him. She nearly tripped, colliding with the man behind her. She had forgotten he was there. His arms moved round her. But it would do no good. He would not be able to hold her. She was falling, such a long way. She could see the darkness and she knew that she would never escape it.

Berg was talking to her. She thought he said that Kraka was dead. He kept speaking, trying to tell her something. Something important. Then he said she was ill, but she could not be. That was not right.

She looked down and saw the small red stain on her skirts. Fear clutched at her along with the pain. But she could do nothing about it. She was still falling and the blackness was waiting. There was only the sound of Berg's voice, and hands holding her. She did not know whether they were his hands or the other man's. Her last thought was that she had not moved to touch him.

THE HALL AT EASHING GLITTERED, as everywhere did that held the king. Berg loosened the leather belt that held the emblem of a dead country. He moved to set the sword aside. Something impeded him, jarring numbing pain through his arm. It was the boy, clutching on to him, hanging off the edge of his tunic.

"What was the battle like?"

"Won."

He undid the buckle, the movement of his fingers deft. Remote. Made without conscious thought.

"Yes, but what was it *like?*"

"I told you." He reached round to set the newly cleaned sword aside, but the child clung to blood-soaked cloth with one hand like a limpet.

"Yes, but... I can do that."

"Leave it." Berg untangled the linked straps that held the sheath to the belt. Bits came undone. The sticklike fingers scrabbled.

"Look out."

"Oh. I did not know the straps would do that. But about the battle—" Berg took a breath that burned. "People said...the lady Judith your sister who wears trousers said—"

"Will you stop that!" He snatched the hilt before the sword plunged over the edge of the table. Instinct over thought. There were no thoughts in his head. It was not possible.

"She said you might die."

Something cut through the blankness. The boy would be frightened in a large place like Eashing, left alone. *Viking's brat.* Such bitterness in the air, the kind that had changed his own life.

"I thought..."

Poor bastard. His arm closed over the boy's shoulders.

"Ouch."

He loosened his hold.

"I knew you would not die. I told her."

But he could not think, not now. He turned.

"Have you seen all the blood on your tunic? It is your shoulder." The boy meant well. "Can I watch while they stitch it?"

He took a step.

"Can I? What was it like when—"

There had been enough time, whatever the midwife and the other women said.

"I mean when the other man's horse came down and… What was it like? Can I look after the sword? Oh. There is Wistan. They say that it was you who took the big Viking, Kraka, even though it was a thrown spear that killed him. They said it was you who cut him out of the battle and held him off."

The spiky fingers stabbed into his blood-crusted sleeve.

"They are going to make a song about it. I heard—" Berg stayed the uncontrolled movement. "What is the matter?" There was silence after the boy's question. The stick fingers held his arm.

"It is all right," said the small child. "Honour to a dead enemy. You taught me that."

He turned away, blinded, seeking the chamber that held Elene.

KINGS WERE THREE PARTS MAGIC. Their powers ran far beyond the scope of ordinary men. Everyone knew that. It had been so from the beginning of time. The future of the land, its prosperity and its fertility were bound up in the measure of their luck. The fate of people.

Judith considered the fact that Alfred was a Christian king could only make the power stronger.

She forced her way through to see him. More bribes to the guards who knew her. She would have spent all Berg's hard-won riches soon.

Berg.

"Lord." She knelt, always a good move. Her knees had a tendency to be unsteady anywhere near Alfred in any case.

"Lady Judith." The voice was full of gravitas, the seriousness that belonged to a king's face of power. She swallowed.

"I am told you have a request?"

The efficiency of bribery. At least he would never guess about that. She folded her hands formally and looked up. *Perhaps* he would never guess. A small fluttering began round her heart. She considered the consequences of royal wrath. *Gravitas.* He was watching her. She thought she detected a thread of concern, which made her knees weaker. But mostly she read patience and curiosity.

It was the same expression he reserved for his eldest daughter, a maiden of five winters who showed exceptional promise.

The light caught both the embroidered hanging on the wall behind him and the brilliant goldness of his hair. Her heart formed one solid painful lump in her throat. The subtle speech and graceful gestures she had practised before the polished sheet of brass in the women's sleeping quarters flew out of her head.

"Lord, would you speak to my brother?"

He stood up.

She regretted asking it. The great hall still swirled with

the aftermath of bitter fighting. She had watched for nigh on five years how much he had to do.

But there was nothing else, nothing short of this.

"SO THAT IS BERNFRITH the moneyer's niece?"

"Aye."

Berg watched the white face, the small still body. He had sent the clucking women away, even Judith who was distraught over letting her charge escape. Judith needed sleep.

There was nothing more the women could do.

"And her parents dead. So little news comes out of Mercia now that the Vikings rule it. I did not know. Nor you."

Berg did not look at the man sitting across from him.

"No."

"And Kraka…"

Berg's hands fisted.

"Kraka," said the voice into the quietness of the chamber, "who is now also dead thanks to—"

But he could not let that pass. "I let him go." The monstrous blackness locked inside slipped a notch. "I did not kill him. It was he who chose death. I would have let him run. Back to East Anglia."

He looked up. Lamplight caught gold, gems, the shape of a dragon brooch.

"He would never have got back to Earl Guthrum."

"He did not try. He turned back toward you."

The incalculable blue eyes did not change "As you said, he chose death. He was lucky it was quick."

The contorted face of the dead king of East Anglia seemed to fill the room between them. That death had not been quick. The voice of the king of Wessex spoke across it.

"The battle was already lost for Kraka. He knew that, just as you knew it. Because you made it so. He could no more have touched me than that stray child could, the one who has so attached himself to you."

The Viking's brat. Berg turned away, watched Elene's face, how she breathed and the dark circles under her eyes.

"It is not your babe she carries, is it?"

"No." He stared at the thin skin and the frightening quietness. "It is Kraka's."

Silence while the other mind absorbed the truth that hid behind what had happened. Berg spelled it out for him.

"I broke my oath."

Somewhere in the shadows was the unquiet glitter of gold. Restlessness, the quickness of thought driven onward to anticipate the next move, the next danger. Always. But there was no going forward from this. This was an ending.

"Did it ever occur to you," said Alfred, "that if King Edmund of the East Angles had died quietly in his bed instead of being murdered, you would have been one of the better contenders for the empty throne?"

Berg made some movement and then restrained it. This was a king speaking.

"That if the Vikings had not come here for conquest and you were the next King Edmund ruling your pathless swamp—"

"You mean my wide and fertile lands." The East Anglian response was out of habit, made without thought.

"Yes, I am talking about your swamp, which sits just to

the northeast of my own kingdom. What do you think would have happened?"

He did not think. But Alfred went on inexorably, drawing him in as he had once before, like a rope that bound.

"Wessex changed the balance of power when it allied itself with the kingdom of Mercia in my father's reign. Mercia has always been a difficult neighbour for East Anglia. Perhaps there would have been peace. Or perhaps you and I would have been dragged into dispute and would have fallen out over the borderlands, and so would have become enemies." There was a pause. Consummate timing. "I am happy with what I have got."

Oh, you cunning bastard. The rope lay round his neck. He did not look up. He knew what he would see. The man who could look past every obstruction to the vision no one else could grasp.

Futures.

He knew he would never give in until he was dead. There was no other option and whatever duty he could give was Alfred's. But even kings could not hold back death, just as he could not. Death had such power.

You could not express such thoughts of death and despair to a king fighting for survival.

"I suppose you could say Vikings were some use, then," said Berg, former atheling. He let the East Anglian accent lace his words, as though that were a deliberate response, as though everything were all right.

"Aye," said Alfred. He stood.

The king sent someone to stitch his shoulder.

And Ashbeorn.

CHAPTER 16

IT MUST BE NEAR THE TIME of the night office, Nocturns, the first prayers to be said in the dark. Judith and the midwife had come to change the bloodied linen, then gone. Only Ashbeorn stayed with him now.

Berg shifted against the wall bench and watched Elene's hand in his. It was very small, with calluses across the palm from holding the reins of the roan horse. If only she had not had to make such a journey. If he had known the truth earlier. If she had trusted him enough to tell him.

She had wanted to leave him.

He put down the hand.

The firelight flickered. Silence.

The good thing about Ashbeorn was that one need not speak to him if one did not want to. He was at home in silence, having spent heaven knew how many years on his own in the forest like an outlaw. Berg glanced at the dark lump on the floor. Ash could sleep on jagged rocks in comfort.

No words needed. Everything about Ash was seen from his life: the upbringing by Vikings and a treacherous English father, the escape into the forest and living who knew how, and then emerging to become Alfred's most loyal thane. Marrying and taking up his life as though he had always been English, not a Viking at all.

Berg touched Elgiva's hand. He thought she moved. He leaned over the bed and Ash looked up.

"Is she feverish?"

Berg touched the wax-thin face. "No. Not much. I thought—" The stillness defeated him.

Ash fed the fire the physician had scented with lavender and elecampane to promote sleep. The room filled with a welcome warmth, but it did not seem to touch Elene.

"How did you do it?" demanded Berg. The question burst out of him, like something forced. Ash dropped the piece of wood on the flames and the forest eyes stared back at him. There was silence. Berg thought he saw pity. He must sound like a madman.

"How did I do what?" said Ash.

The question would not be stilled. "How did you change from one world to another, move from being English to being a Viking and then back again."

Ash had never said it. Not a single word. It was not an acceptable topic. Berg's fingers closed over Elene's hand.

"It is difficult," said Ash. "There are ties to both worlds. They exist whether I wish them to or not." The hazel eyes never wavered. "Both worlds are part of me and always will be."

The fragile hand lay under his.

"So do you regret coming back here?"

"No. It was what I wished. But even so, it was very hard. I—I did not expect that." Ashbeorn turned back to the fire. "I thought that because coming back here was what I wanted it would be easy. But it was not. It took me a long time." Light flared under the competent fingers. Berg watched the averted head.

"Then what made the difference? What made it happen?"

"I wanted it. Most of all, I wanted my English wife. And I wanted life. I always did."

Berg looked back at the pale face against the pillows. Unmoving. He did not know what Elene wanted. Or even if she wanted life. His hand tightened on hers.

The last word she had said to him had been the dead Viking's name.

"Mayhap she might even speak to you of such things." He kept the lifeless hand held close between his. "Afterward," he said, as though the future were there, waiting.

"Tʜᴇʀᴇ ᴍᴜꜱᴛ ʙᴇ ꜱᴏᴍᴇᴛʜɪɴɢ ᴇʟꜱᴇ you can do," bellowed Judith. The midwife glared at her. Stupid half-wit. She would personally strangle the woman in her own veil. Beside her, the king's physician, Brother Luke, named for the greatest physician of all, laid a hand on her shoulder. Doubtless it was supposed to be restraining, possibly even charitable. She did not care. The lash of guilt and the sight of her brother were too much. She shook off the hand.

"*Something,*" she yelled. It was the blood loss that was the problem, not the fever, which was slight. Just the slow, small leaching of blood that would not stop.

"Lady, there is naught," said the midwife. "We do all we can. It will go as fate wills. God," she amended, with one eye on Brother Luke. "And the patient's strength."

God. Judith crossed herself and stared at her brother's bent head. "I am sorry," she said for the fiftieth time. "If I had known what was in her mind, what she would do…"

Berg looked up. She could see the marks of yesterday's battle, of the battle at the fortress before that, of the journey, of watching all night and a day, of the sum of everything that had happened since the invasion of their home.

"You could not have seen." Her brother took a breath that looked as though it shot pain through him. "It is not your fault, spitfire," he said, as though they were back in the nursery, fighting until he decided he had to put her sins right for her. Stupid, childhood closeness. As though such simple things could still exist.

Berg turned his head. Then he said, "No one can know what is in her mind."

She followed his gaze to the white-faced woman in the bed. *Holy saints,* she thought, *you must come through this or you will kill him. He loves you.* The thought shocked her. It was not some careless dalliance with unforeseen consequences. Love. She had thought she was the only one who understood what hopeless devotion was, but now her skin shivered.

She looked away.

"I can look after her for a while. You have to rest." Or you will go the way she does, down the road with no turning. *Fæg*. Fated. The word terrified her. The light was almost gone. Dusk. The time of change. She crossed herself again.

"What the patient needs is to heal herself, in sleep," said Brother Luke.

She glared at the priest. How could anyone accept that? But no one spoke, not even Berg. She could not bear her brother's apparent calmness when she knew what must be hidden inside him. Things he would not utter. Why would he never speak?

"Berg—" But her brother did not even see her. His gaze was fixed on Brother Luke, as though the physician's platitude had made some sense. Something she could not grasp. Chills raced down her spine.

"Berg, I can—"

"No," said her brother. "It is best if I am with her when she sleeps."

The words were final, like the completion of the change in him that must have begun the moment he'd met the unknown woman.

They all left. Nothing else to do.

It is best if I am with her.

Even if she sleeps in death.

He did not have to say it.

ELENE MOVED. Pain jabbed deep inside. Anxiety gripped her. Because she did not know how to stop the pain and if she did not stop it something terrible would happen. Her exhausted mind could not fasten on what it was. Something like death. She could feel the guilt, like a leaden weight. She did not know what to do. Only that Kraka would be angry with her. She remembered his anger and the terrible force of it, and the time he had struck her. She remembered the fear. Hers and his. She knew she must not let him catch her.

She moved again. Something touched her. She stopped. Warmth. Such warmth. It made her think that *he* was there, that Berg who had been Edmund the atheling was with her and she would be safe, even from Kraka. It was as though she could sense his presence through the cloying fog of horror, as familiar as the path of dreams. In her mind, the dream thread spun out into the future, a future in which he never let her go and he did not mind about Kraka.

She could feel his body touching hers, cradling her. She felt every heavy, rough-smooth contour, the richness that had made her blood sing. She had felt such things for him. Mad desire and warmth. She remembered how he had touched her and how he had let her touch him. She remembered the gladness, more than anything. She moved against the bright living warmth and it was there, as though Berg were in her bed, as though they were sleeping together as they always had.

Always.

It was an impossible word. But he had said it.

She thought he was talking to her now. She could hear the deep sound of his voice in the darkness, rough and smooth, like him. The accent that made her believe the world had no horizon.

She could not tell what he said because the pain in her body crippled her and she was so tired. The cloying darkness sometimes seemed inside her head and sometimes outside in the firelit room.

Berg...

She wanted to hear his voice, but the nightmare interfered with it. She knew how she should deal with the nightmare. She had mastered the lesson even though it had been so difficult—you shut it out. You shut everything out. That was what you did.

But if she shut everything out, she would not be able to hear the voice.

She stirred restlessly in the pain, but the warm body moved with her, and the voice, the voice like Berg's. She knew what he said was very important, as important as stopping the pain inside her, somehow bound up with it.

She had to listen.

The words came out of the dark. Fragments, like her dreams. The childhood dream path where her perfect man told her that he loved her and he did not want to leave her or her to leave him. Two halves of a coin. Her breath caught and the dreams mixed with the other feelings, the lover's feelings, hot and urgent, yet somehow full of despair.

She did not like the despair. She thought at first it came from her lover because she could sense the pain. But then she realised the despair was in herself, bound up with the terrible things that waited at the edges of her mind. She did not want to see them. She would rather keep the dream, even if she never woke from it and it became eternal, part of that other world beyond this where nothing perished. That other world was so close and her lover would follow her into it. He said so.

But he said something else. That there was a child. That was the frightening thing, the thing she had to take care of. It was why she had to try and stop the pain. Because of the baby. It would have no life without her. She had to keep it safe from everyone, even from Kraka. She could not take account of the cost, even if it took away the dream that she wanted.

She thrashed against the pain in the darkness. She was pregnant with Kraka's child. The truth was there, in her mind. The dream was gone, killed. It did not belong to her. She moved away. Yet the warmth seemed to stay with her.

She did not believe in that. Or the voice. She could not.

The darkness was waiting. It was so strong, worse than that, it was familiar. It engulfed her, whatever she tried to do. She would be alone. That was what she expected. But something had changed.

He was with her.

She became very frightened, because she knew what he could not. This time there was no way out. She tried to tell him but he would not let go of her, her or the child.

SHE WOKE UP, COMPLETELY. No dreaming. It was dark, but there were glimpses of light. The light hurt her eyes. The brightness came from a fire and the glow of a brass lamp. She was in a room, a comfortable room. It looked familiar. But she could not think about that. All she could think about was the warmth behind her. It surrounded her, molding against her back, the curve of her hips, her thighs. Solid, like a wall. Seemingly indestructible. She let herself lie against it because it was all that she wanted, to feel the warmth.

But the pain jarred at her and the light hurt her eyes. The brass lamp was so bright— The lamp in the room they had given her at Eashing. Her breath made a faint sound. The warmth behind her moved, a living sheet of harsh muscle and smoothly gliding skin. The stuff of her dreams.

But she was not dreaming. She had been, was, ill. She knew that because—

"Elene."

She heard the sharpness of the man's breath, the rough edge to his voice. Real. Everything was real.

"The baby…" The sound was a whisper, forced past the rawness of her throat, but he heard it.

"Still there. It is all right. Elgiva," said Berg.

He knew. Everything. Who she was, what she had done. About Kraka's child taking life deep inside her. His arms moved. She shut her eyes. But he did not let her go. He was lifting her. Her muscles would not work but he took her weight, all of it.

"Here, you must drink this. The physician left it for you."

The physician. She remembered that, and women's voices, moving in and out of her dream. But nothing they had said or done had been able to cut through the darkness, whatever they had tried. Only Berg's voice had such power.

A glass beaker touched her lips. The draught was strong, bitter. She could not hold her head up. Berg pulled her back against his chest.

"You must drink." He tipped the glass.

"It will make you well," he said. The words held a meaning beyond her grasp, like the physician's care, something that should have been able to help her but could not. Perhaps the physician and all the others had understood that in the end, because they had left her with the only thing that had any meaning in life or death.

She lay against his body.

"You must drink more. It will help you. And the child."

The child. She shut her eyes. The tears rolled out from the corners of her lashes. The tears touched his naked skin. She could feel his body heat, the touch of him against her bare neck and her shoulders. His hair teased her cheekbone when he bent his head forward.

She swallowed the draught because that was what he wanted her to do. She drank until there was nothing left but the only thing that existed for her was his touch.

He set the glass aside.

He had no reason to stay with her except… *He knows what obligations are.*

She should ask him to leave her. There were a thousand reasons she could give. He should not stay with a sick woman, one pregnant and ill with another man's child, a Viking's child. She could ask for the physician to come, the other women, the strangers who had been kind to her.

Her hands were shaking and she could not form the words. She was so afraid of the dark, of helplessness. He was the only one who understood that. He had once said *always*.

She knew it was not fair. She knew it was not right and what she asked held no honour. But he understood what it was like to be beyond the limits of honour, caught in the wasteland where such a thing did not exist. They had understood that for each other.

"Will you stay with me?"

The fractured moment spun out, as though the whole of her universe, darkness and light, dreaming and nightmare, were compassed within its limits.

"Aye."

There it was, all the assurance her spirit craved.

She stretched out her arm in the darkness. Their fingers tangled. She touched him the way she had wanted to when he had stood before her after the battle and had offered his hand, and she had not taken it.

He accepted her touch.

His hand closed over hers, held it in his huge scratched fingers. When she was stronger, she would have to let him go. When she lived through this. If. But for now there was nothing in any of the three worlds, in the past or the present or the future, except the two of them.

Her eyes closed. She lay against his heated skin. She tried to hold on to the sense of that. She tried to feel it through flesh and through the spirit. But the darkness closed over her like a wave and she was drowning in it. It would kill her. She tried to struggle against it. But she was powerless, like someone mad, like someone dying.

People were alone when they looked at death. But her mind knew he was still there.

WHEN SHE WOKE AGAIN, the darkness was deeper. The flames in the hearth had turned to heated embers, the scented wood almost consumed.

But she felt hot, like someone with fever. It made her shift restlessly in Berg's arms. For a second he did not move. Her heart stopped. And then he spoke. Just her name, and he leaned away to pour more of the herbal draught. She drank it, locked in his arms, so thirsty she would have drunk anything. But she was shaking, the tiredness so strong she would die of it. She thought she had faced strength's limits before, but never this.

Her head fell back against him. But the side of her face touched not the smoothness of his skin, but rough linen. She forced her eyes open. The burning lamplight showed her the cloth bound high across his arm and shoulder, stark white in the shadows, bloodstained.

She caught the thick width of his forearm. He stopped, the soothing words he used to her in the dark still on the warmth of his mouth.

"The battle…" Her words died, but he saw all that she did, more. The rawness of it still lived in his eyes.

She could not give it speech. The horror of the battle was there in front of her eyes, blocking out the warm chamber: the screaming nightmare, the way he had stood afterward, half-covered in blood, the broken chain mail.

"It is over. Done with. Elene? You must rest. Sleep." His hand stroked her hair. The gentleness of what he did stole sense, struck through her heart. But she could not tear her gaze from the dark stain. She felt the way his skin burned against hers with the same heat. Fever. The nightmare was all round her, filling the shadows of the comfortable chamber at Eashing, tearing at numbed mind and aching flesh.

"The wound," she said. "Kraka—"

"No. It was not Kraka. Just the chance of battle. Hush. Sleep now."

But she had spoken the name out of her nightmares. She had given it shape and force. She had to know.

"But you fought with him." The effort of the words was more than she could force. His hand caressed her loose hair, cradled her head when she could not support its weight.

"Yes. I fought with him."

She turned her face into the broad heat of his palm. Her breath touched his skin. "Did you kill him?"

The hand stroking her hair went still.

"People will tell you that I did."

The tightness inside her chest stopped breath. She tilted her head so that she could see his face.

"What do you say?"

She knew he would tell her the truth. The starkness of the beautiful bones that made up his face, the scars, the shadows round his eyes were enough to make her weep. But she did not show that. He did not move away from her and she did not move away from him. They stayed, in the dark, locked together by a strength too deep to understand.

"I did not kill him."

"*Why?*" The terrible question burst from her, unstoppable. Did he not know who Kraka truly was? Had he not made the connection she had been too horrified to tell him, that this was King Ivar's man? That Kraka would have been there on the day his cousin had been murdered, the King of East Anglia made a sacrifice to Odin?

Her gaze was caught in his and she saw through to what lay behind. He knew what the truth was. He felt it through blood and bone and ruined flesh, through soul and mind.

"You knew about the baby. You knew I was with child by him even before I began to miscarry."

The endless restraint broke.

"You will not miscarry." His hands were on her bared shoulders, huge, their grip like iron. Her heart jolted. But he did not let go.

"You will not lose the child, do you hear me? Elgiva?"

But she could not stand that name, not now, not from him, the other half of her soul.

"What do you want of me?" she yelled. "Do you truly want me to fight so that another man's child will be born? Kraka's?"

"Yes."

The world began to spin, out of control. She was weeping. No, not weeping. The harsh sound she made did not belong to a human being, to someone with a mind and a soul. She did not have such qualities, not any longer. They had all been lost, stripped away from her the day Kraka had taken her from her home. There was nothing left but the wildness of a creature blinded and maddened. There was only the dark. She heard Berg speak. She had to get away from him, somewhere where she would not wound him with what she was.

She did not know she had moved until he caught her as she lurched away, crawling across the finely woven bedcovers like an animal. She lashed out. There was no thought in her head, no rationality, nothing that made a person, only the desperation and the dark. It gave her strength, such frightening strength.

She struck out again, but he had such power. There was nothing she could do. He subdued her the way Kraka had. She lay, trapped beneath his weight.

There was silence. No movement in the beautiful chamber. Nothing except the harsh ragged sounds that came from her. Suppressed sobs, or the sounds of madness. She could feel the numbness growing in her arm where he held her. She knew he would not let her go. She read the determination quite as easily as she read the necessary physical force. She had used all the force that she was capable of on him. It was not enough.

It never had been nearly enough against a man's strength. She had only tried fighting once. She knew what the end of it was. She lay still.

She could feel the deep roughness of his breathing in the dark, the iron band of his thigh across her legs, the whisper of his hair across her neck. Berg…

His hand loosened. She watched it happen. *Only one ending.* The broad hand spread out beside hers on the woven cover. She could see the ring shaped to form the eagle with the fish in its claws. New life. If you could only believe in it. Suddenly she could see him in the forest chapel, waiting while Kraka carried out his desperate ambush to get the silver.

The thoughts came back to her out of the darkness. Thoughts of what Berg had struggled so hard to express to her. Thoughts of all the things he must have felt and never said. Her mind filled with how they had lain together; the feel of it filled sense. The power of thought unfurled. Thoughts of what his actions had meant.

He did not want to hurt her.

The blindness shifted. She moved. He must have felt it, because he drew back, just enough to let her breathe. But no farther. No farther than that. She spoke into the dark.

"You will not let me go."

She felt his breath against her skin. "Not now."

She could read anything from that. Past or future. The useless thoughts beat in her head. She watched his hand beside hers and it was then that she felt it. The warm dampness at his shoulder. ...*the chance of battle*. That was all he had said. No complaint.

He did not deserve this, any of it. Least of all a madwoman like her.

"Why will you not let me go?"

"That is how things are. We both know it now. We should have known it always."

The shivers chased each other across her skin. *Always.* The thoughts crowded her head, so many thoughts that there was no room to feel them, only the heat of his skin and the bond that had been broken. The pain lapped at her.

"Suppose I cannot do it?" *Suppose I cannot live?* The words unsaid vibrated in the darkened air.

"I have told you the answer. I will not leave you. I will not let you go." He rolled round, taking her with him, bond unbroken. She knew now what he meant and the unnamed fear that had touched her before came back, fear for him. But with it all the myriad thoughts crystallised into one. No room for the doubts that crowded in the darkness. *Not now.*

She would not let such harm happen to him, not through her fault.

She lay close against him, the heat of his skin felt through the senses, the pain hidden in mind and body guessed. Like a reflection in shadowed water, like something shared. She could feel the strength that met such pain. The recognition was soul deep. The strength was in her, too. He had made her see it, something inside her that was truly worthwhile. She would use it.

She could not let the frightening void take her, with its terrible power and its dark promise of oblivion. Because then it would take him.

Her fingers laced with his and the endless well of his strength was there. But for the first time in her life with a man, the gesture she made was also possessive. She felt her own strength, not physical, but inside. A match.

She bent all of her mind and her will to what she wanted.

CHAPTER 17

THE LIGHT WAS BRIGHT. Everything had changed. Everything. Life.

Elgiva could hear the women's voices fussing about her again and feel their hesitant touch. Somewhere in the background was the physician's deeper voice, directing them. All the forces of the outside world, doing what they must. She let them finish until only Judith was left with her. Berg's sister was praying. It came out in commendable Latin. She was a king's cousin, after all.

The outside world was so close.

The solemn prayer was followed by much striding about the room. She wondered whether the girl was wearing trousers again. There was an unladylike curse. The wench was worried. She must speak.

"Judith?" said Elgiva.

"Lady, you are awake. Athelbert's bones!" The name of

an earlier martyred king of East Anglia cut through the bright Wessex air. The royal kinswoman in a swirl of blue embroidered draperies sat down. The outside world came back.

"I am glad," said Judith. Her eyes were deeply shadowed. The light in them reminded her of Berg. "So very glad." Judith's decorous veil got caught in the ornate rings on her slim fingers and she said something that had nothing at all to do with martyred saints. Then she cried a little.

Elgiva took her hand. Her fingertip slid over twisted gold shaped into a boar's image. The East Anglian kings.

Judith raised her linen-shrouded head.

"He is with King Alfred."

Elgiva nodded her head. She knew the moment he had gone, when he knew she was safe. She knew what he had said and what he had done. But all that had belonged in the dream world.

"He and the king are talking. They have to plan what to do when Earl Guthrum finds out he will not get the money. Oh, it is all right. Guthrum is not going to invade. He does not have the strength."

Not yet.

Neither of them said it. Elgiva smiled. "Do you bribe people to bring you intelligence of the king's councils?"

Judith blushed. "I would if I could." Her small decorated hands clenched into businesslike fists. "But all those who are oath-sworn are as closemouthed as the grave."

Oath-sworn. Her mind had moved forward. In truth it had done so since the moment of waking.

"He will come and see you," said the late King Edmund's cousin.

Thought had not come with the moment of waking, but with the moment the outside world had come back. She waited.

"DID YOU REALISE he does not even know how many swine are in the herd?" Chad hopped from one foot to the other in Berg's wake. "Not knowing how many. Imagine that!"

They crossed the great hall. Berg imagined Ashbeorn, one-time Viking and newly restored Wessex thane, personally counting the exact number of swine he now owned.

"Careless of him," he admitted.

"Must be an enormous herd, though," said Chad, expansively inclined to be generous. He skipped with nervous energy. The brat should have been sick after being caught this morning trying to soak up the spilled dregs of mead from last night's victory feast. They stopped at the door. Chad kept skipping.

"Ash has his own forest for them. They can eat—"

Judith let them in and left them together.

"I have seen one sow eat— Lady, you are well again." The boy launched himself forward with unexpected speed. Berg caught him. The pain jarring down his shoulder blackened sight.

"Sit."

The boy dropped. "Lady, did you know what—"

"We were speaking of someone's favourite animals." If the boy mentioned the battle…

"Swine?" asked the moneyer's daughter. He could see, in the daylight, what illness and grief had done to her.

"Aye," he said. "Some reckless idiot mentioned this herd…"

The boy's gaze moved from one to the other of them, the hidden core of uncertainty that had overtaken him at Eashing painfully apparent. They soothed him with words, working together without thought. It seemed natural.

"The swine belong to Ashbeorn," said Chad. "He is one of King Alfred's thanes. He used to be a Viking but they still let him be Alfred's man. It is true."

"Aye. It is true."

When the child had gone, there was silence.

Berg sat down on the wall bench where the small swineherd had been. He tried to seek what had never come easily—words. It had seemed possible in the dark, facing death, to say what was inside him, even if Elgiva had not been able to hear him. In the light, nothing seemed possible.

"Elgiva? You will be well."

Her eyes sheened with tears. "When did you know about—"

"Who you are?" *Always.* The word echoed in his head but he could not get it out. He did not know what she wanted. He watched the daylight on her face.

"I cannot say the exact moment. Perhaps that first night we slept together—" He could feel the force of that moment through aching flesh and bone, the small, close room at the half-finished fort, the silence, the smell of despair. And her touch.

"When we lay together in the bed and I touched you, my hand caught the half coin sewn into your clothes. There was no reason for me to guess what it was, but the thought of you was there in my head. I had seen you and there was something that could never exist between strangers who have never met, who are nothing to each other."

He stopped. How did he explain all that lived in his head? The questions and the possibilities that had driven him mad? All he could remember was lying outside in the dirt with the light of the stars overhead and his body aching from fighting, and thinking, what if it was her? *If.*

"I set myself to find out."

"Is that why you would not let me go after I came back to the battle at the fortress in the Andredesweald?"

"In part." *I would not have wanted to let you go anyway. I could not have done it. Except if it was what you wished.*

"Did you come back because you wanted to find death?" He watched her face and thought about what had so nearly killed her on the battlefield, in the journey, even last night. The black force that ate souls. Despair.

She shook her head. "In part."

He got up. It was impossible to sit still, the pain of movement welcome. Her voice followed him.

"I came back for you."

He stood still. Thought and will and the heavy beating of his heart seemed to stop with the movement. Outside the open shutters, he could see light that blinded his aching eyes. The wooden palisade of the fort, the hazy blueness of the forest and the hills that cut off the sky.

"I thought of you," said Elgiva. "I could see you down

on the battlefield. So much danger, the noise and the death all around you and you never stopped. You never once faltered. You had such courage."

He grasped the window frame and the wood bruised his palm.

"You made me think, all sorts of things. All the worthwhile things I had pushed out of my head. I watched so many warriors surround you and I thought you would die, and I could not stand it."

He let go of the window ledge. "But I am not worth it." The words came out now, all the hidden blackness that had been there for so long. "I never saw a future. Everyone knew that. Even Alfred when I swore that useless oath to him. He wanted to fight for a different future. I fought, but I could not see the future."

"But you did see it. You saw it for me."

Across the yard someone was herding the geese out to feed. It was all so ordinary, a small and ordinary life, not destruction. A life that led forward.

"That is what you made me see last night," said Elgiva. "A different future. I wanted it. I could not remember wanting anything for so long, but I wanted that. You—"

"I left you."

"You?"

It made no particular sense or reason. But that was what was in his head, all the unsaid things.

"If I had not let you go from the start, when we were promised to each other. If you had been with me, none of this would have happened. I knew I would spend my life fighting and I told myself that was too great a danger for me to be responsible for anyone. But things might have been different. I could have made sure you were safe, in the king's protection like Judith. Not left to face someone like Kraka with no one but your father. Only yourself to take on the burden."

"But it is not right for you to think that. It is not—"

"Can you say that you have never thought that of me?" He turned round. She was lying against the pillows, watching him. He held the gaze of her eyes and spoke.

"When I held that half coin and we shared a bed, I asked you what that token meant. You said it could have no meaning beyond bitterness and sorrow, that you would never want to go back to the past it represented because to trust in that would kill you."

"You forget. I left you. You told me so that night in the forest when I asked you whether you had ever wed. It was I who left you."

He could still see the shining tears in her eyes and behind it the pain.

"It was because of your lost fortune, was it not?" said Elgiva. "Because although you were a king's cousin, there was no throne. Because you were so damaged I would not want to look on you. Most of all, because you could not give the morning gift to me that you had promised. That is what he must have told you, my own father. That is why you thought you had to let me go. You thought it was best for me. You tried to explain that when I asked you about marriage. I scarcely believed you. I did not want to."

She sat up. The skin on her slender arms looked like glass.

"Do you know what my father told me three years ago? Do you guess? He said that you had never wanted a betrothal to me. That you only agreed to please your family and because we were rich. But that you did not think that a prince of East Anglia should be marrying a moneyer's daughter, and you were still an atheling, a prince, even in exile. That since the misfortunes of war in Mercia had made us less rich, what I would bring to the marriage would not restore your wealth. You needed wealth even more, now. So you would rather find a rich bride elsewhere. That is what he said. I believed him. If you are talking about keeping faith, think of that. I believed my father and so he was able to break the betrothal with my blessing."

"Elene—" He had no consciousness of recrossing the room, but she was holding him, her thin fingers buried in his sleeve.

"He lied to me, my own father, and I can see it only now. If I was angered over you, if I was bitter, it was because of that. I wanted someone to share the blame for what happened to me afterward. But I still used to dream about you. Sometimes I would be lying in the dark, terrified, and I would see you. I would think of you coming to find me. But even with all the power of my dreams, it was not like this. Not with such…" She stopped. He watched her bent head and thought of all the damage that was inside. Endless. The anger choked him.

"Elgiva—"

"How could my father have deceived me? How could he have lied so to me and had me believe him? I loved him and I trusted him. I thought he loved me. I was all that my parents had, no other children, and I came so late in their lives that they had given up hope. The rest of our kindred were scattered through different lands, wherever they were needed to strike coins from silver. But we were so close. Just us."

He swallowed the rage.

"Your father made the decision for your sake, so that he could find you a better husband than me. He did love you." That much had been true. Berg had seen it when the man had spoken to him. That was what had made the request to end the betrothal so impossible to refuse. "He said nothing I could truly argue against."

"Aye. Marriage is supposed to be a practical arrangement. It was I who—" She stopped on whatever she would have said, and when she spoke again her words were different.

"Aye. My father did care for me in his own way, for all that he was so ambitious, so proud. Sometimes I think he gave me that dangerous pride. But not the ambition. Never that." She looked past him. "Pride has such a price." Her small hands plucked restlessly at his linen sleeve.

"I thought about going back to my parents when I left Kraka. I did think about it but I could not face them. Not after—" Her voice made a small choking sound and the tensed fingers dug into his arm.

"They would still have loved you."

"Would have?"

Christ's mercy. What else did he have to say to her? What else had to happen to her because of that insane bastard—

"They are not… Are they dead?"

He covered her hand with his. He could not prevent that much.

"Dead." Her voice no longer held a question. The cold hand turned under his.

"I think I knew," said Elene. "I knew in my heart but I would not admit it. I found her brooch, my mother's brooch. It was with the plunder you took after the battle at the fortress. The plunder from Kraka's men should not have contained that, not something so personal that she always wore, not if she was safe. I wanted to get to Winchester because that was where they would have gone. I had to go there to find out, even if I could never stay with my parents again. But now I do not have to go there because—"

"It was not intended." Kraka's appalling words came out of his mouth. He watched her horror-filled eyes. "Such deaths should not have happened."

"Did it happen when I was taken? When—" The words stopped, but her gaze never left his.

"Aye." He took a breath. "Such things are hard to control." Heaven knew he had seen enough fights, enough raiding. "There is always confusion."

"Kraka." Her bloodless mouth formed the word. He could not hear it. There was no sound. But he knew.

"He told me. When I took him out of the fight." He could still feel the urge to ram the sword through the Viking's throat. The force of it lived in muscle and bone. "I made him tell me what had happened."

"He knew my mother and father were dead and yet he let me believe they still lived?"

"Aye."

"But he—"

"It happened after you made your agreement with him."
He said the words that defended the creature. Kraka's
words. He let none of the anger show in his face. But she
did not see him, only that other world with Kraka.

She will always belong to me. I made sure of it.

"He knew they were dead?" said Elgiva.

The anger would kill him. Kraka's voice mocked in his
head. *You understand that kind of anger, East Anglian. It is
like madness. You have known it.*

He watched the blank eyes. All the useless anger no
longer mattered. What mattered was breaking through
that terrible blankness and easing the pain behind it.

"When people go raiding," he said, "when they start any
kind of fight, it is like unleashing chaos. You have been
on a battlefield. You have seen something of what can happen, understood it, felt it." He took a breath. "It was not
something Kraka had any control over."

Elene made a small gesture of acknowledgement, turning her head so that he could not see her eyes. She said
nothing. The only connection between them was the
touch of her hand on his arm, like something lost.

"Kraka," she said again. Then she raised her head. Her
eyes were suddenly focused, as keen and as far-seeing as
when she had held an armed man at the spear's point like
a Valkyrie. "It was Kraka himself. He killed them. That was
what he could not control."

Her eyes sought his. "You do not have to conceal the truth
out of honour, or to spare me. I can see how it must have

been with Kraka and my father. My father must have refused him the money, out of pride and anger, and so Kraka killed him. Then he must have killed my mother, too."

"Elene, listen to me. That might have been how it was, but it was not what Kraka intended. What he intended was what he first told you in truth."

"He killed my parents. I stayed with him. We made the bargain and he treated me well, and all the time—" Her gaze slid past his, until she was lost in that other world. But not entirely in the other world. He could feel her pain through the touch of their flesh.

"How could he have treated me well? It was such falseness."

He could not let her take that pain.

"No. Not falseness. Perhaps it was atonement." *I treated her well…. I wanted to. It wiped out the debt.* "You said you understood him." He thought of the madness locked in Kraka's eyes and the fear. "Then you will understand what he could control and what he could not."

"He killed my parents, my own kin, and yet I stayed with him. I shared his bed." She stopped on the word. Her gaze hit his for one instant then sheered away. "I lay with him." But he was beyond caring about that, only about what she felt.

"You did not know what he had done. You wanted to save your parents. That is why you went with him."

Her head stayed turned, away from him, the tension visible in the vulnerable line of her neck. The pain was palpable. He had shared so much with her, not just the bond that he had wanted, but the despair.

"Aye," she said. "He did not tell me, and so I did not know. I stayed and I felt… I felt gratitude to him. He made me feel that because he spared me too much ill-treatment. He wanted me to feel that gratitude. But it was complete falseness, everything he did, everything he tried to take from me."

"It was not complete falseness. Can you not understand what he felt for you? What was there despite all the selfishness and the brutality and the black spirit he could not leash? If he was capable of caring anything about another human being, he cared about you."

She did not look at him. Only at the other world, the nightmare. She did not bend her head. He watched the proud arch of her neck. He could feel the trembling through her touch.

"How can you say that?"

"Because I spoke to him when he knew he was going to die, even if not at my hand. Because in the end I could read him like my own reflection. I can feel what he felt and a thousand things more." There was a stretched moment of silence. "I do not think anything exists that I would not do for you."

The fiercely held head bowed as though she could not support it. As though she could support nothing. He caught her fall.

CHAPTER 18

HE WAS THE ONLY POINT of warmth in the world. He let her touch him. There was nothing else Elene could do, nothing she was capable of, not thought or knowledge of what was right. She felt his arms close round her so that he was holding her the way he had in the dark. There was nothing but the feel of his body close to hers, sharing her bed, lying with her in the blackness.

Nothing but the awareness of him. Her hands sought the supple turn of his back, the broad width of his chest, the harsh laboured feel of his breathing. She felt the dark heat of his mouth.

The kiss was gentle. It held everything she wanted, kindness and strength and reassurance. Life. And behind it all, the passion. She let it seep into her soul.

Her hands slid across his chest, the smooth lines of his torso. He was so solid, heavy bones. She was lying half across him. Her fingers traced his flesh through the restriction of clothing, felt the solid power, the strength of life. Her fingers stilled.

Nothing said. No words possible for them, no expression for all that was felt. His broad hands cupped her head. He would not touch her because she had been so ill. She knew that. They did not need to speak.

Yet she wanted to know his closeness, needed it, needed *him*.

Her hands moved lower, cradling his hips. She was shaking. He would know how much she wanted him. How much she needed him to want her. She needed his desire. It was the only thing that could join past and future. What she wanted was the prize she could not deserve, his love.

It was a madwoman's action, to touch him now, like this. It was the only thing she had. She pressed closer until the heated touch of his mouth on hers strengthened. Her fingers sought the hard quickness of his body. The kiss took her breath. The passion was there, felt through breath and sense and blinded touch. She let it take her, the power of his kiss and the heat of his body.

Let me touch you.

She could not manage the words because she was nothing, a lost spirit with no home and no place. No life.

Please.

She could feel his strength. He did not turn away from her. He let her feel the power of strength undisguised, the harsh beat of his heart against her breast, the force of his life and his warmth. It overwhelmed her. She followed it, with her mind, with the movement of hand and body and desperate sense, her fingers tearing at his clothing, seeking closeness, shared need, the elemental completeness of it.

She was so afraid he would reject her, that he would not accept her touch, born of the love that was not good enough, even though it filled her mind and her being. This was something she wanted, needed, to show him, an explanation on a level different from that of words. Between them, after all that had happened and all that she had done with Kraka, it was necessary, as necessary as the words had been. Touch and the power of it was something she needed to give him, even if her love never could be right.

She sought the intimacy of his body, the heat of hidden skin, hands desperate until she touched hard, smooth flesh, the burning power of him.

She gasped against his mouth, the sound taken, subsumed by his power, the need and the closeness, and absorbed like all that she was, her whole being, bound up in him. She touched him, hot male flesh. Her fingers moved across his hard length, the heated tightness, the moist slip of smooth skin. The desire for him burned her, consuming fire.

There was such need, all the fear and isolation and wanting, all the madness and bitterness and the despair of death packed behind it. She wanted the force of life to overcome it, the possibility of happiness, even if it was only for an instant. He carried that possibility in himself even if he denied it. He was meant for the warmth of life. She wanted the possibility to be there for him as much as for herself.

His body moved, carrying her with him. The kiss broke. There was nothing but the hot flesh under her hand, the sense of power, bright and fierce and overwhelming. Nothing but his strength, vital and complete, surrounding her so that the harshness of the sound he made was sensed through her flesh as much as heard. She felt his tight movement. Power. She felt the life flowing from him to her, the stark, primitive completeness of it, the hot gush of his seed against her hand.

She lay against him, boneless, her bent head resting against the heavy rise and fall of his chest. She could feel his hand cover her shoulder.

He said her name, her proper name. *Elgiva.* She could hear all that lived in his heart, all that they had shared, all she had taken from him, in the rich sound of his voice. Her eyes filled with tears, all the press of the tumultuous feelings.

She bent her head lower. Her hand still touched the slickened heat of his flesh.

She touched him with her lips. The intimacy was beyond her reckoning, more than she could bear. She could not stop what she did. Her mouth touched the powerful blood-engorged flesh, as though she could take that power deep inside her, so deep, as though—

She felt the shudder of powerful muscle beneath the lightness of her body and she drew back. But her fingers still held him, rested against male flesh, the hot moistness of his seed. She was mad, beyond the reach of what was civilised. She said the words in her heart.

"I wish it was your child I carried."

His hand on her shoulder tightened. Then it moved to light on her hair. Gentle.

"It is your child, Elene. I would look after it. Him or her. Just as I would want you."

A promise, like an unbreakable obligation. But what that meant—for him.

"But how can you want me? How could you make a promise like that? Now?"

"Now? I made it many years ago when I was fourteen winters old."

The tears stung at her eyes, heated and full, too full for her to contemplate. She held them back. The intimate warmth of his body shifted, not away, drawing her closer, like something valued.

"We have already made our promise."

The tears pressed.

"But that was a dream."

"Aye." It was all he said, just that, as though dreams and reality could exist together. She lay still against the rock-solid strength of his body.

He said nothing. But the silence was not despair. It seemed full of the possibilities she had wanted to feel, just by touching him. The possibilities she had wanted to take from him.

She made herself think, forced herself to see what was.

"Suppose I bear a son. How would that be? A boy brought up in the house of a prince of East Anglia?"

The hot-muscled flesh moved. He shrugged, as though such a thing did not matter.

"A prince with no throne. Besides, it may be a girl. A

Valkyrie like you." He made no further move, just stared deliberately at the roof. "Judith can teach her swordplay and you can teach her how to fight with a spear. How could she lose?"

A small sound broke from her throat, halfway between laughter and the burning press of the tears. She thought of the first time he had made her laugh out of despair. Despair over Kraka, who was dead.

"It will be all right." His voice was endlessly steady, the solid bulk of his body richly warm. "Either way, boy or maiden, it can make no difference." There was a small space of charged silence. "I have made my peace with what is done, with Kraka."

She stared at his mutilated face.

"Because you let him go?"

"Because I would do nothing else."

The finality in his voice was complete. But she had lain with him much like this and felt the bitter pain of the way he had been damaged, the pain of the savage destruction King Ivar's men had wrought in his homeland. The same destruction the Vikings sought in Wessex.

"I took away your right to avenge the honour of both the dead king and the living."

"They will make a saint of my cousin. They speak of miracles at his tomb already. His spirit must be with God, not on this earth. It does not need deeds from my hand. As for the living, Alfred bears no grudge. That is not what he sees."

"Is it true what Chad said?" Her breath tightened. "That one of King Alfred's sworn men was a Viking?"

"Aye. Ashbeorn. He was born English but was brought up as a Viking. Then he came back here. He was like a creature with no home. Now his home is here. That was what he wanted. But it was hard on him, moving from one world to another. You could speak to him one day, if you wished. He has an English wife, Mercian."

She looked away.

"And they accept him here?"

"Aye. He has the king's trust. Alfred's mind always looks to the future. That is his gift."

"And yours." She turned her head against his warmth. "You cannot deny that now, after all you have said. You could not have denied it before. I saw that in you from the start. That was the true source of my bitterness toward you. I did not want to see what you saw, but I could not help it." Her aching body tensed. "Just like now."

"Elene—"

"I wish I were someone better," she burst out. "Someone who could deserve what you give. I wish I were the person you dreamed of, like summer, like the sun in the sky. That is what you said. That is what you dreamed of. Not someone who has done all the things I have. I wish I were that person."

He moved, smooth power, his hands catching her shoulders, lifting her up, trapping the curve of her face so that she had to look up.

"You are still all those things to me. I do not wish for anyone different." She watched his eyes and saw the sudden burning heat. She felt the touch of his fingers against her tear-damp skin. "If I had someone different, I would lose half of myself. Can you not know that?" His gaze looked straight through her as though he could see to what was hidden. As though—

He turned away and the sharp sob, the harsh breath, caught in her throat. But then his hand touched hers. She felt rough warm flesh, something hard, metallic. She looked down.

A perfect disk of pure silver, minted by her father. It was broken and yet the two halves fitted together. Matched.

"The coin. You kept it. You found the half that I lost that night at the monastery guesthouse."

"Aye. You are careless for a moneyer's daughter."

"You kept it."

"And if you leave me for a third time, I shall have wasted my trouble."

Her heart beat out of time.

"I did not mean to leave you the first time. It was only because of what my father said and because…because I believed him. I believed you might not want me. I believed even a prince in exile might truly not want a mere moneyer's daughter, and no longer a rich one—" She caught the hand that had moved.

"No, let me say it. I must say it. You see, it was more than that, much more than practical things. I had seen you and I had loved you, even then, even when I was still a child. You were my dream and somewhere deep inside I must have feared that dreams like that, dreams like *you* did not come true."

Her hand closed round his, over the sharp ridges of the coin.

"I left you the last time for the same reason. I knew for sure then that I was pregnant. Even I could no longer disguise that truth from myself. Judith guessed it. She made it real. I do not know when I first knew. I could hide the truth from myself so well. I could blame what was happening to my body on illness, on the terrible strain of the life I lived."

She stared at their joined hands.

"I suppose that must have been the truth behind why I left Kraka. I must have known deep in my heart that I could not leave a child to his mercy, and yet my mind could not cope with the truth, with thinking things through. Nothing much mattered to me by then, not the bargain, not honour, not myself. I could not see those things. I could not see anything. I was so weak."

"No."

She could feel the tightness of his hand round hers, the closeness of another being who had been pushed beyond the limits, far into the wasteland and into the bitter sin of despair.

"And so I left. There were enough reasons. Kraka had gone back into East Anglia, reporting to Earl Guthrum and receiving his orders. There were only his brothers to look after me and I was afraid of them. In some twisted way I meant something to Kraka, but nothing to them. I knew what they would think. His property was theirs."

The fierce strength beside her moved.

"It is all right. Nothing happened. I fled before it could." She hated what she had to say to him. All that had to be done to bury the past. If he would still have her. *If.*

"I ran away and I found you and everything changed, all that was in my mind and my heart, everything I was. Everything good that happened I owed to you." Her hands moved against the skin of his hand, hesitant. "That is how it was. You made me love you all over again." She felt the tightness in his body, the harsh control that held back what he felt. *What did he feel?* She kept speaking.

"When I left you the last time, I could not hide the truth. Your sister had spoken of it and so you would come to know. Perhaps you half guessed it already. You took such care of me. And perhaps you would go on taking that kind of care. Judith must have thought the child was yours. She said you were a man who understood obligations. But I had already come to know that. I could see it in everything you did. Then I found out from something she said exactly who you were."

"You found out. You knew all that and you still left me."

She could feel the burning force of what was held back inside him.

"I had to. Because the truth was exposed, and there were no excuses. I knew the sense of obligation would tie you completely. Honour. How could I do that to you? I knew I could not burden you with a child that had come from Kraka, from one of Ivar's men whom you hated for the wrong they had done. I found out that Kraka had left. I thought he had gone back to safety in East Anglia after all, because there was no other choice for him. I thought—"

She took a breath. She watched their hands. Two hands. Joined.

"So many thoughts went round in my head. Like the onset of fever and I had no time to sort them out. And so I fled."

"But you must have known I would still care for you. You must have known that much. I tried to show you. I wanted you to feel safe. I tried to make you feel safe again because I thought that was what you needed. I wanted you to feel that from the first, even before I knew who you were. I wanted you to trust me even though we met like strangers, enemies, and then I began to guess who you were."

She watched his great heavy fist round hers. So many feelings locked in his heart and he had never been able to let them out. She, of all people, ought to have been able to understand what it was like to be locked in silence, isolated by thoughts and emotions far too dangerous to express.

"I should have told you," said Berg, one-time prince of a lost kingdom. "I should have said all sorts of things I held back. But I did not know whether you would want to hear it. You seemed so hurt by the past. I did not want to add to that and I could not offer what I had offered you once. Only a life to be spent fighting. You have seen how lethal that is, how destructive." The grey eyes narrowed, facing something unseen, something that lived beyond the four walls of the quiet room—the future rolling out in an endless wave.

"I have given my oath to Alfred. I cannot take it back. He is a king who sees what will come. He will meet it." The keen East Anglian eyes focused. "No one could leave a man like that to be alone."

Ælfred Rex hanc fecit. The circle closed, the thread that had begun to roll out in the Andredesweald, before that, from the time she had been taught to think or to read, from the first time she had met Berg under a limitless sky. Complete.

"You understand," said Berg. The words encompassed everything, honour with dishonour, despair with hope. Kraka. The madness with the Valkyrie's spear. The death of the East Anglian king. The spirit of the new king.

Past and future.

A thousand things more intimate.

She became aware that his gaze was focused completely on their joined hands. The awareness flowed round her, deep inside, tingling through the barrier of her skin. The rough voice kept speaking.

"Even if I turned away at this moment, in the end the war would come to me. I would have to fight."

"I know that."

"Aye. So you do." The simple statement went bone-deep.

"I would want to be with you," she said. "I would want to share whatever the future brings, with you. Besides, I do not think you have thought about how useful I could be. I could make you heartening speeches like Hildegund in the story when she was betrothed to Waldere. She was very good at that. I could address you as the Right Hand of Attila the Hun and polish your armour for you."

"That would help."

"See? We agree. Although she worried about him being overly brave, she never truly wanted to be parted from him and their betrothal survived everything, flight and battle…" *Everything.*

"Elgiva."

The name whispered through the air. She took a breath. It hurt her lungs. She stared at their joined hands. She thought of how he had stayed with her as far as the edge of death. That he had said in the terrible power of the darkness that he would not leave her, even then. What he had said in the darkness was now here in the light. Real.

"You have my love," she said. "You always did. I still loved you, even when I fled. I cannot stop loving you. I was only afraid of being a burden." The beating of her heart would kill her, choke her breath. He still held her hand. She had only to believe. "Will you still have me?"

She felt the abrupt movement of his body, heard the sharp intake of his breath. Felt the strong touch of his fingers.

"Is that an offer of wedlock?" He still held her hands. She could feel his strength. "I thought I was supposed to make the offer."

Abruptly, she was trembling. "Perhaps it is a Valkyrie's choice. Life." It flowed into her through the touch of his flesh on hers. "A future. Besides, you made a mess of it last time. No morning gift."

"Then it is as well we are still betrothed and I do not have to offer a new one. Except—"

"What?" Her breath caught. He was so close, so very close, in so many ways.

"Maybe enough of my fortune is restored to find some

land in Wessex. If that would be what you wish. I might even run to buying a few swine."

A job for Chad, the Viking's brat.

"It might do." The words choked. Tears.

"And then there is my princely name. You seemed to like that."

"If it is all you have."

"Well that is not exactly what I would call a heartening speech."

"I need practice." The closeness was so strong, overwhelming. She let her head lean against the curve of his neck, the bright fall of his hair, so that he would not see the tears. "So, are we still betrothed then?"

"Aye."

She lay in the bed beside him and tried to envision what a future looked like. He held her. Truly. She kept speaking to stem the tears. "Do you think we should wed, or is that rushing it?"

"The child might like it."

Her heart held still. He must sense it. She knew he did because of the care with which he held her. Then his head bent and his mouth brushed hers, tantalising, like a promise of the future. Her tears touched his skin. She took a breath.

"Can you begin to know how much I love you?" Her lips sought him, touched scars, warmed skin, the fire of his mouth.

"If you are my wife. If you let me love you as I wish." She could feel in the words, in his touch, all that had been held back, the strength and the power of it. She could see all that she had been blinded to. It lived in his kiss, in his touch, in his mind. It lived in her.

The future.

EPILOGUE

"What will you call her?"

"Brunhild."

Elene looked from her husband's bent head to that of the swineherd. The babe in her painted cradle made crowing noises.

"Brunhild?" said Chad. "What sort of a name is that?"

"Appropriate. You watch, another fifteen winters and this one will be attacking me at the spear's point. Just like a Valkyrie."

Just like her mother. Not said. But Elene, Elgiva, had seen her husband's glance.

It seemed so long ago, the desperation in the summer heat of the Andred Forest. Another life.

"A Valkyrie?" said Chad dubiously. He scented some adult undercurrent he had not fathomed. "Why—"

But Berg picked him up and lugged him toward the

door. There were squeals of undignified protest. It was a game Chad never tired of. Just as he never tired of Berg. Or the herd of prime swine that had come with the estate.

"Why—" Punctuated by squeals. "But—" The door shut.

Berg came back. He was watching the child. She was almost afraid to touch him. But it was fear that had nearly made her lose him. Fear and silence and so many things held back.

"What are you thinking?"

She touched his hand.

"Whether or not to broach the new barrel of ale tonight."

"*Swine.*"

"I would not let Chad hear you say that. Although he might consider you meant it as a compliment." His hand closed round hers. "I was thinking about the future. With you and the other Valkyrie."

Elgiva stared at the tiny child in the ornate crib Berg had had made for her.

"Not about the past?"

He shook his head. Morning sunlight glinted over the damaged skin of his face. All she saw were the grey-flecked eyes that looked beyond horizons.

"I like now," he said.

"Aye." She turned against the warm strength of his body. She touched him, the way she had once denied herself for so long, the way she wanted to. She felt the response, instant, like part of herself. His arms closed round her and she let herself give all that was in her heart, all that she wanted him to know and feel.

"Will you keep us both then?" Her lips touched his, the soft sigh of her breath.

"Aye."

She appeared to consider this.

"Even if we attack you at spear point?"

"I have told you. I am good with a spear myself."

"So…so you are."

She watched the hidden laughter that now came easily to him, the echo of joy. That was what she wanted for him, the same gift that he had given to her. He was so close, as close as the other half of a coin. She could feel the touch of the small piece of beaten silver between their bodies. She wore the lost token openly now.

The heat of his mouth took hers. There was no thought, no doubt, only life and the strength of it.

HISTORICAL NOTE

THE FIRST ENGLISH LAND to fall to the Viking invasion was Northumbria, followed by the kingdom of East Anglia. The death of King Edmund of the East Angles is traditionally held to have taken place on November 20, 869. No one knows for sure exactly how the martyred king died. Legend says that he met a grisly fate as a captive after battle at the hands of the Viking King Ivar (the Boneless). He was revered as a saint after his death.

It is thought many English warriors from the defeated lands escaped to Wessex, the last unconquered kingdom, which had fought and bargained its way to an uneasy peace.

The far-seeing King Alfred began to build fortresses. Some were new and some improved on existing centres. Berg's fortress is imaginary, although a genuine Andredesweald fortress (unfinished!) was the site of a battle later in Alfred's reign. The forts played an important role in protecting the kingdom. Some housed a mint, at which silver coinage, vital to the economy, could be struck and stored.

The peace broke completely in 876 and it was two years before Alfred finally beat back Earl Guthrum's invasion.

The rulers in the story are real: King Alfred and King Edmund the Martyr, the Viking King Ivar and King, or Earl, Guthrum. All of the other characters are imagined (although an international family of moneyers whose names began with *Bern* did exist).

*Turn the page for
an exciting preview
of
Helen Kirkman's
next dramatic novel
FEARLESS
A sweeping tale
of destiny and desire
coming
July 2006
from HQN Books*

CHAPTER 1

Kent, England—the South Coast, AD 875

"How can you refuse what I ask? How——"

The man did not stop. Judith was left, watching the broad back and the dazzling fall of hair dislodged by the decisive force of his movement. Desperation flooded her veins.

Never, he had said. *Never…* The word echoed in her brain.

Never.

She caught her breath. It choked her. She could not fail. The consequences were too great. Lethal.

She would make him do it.

She followed him, her arms pushing through the press of people in the great timbered hall, through foreigners, pirates, mercenaries for hire. Men. None of them could stop her. The fierce anger inside her was stronger than a shield, burning, its raw newness overlaying something much older, unhealed.

She would not think of that. Only of her goal: the broad back, expensive blue linen stretched tight over moving flexible muscle, tangled gold flooding across it. Improbable beauty. Whoreson.

He moved through the crush as though it were not there. Strength. Such strength. She would reach him.

She must—

Suddenly, her gaze caught a bright flash of unsheathed steel. Death.

He did not see it. No one saw. Not one prideful, highly trained warrior in the crowded hall moved, even as the carved blade caught the narrow beams of the sun.

Her muscles froze. She wanted to cry out, but the sound that emerged from her mouth was no more than a strangled gasp. A head turned, a warrior. But the face was blank, uncomprehending. She caught a flash of scorn for a woman's megrims. Dismissal, as familiar as gall, and all the time the blue-covered back kept walking. Walking. The black shadow after it. No one could see.

"No—" Her brain could not find words fast enough for thought in the tiny, fractured instant of time.

There was no one, no one to prevent it.

Except her.

Judith screamed. This time the sound was full throated and shocking. He turned, the man who had refused her. He actually turned. She thought he realised, not exactly what was happening, but danger. She saw the thick muscles under the blue linen bunch, rearrange themselves into a tight line of power. But for all his vaunted strength, he would be too late. Too late.

She had no sense of making a decision, right or wrong. She only knew that her body was moving toward the wall of coloured linen, the expanse of vulnerable unprotected flesh beneath it. The dark shadow lunged for its target, off balance now, because of her scream. She brushed past a bright blue shoulder and hit the black shadow in the sunlight full on.

The impact smacked through her, jarring bone, worse than she had expected, like hitting a wall. But the whole of her weight thudded home. There was a moment of recoil in the assassin's movement, a moment beyond time, full of the pounding of the blood in her ears and the wild beating of her heart. The black shadow wavered, but then it collected itself. No shadow now but a solid body of muscle and bone, more than that, as hard as stone.

He was frighteningly strong.

She struck out, knowing the knife was still somewhere, twelve inches of fire-hardened steel. She saw it, trapping the high sunbeams. The light through the open window blinded her eyes. She hit out again, reaching for his arm, but he had hold of her. So strong. She twisted in his grip, knowledge and primitive, terrified instinct. Her muscles bunched, the way her brother had taught her, as though she were back in childhood wrestling with Berg in some nursery fight.

She always won.

But Berg had never used all of his strength against her, the way this man did. He would crush the life out of her.

She hacked at his feet with the sharpness of leather heels. He cursed. Foreign. She hacked again, harder, heard a grunt, felt the involuntary shift in his weight, got an arm free. If she could use an elbow— He fell.

She must have taken his balance after all. He collapsed, hitting the rush-strewn floor with a sickening crack. Gone. But so was she. Falling. She tried to roll under the impact, half succeeded. But she still lost her breath, felt the hard thud of seasoned oak wood jar the side of her hip, her shoulder, her head. She gasped, the pain shooting through her. It felt sharp enough to cripple. She forced movement, twisting over, scrabbling for purchase like a drunk under the mead bench.

Outside the harsh rasp of her own breath, she could hear the beating swell of disturbed voices, see a forest of feet. Someone grabbed her. This time she wanted to scream in panic. She hit out, backward. There was a suppressed grunt of pain. She had struck him.

"Murderer…" she yelled. Her voice cracked. *Deliberate, cold-blooded killer.* The knowledge hammered inside her throbbing head.

She could not move. She could not understand exactly how he held her, but she was helpless.

"Nithing." The accusation of cowardice, of utter and unredeemable lack of worth, struck round the packed hall.

There was silence, no movement, nothing. She became aware of his heat, of the unforgiving closeness, of the long, stark lines of his body on the wooden floor with hers. Of the sharpness of his breathing. She could hear it in the silence. The sound of it mingled with hers. And then the background noises began again, the hissing roar of dozens of voices like the sea, like the dizziness behind her eyes. The hall was full. Someone would help her. Someone...

"*Nithing.*" It was a breath of sound.

"Nay." The foreign voice cut across the noise, slicing through the swirling currents with the strength and accuracy of a forged steel blade. "Not an entirely worthless life. Not if you saved it."

A different voice, even though the flat accent was the same. Not the assassin's voice. Deeper. Her eyes focused. She saw the bright blue cloth first, even before his hand where it curved round her rib cage, stopping movement. Breath. The bright gold swing of his hair touched her shoulder.

"You..." The burning heat from his body struck through her, the feel of a man, not the anonymous barrier of the assassin, as hard and frozen as stone, but the close human contact of male skin burning through the linen, the smoothly shaped flexible lines of muscled flesh. Not the assassin with the knife, but the man who had refused the desperate boon she had asked of him. The victim.

Alive.

Living. Like her. She felt his warmth and the dizziness beat through her mind. She was shaking, now that it was over, trembling like a child.

"The man was an assassin. A murderer—"

"He is dealt with."

Dealt with. "I thought you were dead. I thought he

would kill you. He had the *seax* blade and you did not see. You did not know. You—"

He said something. She did not know what. The sound of it breathed against her hair and her face. Warm against her cold skin.

His deep voice was harsh, like his strained breathing, and then it became steady. An act of will even though she could feel the laboured movement of his ribs against her back. Such control. It negated everything that had happened in those few desperate moments when he had been attacked. It blocked off the primitive, visceral turmoil of those minutes and she thought it covered much more. That there was fire beneath that ruthless covering, something depthless. Anger?

What lived in his mind?

She had to know.